Leviathan

Viking Ancestors
Forged in Fire
Book One

Sky Purington

Story Overview

The only thing Destiny knows is her name, but who's complaining? She lives in a beautiful million-dollar seaside chalet without a care in the world. At least until a psychic shows up at her front door claiming Destiny's true identity is remarkable. She must remember who she is. What she's meant to do. If that isn't enough, her house isn't her own, and her fate tied to a man in the distant past. A fierce, brooding Viking who's too arrogant for his own good yet sinfully alluring.

Leviathan doesn't believe in love, so the woman he saved shouldn't be haunting his thoughts. Especially considering they barely got along. Yet now, thanks to the fire he used to keep Destiny alive, the feisty, stunning redhead is put in his path once more. Worse yet, she might be the foretold Sigdir who sparks the next Great War. That means she must die by his blade once and for all.

Will Leviathan be able to sacrifice Destiny to save everyone? Or is it already too late, and she's found her way into a heart he didn't know he had? Find out as they embark on an epic dragon shifter romance adventure across time in Viking Ancestors: Forged in Fire. Expect through-the-roof passion, a host of nasty villains, and an array of happily-ever-afters that won't come easily.

Pronunciations

Eirik (eye-rick)
Frida (free-duh)
Håkon (hawk-ohn)
Helheim (hel-himm)
Leviathan (luh-vie-uh-thn)
Loki (low-kee)
Midgard (mid-gard)
Mórrígan (more-*i*-gen)
Múspellsheimr (moo-spell-shay-mm)
Mt. Galdhøpiggen (gall-ter-peegan)
Naðr Véurr (n*ah*dr vuu-*ah*)
Níðhöggr (neathe-högr or neathe-herd)
Valhalla (val-hal-uh)
Valknut (vulk-noot)

Dedication

For my Ancients and most especially, Leviathan. I first met your kind a few Viking series ago and became intrigued. Since then, you haven't let me down. Here's to your continued success adapting to life on Midgard!

Series Overview

As foretold by the great serpent Níðhöggr, a Great War simmers on the horizon. This time, the Sigdirs and their allies are caught in the lethal crosshairs of battling gods. Determined to keep their fellow dragons and human counterparts safe, they will do whatever it takes. Even if it means tapping into the ancient power of a blade nearly as old as the gods themselves. A dagger that requires five male dragons be forged in fire with five females, harnessing the power of fated mates. First, though, their mate must agree to be together for all eternity…

Prologue

D ESTINY *HAD* TO get there before he appeared.

Every step in the cloying darkness brought her closer to the end of the tunnel. Toward a terrifying outcome. Something truly sinister. Evil. Yet, she had to keep going. Save her. Who, though? Why did she care so much? Who made her head toward danger rather than away from it?

She never found out because she never got that far.

Instead, *he* appeared. Held something out. Insisted she take it.

Sometimes she raced past him toward the looming cave. Other times, she flew, then sometimes even crawled, dragging her stubborn body forward. Icy spray coated her face. Cold, hard rock cut into her bare feet, knees, and hands.

"Take what he gives you and come home," whispered on the frigid wind. "It is your destiny. Your salvation. Their only hope."

Who's? And where was home? Only one part made sense.

"Destiny," she would whisper in return, drawn to the word. "I'm Destiny."

Or at least that's what she had named herself.

"Closer," the voice urged. "Do not stop. Not for anything."

"I'm trying," she ground out, walking then running only to slam into him again. The mysterious man in the darkness. He who haunted her dreams. Plagued her with lust and desire. Excited but frightened her. Because he meant to end her, didn't he? Help her then kill her?

So she never took what he held out but ducked around him and kept running.

Sea spray stung her eyes. The wind grew colder. Her vision hazed red.

I'll get there. Nothing will stop me this time.

But it did when she ran into him once more. An impregnable wall of muscle. He grabbed her wrist and pressed something into her hand. Something that would help her see past the fog. Past all she had forgotten.

Flashes of something came through. Bits and pieces just beyond her reach.

Raging fire all around them. Searing metal. Roaring man.

Then he was gone, but not whatever she held. Yet somehow, she felt empty. Lost. More terrified than before. She had to reach the end of the tunnel. Had to save them. Not just *her* but *him* now. Finally see the face behind the voice. Finally touch who teased her dreams and aroused her ruthlessly.

So she bolted. Raced after him. There. Almost there. Then *slam*, everything snapped shut, and she jolted awake.

This time, however, all wasn't lost.

Rather, based on what woke her, things were just about to get interesting.

Chapter One

Winter Harbor, Maine
2021

DESTINY BLINKED A few times, trying to place what woke her only to realize it was her doorbell. Usually, she only dreamt about the man who haunted her at night, but it seemed he'd decided to visit during the day. Or late afternoon, by the looks of it. She yanked off her hoodie and fanned her overheated skin. As usual, despite the terror of that particular dream, she was aroused as hell.

She opened her phone's Ring app to see who stood out front. While some might at least ask the stranger who she was via intercom, Destiny did no such thing. Not only because the older woman looked kind but because she was flat-out bored. Not to mention restless thanks to her reoccurring dreams. Him. The elusive stranger just out of reach that seemed to lure her and push her away at the same time. Who *was* he? Moreover, why did she get the impression he was Viking of all things?

Crazy dreams aside, she'd grown edgy. Needing something she couldn't quite put her finger on. As if maybe, just *maybe*, someone would show up and finally tell her what was going on. And she wasn't talking about repetitive dreams.

No, she was talking about her identity.

Who *was* she? Where did she come from? Did she have a family? Friends? A name other than the one she'd given herself? When did she buy her sprawling million-dollar seaside chalet? Did she ever have a job? A passion? Hobbies?

Thinking a strange woman who was either lost or selling something could enlighten her was silly. Ridiculous even. But, hey, at least it gave her hope on her short commute to the door. A mini-burst of much-needed excitement and anticipation that got her mind off phantom Vikings.

She opened the door and smiled, pretending for a moment the woman came bearing Destiny's shrouded life story. "Hi, can I help you?"

"Hello, dear, I'm Elsie." Full-figured and lovely with youthful skin, white-streaked chocolate brown hair, and warm, friendly blue eyes, the woman smiled. "Or Auntie, Aunt Elsie or Auntie Elsie." Her smile widened. "Whatever you prefer." Thin, metal bracelets of varying colors clanged together when she gestured at her cell phone. "I'm here about the ad."

What ad? Destiny cocked her head. "Excuse me?"

"The ad you placed." Elsie noted the number on the house then perked a brow. "Are you Destiny?"

"I am," she replied slowly. "But I didn't place any ad."

"But of course you did." Elsie's smile never wavered. She held out her phone. "See, it says right here you placed an ad for roommates."

She began to shake her head when the strangest feeling rolled over her. Though she'd never placed an ad, she *had* been thinking about roommates lately. How nice it might be to have some people around.

"Not just that, but we spoke on the phone," Elsie continued, stating something she might have led with. "Arrangements were made for me and my nieces to move in tomorrow."

"*Tomorrow?*" She frowned and shook her head, caught off guard, mainly because something about this felt familiar. "I'm sorry, but I don't remember us talking on the phone."

Or *had* they? Suddenly, she wasn't so sure. Trying to gain her bearings in a world that felt off-kilter, she leaned against the threshold. What was happening? Why did she feel so out of it?

"Are you all right, dear?" Elsie peered at her in concern. "You've gone a tad pale."

4

"I don't know," she whispered.

"Come, let's sit you down." Elsie ushered her down the hallway, sat her at the kitchen island, poured some water, and urged her to drink.

Honestly, the last thing she wanted was water. Not with the bizarre mix of panic and acceptance taking hold of her. She felt like she'd been adrift at sea without any direction until now.

"Ah, yes," Elsie said, almost as though replying to her thought. "Perhaps something a bit stronger is in order?" She kept a close motherly eye on Destiny while she pulled out wine glasses and a bottle of chilled white wine, admiring the brand and year. "You have good taste."

"Thank you." She narrowed her eyes. *Had* Elsie just read her mind? "Did you..."

She trailed off and shook her head again. Surely not. Yet even as she denied it, she noted other oddities. How Elsie seemed to know her way around Destiny's kitchen. She hadn't opened various cabinet doors looking for glasses like most people would but seemed to know right where she was going.

Pure coincidence, Destiny assured herself. *Lucky guesses.*

"They weren't," Elsie said gently, her tone soothing. She poured Destiny a glass of wine. "I have what some would call a gift."

Destiny perked her brows. "Come again?"

"I'm a bit of a psychic sweetheart," Elsie revealed. "And everything about you comes across more loudly than most."

What was this woman talking about? Yet, she got the feeling she knew. That somehow, someway, this was normal to her. Or had been at some point. Back before she forgot everything.

"Yes." Elsie tapped her temple. "I sensed it when I first saw the ad, then more so over the phone, and now..." her brows fluttered up, "let's just say, there's something very special about you."

"Other than that I have no idea who I am or how I got here?" she blurted before she could stop herself. But then, there was something about Elsie that made it easy. Natural almost.

"Ah, yes," Elsie said softly. Her gaze swept over Destiny in a whole new way. "Special indeed."

"How so?" For a split second, she got the overwhelming sense Elsie might be right. That she'd forgotten something far bigger than her name or where she was from. How she ended up here. Why she forgot placing an ad or speaking with Elsie on the phone.

"I'm not sure what makes you so unique, but it's there," Elsie searched her eyes, "hovering right beneath the surface just waiting to reveal itself."

"Which means it will soon enough," came a tentative voice from down the hall. A woman peeked her head in the door and smiled. "Hi, you must be Destiny. I'm Elsie's niece, Maya. Mind if I come in?"

Make-up free, with enviable creamy smooth skin, Maya was a natural beauty, her braided hair a stunning mix of golden honey and light blonde. Her eyes were such a light shade of brown they matched the gold in her hair.

Before Destiny could respond, Maya said something over her shoulder, slipped in the door, and shut it fast but not before a crow zinged in after her.

"Oh, dear, don't mind the bird," Elsie assured Destiny.

Moments later, Maya opened the door, made an 'out' gesture, and off the crow went.

Destiny's jaw must have been hanging open because Elsie patted her shoulder and went on. "I'll explain all that in a moment. It's quite the thing and—"

"And nothing." Destiny finally got her wits about her. "Who were you talking to, Maya?" She headed that way. "Who's out there?"

"Nothing I can't handle." Maya angled herself so Destiny couldn't open the door. "Just give it a few minutes, and they'll disperse."

She frowned. "Who?"

"Them," Maya said vaguely. She tucked her hands into the pockets of her woodsy plaid jacket and braced the heel of her hiking boot against the door. "Trust me, all's well. They're just more riled up than usual…" Her eyes widened on Destiny as though she recognized her. "And no wonder! I'm surprised you don't have the entire Arcadia National Forest roaming around here with the energy you're putting off. It's very…magnetizing."

"Isn't it, though?" Elsie echoed.

What on Earth were they talking about?

Maya shrugged a shoulder and went on. "Usually, my kind turns them off, but I run a little different."

"Turns *who* off? And *what* kind are you?" Destiny scowled, about done with this. "Open the damn door already!"

Rather than wait, she sidled around Maya and opened the door only to discover a slew of both wild and domestic animals meandering around her driveway. Everything from wolves and dogs to cats and squirrels.

"They mean no harm," Maya defended. "They're just drawn to my energy...and maybe even yours. Like I said, give it a few minutes. They'll disperse."

"What the," she whispered, looking from the animals to Maya.

"Come, sit back down." Elsie once again ushered her down the hall to the kitchen. "Enjoy your wine, and we'll explain everything." She bit the corner of her lip. "At least as much as we can right now."

"Good idea." Destiny sank into her chair and downed half her wine in two long swallows. "The sooner, the better." She glanced from Maya to Elsie. "Starting with this roommate situation I evidently agreed to."

"Which I sense you're not so opposed to?" Elsie guessed. "Despite the frustrated look on your face."

"An understandable look." Maya plunked a small canvas cooler down on the countertop. "All things considered."

"Very true, love," Elsie agreed. "This has to be a lot."

Seriously? More than a lot.

"She's already halfway there, though, isn't she?" Maya winked at Destiny and pulled bottled water out of her cooler. "You'll be with us in no time."

With them? What was *up* with these people?

Yet, once again, she didn't feel all that alarmed. Rather, it felt like things were going just as they should. She glanced from the cooler to Maya. "Do you always carry water around with you like that?"

"Actually, no. I thought it was going to be a longer haul up there." Maya paused with the cap half unscrewed. "You don't mind, do you?"

"No." She frowned again. "Longer haul up where?" She glanced between the women. "I think it's past time you explain what's going on."

"Of course, darling." Elsie nodded and sat across from her. "What would you like to know?"

"Everything," she replied. "From the moment you showed up to now." She narrowed her eyes. "Because it almost sounds like you know who I am. My real identity."

"Not entirely, but I'm getting closer to seeing it." Elsie sipped her wine. "Closer than you, by the sounds of it."

"Unfortunately," Destiny muttered in agreement.

"Amnesia then?" Elsie said softly before her lips tugged down. A curious light lit her eyes. "No, something a bit more profound. Purposefully repressed." She cocked her head. "The question is, was it by you or someone else?"

Before Destiny could respond, Elsie went on.

"We'll get to that soon enough." Elsie glanced from Maya to Destiny. "Before that, though, it's best you know what my nieces are."

Right. *What* not *who*.

"Because you're something," Destiny murmured, feeling it instinctually. Feeling it as though they had already said it. "Something...very different."

"Yes." Elsie eyed Destiny as though gauging whether she was ready to hear more. "Something different, to be sure."

"Not quite human," Destiny whispered, blinking. It felt like she hovered between two realities. The one she knew and one that seemed absurd...yet not. She narrowed in on Maya and, like it was the most natural thing in the world, followed details that suddenly flittered through her mind. Joy but worry. Happiness yet fear.

Then cat-like eyes.

Wings.

Talons.

"What the *hell*." She shot to her feet but didn't flee. Rather, she stood her ground, strangely on guard yet at ease. Comfortable in a way that made no sense. Instead of fear, she felt curiosity, then certainty.

"I think you know what I am," Maya said gently, remaining still yet somehow moving. Or was that an optical illusion?

"Yes, just that," Elsie confirmed, clearly reading her mind now. She poured Maya a glass of wine and urged her to sit down so she seemed less intimidating. "Come, sweetie, sit so that Destiny can adjust. She's sensing your vibrational pull, which as all those animals outside know, is substantial."

"Vibrational pull?" Destiny murmured, sensing it more acutely now that Elsie mentioned it. Or should she say, able to separate the sensation from everything else she felt. It was predatory and intense. Yet alluring, too, drawing her closer.

"Dragon," she whispered when cat-like eyes flashed in her vision again. Terror spiked through her, then vanished only to be replaced with such a strong sense of relief, she sank back into her chair. Just like that, it was as though a blindfold had been removed, and she saw for the first time. As if the revelation made perfect sense. "You're half dragon."

Not a question but a statement. A cold hard, fact.

"I am." Maya sat beside Elsie and smiled at Destiny. "And you saw that remarkably fast." Her brows perked. "But then—"

"But then she's plainly in-tune with things that most aren't," Elsie cut her off, obviously wanting to navigate this conversation a certain way. Not to overwhelm. In truth, her warm smile did have a way of putting Destiny at ease. "Yes, Maya is half dragon, just like her sisters." She gestured down the hall toward the animals beyond the door. "Where normally animals don't like dragons, in this case, they're attracted to her because she runs on a higher frequency or vibrational level."

She arched a brow. "Come again?"

"Simply put, my girls run on different vibrational levels not just because of when they were born but where." Elsie shrugged. "It's sort of along the lines of astrology for humans, but for them, it had to do with ley lines."

A strange chill swept through her. Why did that sound familiar? "Ley lines?"

"Yes, lines that circle the globe, connecting monuments and sacred sites with undetectable Earth energies." Elsie smiled at Maya, her love for the younger woman obvious. "In this case, Maya and her sisters *are* the energies attached to some undisclosed location or locations. Places they've prepared themselves for their whole lives."

This just kept getting stranger and stranger.

"I see," Destiny murmured, though she didn't. Not really. At least not at first. Not until that strange sensation washed over her again. The one that seemed determined to make all of this normal. Understandable on a level she couldn't quite lock down. "So where and when they were born affected their energies…or vibrational level?"

"That's right." Maya grinned, quite at ease telling a perfect stranger all this. "Some of us run on a higher level, others lower."

"Like good versus bad?"

"Kinda, sorta, but not really."

"Not really is what I'd go with." Elsie gave Maya a sympathetic look. "They can be trying at times, but none of your sisters are evil, dear."

"I know, auntie." Maya shook her head. "Just, as you said, trying at times. At least the one…and the other."

"Yeah, yeah," came an amused voice as another woman let herself right in. With thick wavy sun-streaked brown hair pulled back in a high ponytail, she flicked a pine needle off her black running suit and sauntered their way. "I took care of your pest problem, Maya."

"Oh, no," Maya groaned, striding down the hall past her. "What did you do to them, Jade?"

"Just let 'em know who's boss." Jade winked at Destiny then called over her shoulder. "You know damn well I don't have to do a thing, sis. Animals scatter when I'm around."

"Jade, meet Destiny." Elsie gestured between them. "Destiny, Jade."

They nodded hello then resumed sizing each other up. At least that's how it felt. Where she'd been completely at ease with Maya, setting aside the whole dragon thing, of course, Jade was a different story. Something about her both appealed to Destiny and set her on edge.

"Despite her unusual amount of energy, Jade runs on a lower vibrational level than Maya," Elsie explained, yet again reading her mind. "So she might feel a bit different to you."

"I'm second rung to the bottom out of us four sisters." Jade snorted and grabbed a bottled water. "Maya's the queen bee." She smirked at her sister. "The almost 'transcended one' we like to call her. Super kind, good, loving, vibrational level through the roof." A few chugs of water later, she continued. "Our sister Trinity's next level down from Maya." She opened the fridge and looked around, grumbling about the lack of beer. "Then there's Raven, the darkest of us all."

"You mean lowest vibration," Destiny corrected, coming to Raven's defense for no explainable reason. "I doubt it makes her a bad person."

"No, but it *does* make her something," Maya replied.

"Yes, something we need to talk about." Elsie's countenance grew serious. "In fact, we've got quite a bit to cover sooner rather than later."

-Leviathan-

Chapter Two

SEVERAL HOURS LATER, Destiny was still trying to process everything she'd learned. All four sisters were half dragon, and Elsie wasn't just a psychic but one specifically suited to dragons. Which, as she would go on to explain, took a great deal of patience. Especially when navigating dragons who ran on different vibrational levels.

"So those bracelets really work, then?" she asked yet again. "They keep your nieces' energy from wreaking too much havoc on your mind?"

"That's right." Elsie smiled fondly at her colorful bracelets. "Trinity, who can tap into both levels more easily, made them for me when she was a little girl."

They sat on plush adjacent sofas in front of the fire, enjoying cocktails and getting to know each other better. Destiny liked everyone a great deal despite Maya and Jade's varying vibrational levels pulling her emotions in different directions. According to Elsie, she was more sensitive to it than most for some unknown reason.

"Do you think I'll need bracelets as well?" she asked Elsie. "Especially when I meet Raven?"

As it happened, the three of them had come ahead of time to prepare for Raven's arrival. That was why Maya had brought plenty of water. Apparently, Destiny had also agreed to rent out the cabin just up the road. Yet another building she had no recollection of buying. Nevertheless, Raven would stay there for a time, so Maya and

Jade were getting it ready. Most would think that meant cleaning but no. They were making sure there was nothing present that could pull Raven's vibrational level lower, making her susceptible to death or, even worse, evil.

"Honestly, I don't think you'll need bracelets like mine." Elsie smiled at Destiny with warm reassurance. "In fact, I have a feeling before all is said and done, you might just make it so I don't need them either."

Maya smiled. "Wouldn't that be wonderful?"

Jade eyed Destiny dubiously. "No offense, but I'll believe it when I see it."

"You wouldn't be you if you didn't," Elsie remarked, still giving Destiny that all-knowing look she seemed so good at. One that somehow put her at ease. "It's already easier being around my nieces, isn't it?"

"Actually, yeah." When they first showed up, it wasn't too bad, then *boom*, it hit her like a ton of bricks. Maya's vibration yanked her up one second, Jade's down the next. It was one heck of an emotional rollercoaster. She couldn't imagine what it would have been like had she met Raven first. After all, she was the sister who'd dreamt of this place. Who told Elsie to keep an eye out for roommate listings in Winter Harbor, Maine.

"When will your other sisters be arriving?" Destiny asked.

"Sooner than expected, I think," Elsie replied. "Likely tomorrow or the next day. It will depend on how you progress."

"She seems to be moving right along." Maya looked at Destiny with approval. "I imagine you'll remember more anytime now."

"I hope so." Tempered excitement flashed in Jade's eyes. "I'm looking forward to finally meeting our fate head-on."

Elsie gestured at Destiny. "Safe to say you already are, darling."

Interestingly, Destiny agreed. But how could she not considering what she'd remembered since the women arrived? Memories that came out of nowhere. Bubbled to the surface, repressed all along. Though it still seemed dream-like, she now recalled placing the ad and speaking on the phone with Elsie. While some might be freaked out by recalling such out of the blue, it felt oddly freeing.

As though it marked the beginning of many mental doors unlocking.

If all that wasn't enough, the ease and comfort she felt with her new arrivals was unquestionable. It was as though she'd known them for years. As if on some strange level, they were family. Elsie assured her they weren't, though. Not via DNA anyway.

Either way, Destiny thought nothing of letting them settle in. For Maya, that meant kicking off her boots and helping Elsie whip up some tasty munchies. For Jade, who had evidently run around both properties burning off any lingering negative energy, taking a hot shower was in order. Now, wearing tiny black cut-off shorts and an equally skimpy black t-shirt with fuzzy hot-pink slipper boots, she paced restlessly like a caged tiger.

"I'm surprised running on a lower vibrational level doesn't zap all your energy," Destiny commented.

"Normally, it would. *Should*." The corner of Jade's mouth shot up. "But it seems I'm an enigma."

"It's her gift or dragon magic, if you will," Elsie clarified. "She balances out the energies of her sisters, so they don't go too high or low."

"Yup." Jade continued pacing. "Mostly, I soak it up and let it go, depending on the energy." She eyed Destiny. "Your energy's definitely unique. I can't quite decide where it's meant to go."

"Meant to go?"

"Yeah." Jade narrowed her eyes. "It's almost like it's not quite human energy. Like it's spiked with something..." She searched for the right word. "Something a little addictive, actually. Yet I have a feeling it's unnatural for me to hold on to it for too long."

"It really is intriguing." Maya gave Destiny a reassuring smile. "It's also very warm. There's a lot of goodness in it."

"Right," Jade agreed. "There's also a touch of dark. A naughty element I can't quite latch on to."

Naughty? Her mind went back to the Viking. The feelings he invoked. The almost unnatural allure he possessed.

"Ahh," Jade said softly, undoubtedly sensing a shift in Destiny's energy. "Naughty indeed."

"Who is he?" Elsie's brows flew up in surprise. "You had him well hidden in your mind until just now, Destiny." She tilted her head curiously before she seemed startled. "A *Viking?*"

Maya and Jade narrowed their eyes.

15

"That doesn't sound promising," Maya said, alarmed.

Relish lit Jade's eyes, and she grinned with anticipation. "Oh yes, it does."

"I should have known," Elsie said softly, seemingly lost in thought. "I should have seen it long before this."

"Seen what?" Maya asked.

"You were all born in or on water," Elsie murmured. "Drawn to it. Compelled from your mother's womb." She focused on Destiny, her gaze once again kind. "If you're ready, I think it best you learn more. Perhaps who you are and how you're connected to this Viking." Her eyes flickered over her nieces. "How all of you are."

"Do you mean to tell me the time travel we've prepared for is back to…" Maya began only to trail off, clearly stunned and perhaps dismayed by the possibility.

Jade, however, had no such reservations. "*Damn*, back to the age of the Vikings?" She rubbed her hands together in anticipation and actually smiled. "Can you even imagine?"

"The amount of negativity in ancient Scandinavia with men the likes of that?" Maya's brow pinched. "Yes, I can. Very much so."

"Big vicious fightin' men." Jade seemed downright giddy now. "Heck yeah, sign me up." She looked at Destiny eagerly. "Are they dragons too?" She shook her head, grinning from ear to ear. "Tell me they're Viking dragons," she groaned. "Because that just gets all my girly parts—"

"I imagine they are dragons," Elsie cut her off and focused on Destiny. "Which means my girls and I are heading in the right direction. That this must be what I sensed coming."

"So you think this Viking has something to do with what your nieces have been preparing for?" Destiny surmised. "That he's related to the location or locations they're connected to?"

"Yes." Elsie squeezed her hand. "And, as I told you, I think you're the one to lead them."

Apparently, from the moment they were born, the sisters knew they had a great fate, or destiny, so to speak. One that involved traveling through time and helping humankind in some monumental way. If that weren't crazy enough, they knew their path lay solely with someone who was a stranger to herself. She and another had put them on this path. One they must see through. Now, putting the pieces together, considering Destiny *was* a stranger to herself, they could only assume the Viking who'd been haunting her was this mysterious *other*.

"What other?" Destiny had asked earlier. Could it be him? The man from her dream? Her skin had warmed at the thought. Her heartbeat had kicked up a notch.

"I sense masculine energy affiliated with it," Elsie had responded. "But I'll know more once we have a session. Once you let me in all the way."

Once she did that, they would all learn more. How much was yet to be determined. She was ready to find out, though. To open more doors in her mind and get answers.

She could have mentioned the Viking earlier when they were discussing it but chose not to and wasn't totally sure why. Maybe because he seemed so far-fetched. Preposterous even. Yet she realized soon enough it wasn't that. No, her evasiveness turned out to be pitifully basic.

Blatant possessiveness.

It almost felt like he was hers and hers alone until she deemed otherwise. Which she must have at this point, considering the women had started sensing him. Either that, or he drew closer somehow, so picking up on him became easier.

"How do I lead everyone back in time when I don't know where or when I'm going?" She shook her head. "More importantly, I have no clue how to travel through time."

Yet, she believed it was possible. More so by the moment.

"If you're ready to learn more about yourself," Elsie replied, "I suspect we'll find out." She squeezed Destiny's hand again. "The question is, are you ready for this?"

As she'd learned earlier, *this* meant Elsie would help more memories surface. She would pull back Destiny's mental veil.

"Yes, I'm ready." She'd never been so eager. "The sooner, the better."

"You say you're ready." Elsie searched Destiny's eyes. "But are you truly? As I told you, it might prove very uncomfortable." She shook her head. "We could wait. Give you a few more days to adjust."

"No." She shook her head as well. "I feel like I've waited long enough. Too long."

She was restless and wanted to push past the lull she'd fallen into. The boredom she sensed didn't belong in her life. If anything, dragons and time travel sounded more up her alley. Like something she might have been familiar with.

"You need to understand you might learn things about yourself that are...difficult," Elsie said gently.

"I know. You already told me." She narrowed her eyes at Elsie's hesitancy. "Is there more?"

"There may or may not be," Elsie began, only for Jade to cut her off with a heavy sigh.

"Just rip the Band-Aid off and tell her already, auntie."

Destiny frowned. "Tell me what?"

"It may be best if—"

"What if you were a dragon too, Destiny?" Jade asked impatiently. When Elsie scowled at her, she shrugged and rolled her eyes. "What? She seems pretty open to everything coming at her, so why not be honest? I mean, I'd rather learn I was half dragon from friends rather than in a session." She shook her head. "It might prove damn unsettling, don't you think?"

"Half dragon?" Destiny murmured, not shocked but reflective. She thought about her reoccurring dream. The brief moments she swore she flew.

"Ahh, so you already suspected," Elsie said softly.

"And you don't seem too happy about it," Maya noted.

"I never said that." She was right, though.

"You didn't have to," Jade replied. "It's all over your face."

"At least it's not terror," Maya pointed out, focusing on the positive.

"No, not terror." Destiny shook her head. "I felt a flash of that when I learned you were dragons, but it was quick. And now learning I might be, or am," she paused, thinking about it, "mostly, I just feel frustrated." She narrowed her eyes. "Almost as if I already knew what I was but ignored or repressed it. That I didn't want to be it."

Jade snorted. "Who wouldn't want to be a dragon?"

"It's not a fit for all," Maya reminded. "At least not at first." She looked at Destiny with compassion. "Where my sisters mostly loved embracing their dragons for the first time, it was rough for me."

When Maya hesitated, as if wondering how much she should share, Destiny urged her to go on.

"Well, dragons tend to run a little...intense sometimes," Maya revealed. "So it was hard for me to sync up."

"Just a *little* intense?" Jade chuckled. "More like we're dominant, kick-ass, top-of-the-food-chain beasts."

"Speak for yourself." Distress pulled Maya's brows together. "I feel no need to dominate over others and don't eat animals."

"Which is damn unnatural," Jade muttered, snagging some pepperoni off one of the snack plates.

"What the girls are getting at," Elsie intercepted, "is that as a rule, dragonkind runs on a lower frequency. Their nature is more primal and aggressive. Which, as you can imagine, might take some getting used to for someone like Maya."

Without a doubt. She looked at Maya. "Yet you have."

"Yes, with a lot of hard work, I've found balance."

"Translation?" Jade looked skyward, clearly baffled by anyone denying themselves such satisfaction. "She never shifts."

"So that's possible?"

"Sure," Jade said around her food. "If you want to live a boring life lacking any real pleasure." The corner of her mouth curled up. "Because trust me, repressing our inner beast zaps the fun out of things if you know what I mean."

"You have no way of knowing that," Maya grumbled.

"Uh, yeah, I do." Jade flinched and gave her a look. "So says your sad sex life and the fact you've never had an orgasm."

"Alright, that's enough." Elsie focused on Destiny. "Everyone has their own take on what it is to be dragon. You'll find your way as you go."

Or not, she thought, convinced that at some point, she knew exactly what she was and had no use for it. Yet, she could admit to being intrigued. Curious. Ready, no, *desperate* to learn more.

"Okay, okay, sweetheart." Elsie patted her knee. "If you're so eager, then the time must be right." She rummaged around in her pocket before pulling out another thin bracelet. "First, I insist you put this on. Not only will it protect me from however your dragon might react to my mental intrusion but give me a sense of your energy. Who you really are."

19

"And to connect you two, of course." Maya gestured at her own green rubber band looking bracelet. "We all have one."

"Yup." Jade pointed out her own thin black bracelet. "Each took on its own appearance the first time we wore it. A means to work with our energy." She started pacing again. "And of course, to suit our personalities. Mine works with about every outfit and helps me filter anything negative in the air. Naturally, Maya's looks like it supports Green Peace and helps her from floating off on a righteous cloud."

"It allows in just a smidge of negativity, so I don't transcend too far," Maya corrected. "If that happens, it could damage my inner dragon with too much positivity."

Destiny frowned. "Damage?"

"Yes." Maya sighed. "Perhaps even hurt it beyond repair."

"Which, in turn," Elsie said, "could hurt Maya beyond repair for her and her dragon cannot exist without each other."

"God, what you guys suffer sounds more like a curse than anything else," Destiny remarked, feeling for them.

"It has its ups and downs." Maya looked at her sister fondly. "But we've worked through it together and navigated our way with each other's help."

"Right," Jade echoed.

"And we'll help you too, Destiny," Maya went on. "You can count on us."

Jade nodded. "Damn straight."

Most would think she was nuts for trusting these women so quickly, but she did. Other than feeling like she'd known them for years, there was just something about them. A soul-deep alliance. As though she was connected to them not just on an emotional level but a physical one.

"I'll wear it," Destiny confirmed, nodding at the bracelet in Elsie's hand.

"Excellent." Elsie slipped another bracelet on then gave Destiny hers. "After you put it on, it will shift to something that suits you. Once we do our first session, the connection between us will form, and the bracelets will keep us connected. Then through me, you'll eventually connect to the others."

"Connect how?"

"It varies from sister to sister," Elsie enlightened. "Sometimes it's telepathic, other times, more of a sensation or instinct. With Raven, it will only ever be via some sort of darkness or negativity. Her vibration is far too low to communicate via the mind. That requires an elevated vibration."

Despite her still being a perfect stranger, that troubled Destiny a great deal. "How unfortunate for her."

"One can't miss what they've never experienced," Elsie said softly, her compassion for Raven evident. She gestured at Destiny's bracelet. "Go on, love. Put it on. Then I should have a good idea how to proceed."

"What do you mean?"

"Well, with every sister, it was different. Some needed absolute darkness to continue." She glanced at Maya. "Others needed to be brought out into the sunlight." Her gaze returned to Destiny. "Others needed...something in between."

Destiny glanced outside. The sun was nearly set, so hopefully, she didn't need sunlight. Either way, she had faith in Elsie to handle things as she saw fit.

So she slipped the bracelet on and began a journey she could never have imagined.

-Leviathan-

Chapter Three

THE MOMENT DESTINY slid her bracelet on, the fire roared and screamed up the chimney.

"Do you see that?" she whispered, not alarmed but drawn by the bright crimson at the heart of the flames. "What *is* it?"

"Something deliciously dark," Jade said in awe, drifting toward it.

"No." Destiny blocked her, not quite herself. "You cannot touch that, dragon. Not yet." She shook her head. "Perhaps never."

"What do you mean, dear?" Elsie said gently, coaxing forth whatever she sensed in Destiny. Her gaze went to the sea beyond the floor-to-ceiling windows, her voice suddenly different. Off somehow. "Take care, nieces. She's far more than we anticipated."

The fire roared even more, its flames twisting and curling around something. What *was* that? If she didn't know better, she'd think it a blade. A dagger, to be specific.

"Damn," Jade whispered, her attention on the sea now too. "Is that what I think it is?"

"It is." Maya drifted that way, her skin white as a ghost. "A Viking ship."

"Sit down, you two," Elsie ordered, her voice unnaturally stern. "*Now.*"

Though both were mesmerized by the sight of the ancient ship on roughening waters, they obediently sat. Thunder cracked, and lightning flashed over the phantom boat. Seething black clouds battled with the sun as it inched toward the horizon.

Destiny glanced from the ship to the dagger. The flames grew a fiery red before they centered around the metal and sparked various colors. First gold, then emerald green. Deep crimson simmered down to a glorious purplish-blue. Then, *boom*, turquoise flames flashed so brightly everyone had to look away.

Everybody but Destiny, that is.

As swiftly as the flames came, they went leaving nothing but ashes.

"It's gone," Maya said softly, sounding a little lost. "The ship's gone."

"It was naught but a ghost ship," Elsie murmured, her voice still different. "An echo of things to come."

"Oh hell," Jade exclaimed, awed. "So Vikings *are* our destiny?"

"Destiny is your destiny." Elsie joined Destiny, her gaze trained on the ashes as well. "There is something in there for you, child."

"Yes," she managed, intrigued yet hesitant.

"You must follow your instincts." When Elsie's gaze turned her way, she was met with black dragon eyes. "You must take what he gives you and come home."

Just like the voice in her nightmare had urged her to do.

Though most would be terrified at what appeared to be evil simmering in Elsie's gaze, she wasn't. Not at all. Instead, it felt kindred. Part of her. Egging her on. Trying to remind her. So she went to the hearth, more mesmerized by the moment. Compelled.

It was there.

Just beneath the simmering ashes.

A dagger unlike any other.

Its metal burned red as though just forged. But then, though clearly ancient, in some strange way, it *had* just been forged, hadn't it? She crouched and continued eyeing the embers.

While she knew what she had to do, she was suddenly hesitant.

"It will be all right, my child." When Elsie's hand landed on her shoulder, she knew it wasn't the older woman speaking to her but the voice from her dream. "It won't hurt you now any more than it did then. You just need to take it. Trust it. Make it yours."

The voice suddenly seemed strangely familiar. Loving. Gone from her for too long.

"Mother?" she whispered, emotional. "Is that you?"

Before this, she had no recollection of her mother. Had that been her at the end of the tunnel? The person she'd been so desperate to reach?

"Yes," Elsie responded, her voice more different still. Sad if Destiny wasn't mistaken. "It is time."

Time for what?

The moment she thought it, she was back in the tunnel from her dream. Back to the desperation she felt as she clawed her way down it, then flew, then stopped short.

He was there.

Coming.

Seeking her out to help her. Then end her.

Even as he aroused her.

"No," she growled, her voice animalistic.

The moment she said it, the vision snapped away, and the hearth returned. She no longer felt hesitation. This was right. *Hers.* Unafraid of being burned, she plunged her hand into the ashes and wrapped her fingers around the hilt at the exact moment the sun hit the horizon.

Instead of being burned, a pulse shot through her, and she felt revitalized.

"Sonofa," Jade whispered when Destiny stood with the ancient-looking blade in hand. "What *is* that?"

"The beginning," Elsie got out a split second before another pulse shot through Destiny, and everything exploded in fire.

The same fire that had wrapped around her and the Viking in her nightmare.

She should have been terrified, screaming, writhing in pain, but instead, she only felt courage and curiosity as flames engulfed her but never touched her. Much like it had been since Elsie and her nieces arrived, she felt accepting of everything. As if she were starting a new chapter.

Exhilaration turned to sheer eagerness.

What was on the other side of this? What would she see? Would she still be standing in her living room or somewhere else? She clenched her hand tighter around the blade's hilt and narrowed her eyes, surprised by how much she hoped she ended up elsewhere.

Perhaps wherever that Viking ship went.

She inhaled deeply, enjoying the searing heat entering her lungs when it should be torture. Her vision flared red, and her pulse kicked up about a thousand notches. Anticipation blew through her so strongly she nearly wept. Excitement she had no idea she craved to this degree.

Moments later, the fire faded, and she found herself alone in darkness.

"Destiny?" Elsie whispered, sounding oddly far away.

"I'm here." She remained perfectly still, determined not to panic when the courage she'd just felt vanished. The air turned icy. The darkness more cloying. "Where are you? Where are *we*?"

"I'm speaking to you within the mind," Elsie said gently, calming her nerves. *"You need to take a moment, Destiny. Allow your vision to adjust and let your other senses take over. What do you hear? Feel? Taste?"*

"Taste?" she managed, wishing Elsie was actually here. That she could reach out and touch her. Feel the warmth of human life in what felt like a cold, endless abyss. "What does taste matter?"

"Everything matters where you are," Elsie replied. *"Everything matters where you're going. Every bit of insight you can glean as you—"*

"As I what?" Destiny asked when Elsie's voice cut off and simply vanished.

She swallowed hard and tried to rally her courage. Elsie was right. The only way out of this was to pay attention to details. Rely on instincts that seemed to come alive more and more by the moment.

So she closed her eyes and focused. *Saw* when she couldn't actually see.

Just like in her nightmare, ocean waves crashed nearby. The air tasted of sea salt. Icy wind whipped through a tunnel that suddenly seemed familiar.

"I'm here," she nearly exclaimed but kept her mouth shut and her newfound blade at the ready.

This was it. The tunnel from her dream. The more she accepted that and let her other senses take over, the more her vision adjusted.

She saw her bracelet was now pearly white. Saw the damp stone walls at her side. Felt the craggy, uneven floor beneath her feet.

It became easier to walk without looking down. Without taking care. Rather, she made her way forward easily, not struggling toward something this time. Nor was there any fear. Instead, she walked with a sure-foot and renewed curiosity. She wasn't in twenty-first-century Maine anymore. She knew it without question.

Rather, she was with the Vikings.

While one part of her felt unexplainable disgust, another felt elated. Harsh resentment mixed with a sense of belonging.

"Why?" she ground out when she meant to keep quiet. Yet she said it again, then once more before she slowed.

Was that a glimmer of light ahead? Was that, at long last, the end of her tunnel?

"It is," Elsie seemed to whisper from far away. *"Follow it, child. Follow where your mother led you…"*

So she did. Faster. Closer. So damn eager, she imagined she flew though she didn't. She simply moved gracefully. Without hindrance. As if navigating cold, dark places came naturally. Would she see what had been hidden from her for so long? Understand all the things she'd forgotten? Perhaps find her mother?

Moreover, her traitorous mind wondered, would she run into him? Her Viking? Would he be waiting at the end? Would he finally show his face in the light of day or remain in the shadows like the coward she was beginning to think him?

It just so happened she found out seconds later.

Chapter Four

Scandinavia
960 A.D.

"BLOCK HIM, THORULF," Leviathan warned, watching his protégés battle. "You know what's coming."

Sure as Midgard was one of the Nine Worlds, Dagr's eyes turned black, and he got by Thorulf's defenses. He pressed his blade against his cousin's neck and grinned. "You will have to be faster than that if you ever hope to beat me again."

Though Dagr's father and stepmother were dragons, his birth mother was Hel, Goddess of Helheim. Thorulf grumbled something about an unfair advantage and stepped away before Dagr could gloat some more.

"You have godliness in you too, Thorulf," Leviathan reminded. "You just need to learn how to better harness it."

"Celtic godliness will never be able to compete with Helheim's power," Thorulf grunted, sheathing his blade. "I'll just have to learn to outmaneuver him."

Dagr chuckled and sheathed his blade as well before clasping Thorulf on the shoulder. "Perhaps it's best to accept that I'm the better warrior."

"I'll do no such thing." Over his angst in record time, Thorulf winked at their growing harem of female admirers and shot Dagr a crooked grin. "There are better things to do at the moment than battle, though, are there not, cousin?"

"That can wait." Leviathan gestured that they join him. Because he was an Ancient and aged much slower, he appeared the same age as his protégés. "First, we must discuss the growing unrest not just in our neighboring communities but within the Realm."

Created by their Great Serpent ancestor, Níðhöggr, the Realm was a place on Midgard or Earth for dragons to come together. It was also where Leviathan had been tasked to ready the children born of the last generation for a Great War. Now those children were men, and he sensed the clock ticking down.

More specifically, he feared his actions of late might have somehow set things in motion.

"Have we not discussed it enough already?" Dagr's attention lingered on the women. "We know the Great War might be on the horizon and are prepared."

"Are you then?" Leviathan perked a brow. "More weapons still need to be made." He gestured at the Sigdir's Viking Fortress. "The walls better fortified."

In truth, King Sven had taken good care of things over the years, and their armory was well supplied, but that wasn't the point. Though Leviathan had trained Dagr and Thorulf plenty, and they were almost where they needed to be, the likes of what might be coming set him on edge. Mainly because he didn't know from whence it came. They could fight fellow Viking tribes well enough, but he suspected things wouldn't be that simple when it came to the gods warring above them.

"We could not be better prepared, friend, and you know it." Thorulf crossed his arms over his chest and eyed Leviathan. "Ever since you returned from Scotland, you have been different." His gaze narrowed. "Uptight. Changed." He glanced from the women to Leviathan. "Perhaps because you have not enjoyed the pleasures of one woman, let alone the several you usually indulge in."

"He's right." Dagr shook his head. "And it has you in a fouler mood than ever. One you should assuage so that—"

"I'm fine," Leviathan groused, knowing full well they were right. He had tried to enjoy a woman, several in fact, but could not. Instead, for the first time in his long existence, his stubborn cock remained flaccid, and his mind on the redhead who had affected him too profoundly.

So much so that he feared he might never enjoy a woman's sweet flesh again.

He had no one to blame but himself, though. When he helped his kin in Scotland and Ireland, he'd done something detrimental. Something he thought he'd be able to walk away from, but it seemed he was mistaken. He rested his hand on the hilt of the dagger sheathed at his waist and tried to put her from his mind, but she wasn't budging. Not her long flaming red curls, her bright turquoise eyes, or most especially, her sinfully voluptuous body.

"What happened when you went to our kin's aid anyway?" Thorulf's gaze fell to Leviathan's dagger. One he had obtained in Ireland from that very woman. "You told us some of it, but I suspect not all."

"It was just as I said. I went to help kin." Specifically the Sigdirs' descendants, considering he traveled forward through time to get there. "Things were resolved, but measures had to be taken. Measures that may or may not affect us here."

He knew chances were good that what he'd done there sparked something. Or better put, started the wheels spinning toward something that might change all of their lives considerably. He needed to visit his seer again. Seek her council. See if something had changed with her predictions.

"Are women from the future traveling back in time again?" Dagr leaned against a tree, sighing when Leviathan motioned that the women meandering nearby be on their way. "Is that what this is about?"

Thorulf's stepmother and grandmother were from the twenty-first century, so it wasn't an unusual question to ask. Time travelers were a part of their community, going back several generations now. Each generation of Sigdir men seemed destined for women from the future. So they were prepared for the possibility of mating with one female, be she a dragon or not.

Generally speaking, Dagr and Thorulf, who were as close as brothers, didn't seem particularly worried about it. But then they were of the mind they would continue their carousing ways after. Usually, that would amuse Leviathan because it had yet to work out that way for other Sigdirs, but not today. He was too tense. Out of sorts. More alert than usual.

"I don't know if women will be traveling back, but you best be prepared." He eyed the darkening sky and incoming storm. It wasn't of the gods, but it was off. Telling somehow. "Something is changing."

"Coming," Dagr murmured, gazing at the horizon. His eyes flickered with darkness. "From far away."

"Yes," Thorulf said just as softly. Cool wind gusted. His dragon eyes narrowed on the north as if he sensed something specific. "Something...or *someone*..."

Thunder cracked, and Leviathan's vision hazed red.

Someone *was* coming.

When phantom fire suddenly flared around him without touching his skin, he knew who.

"Loki's cock," he growled when the flames vanished as quickly as they had come, taking his dagger with them. "She's got it."

"Who's got what?" Like Thorulf, Dagr had his blade at the ready. "What just happened, Leviathan? What kind of fire was that? Because it felt—"

Leviathan didn't linger to answer but embraced his dragon and headed north. She was here. He could sense her. *Feel* her. And it was the most he'd felt in months. The most he had felt since last he saw her. When she no longer remembered who he was.

"Do not follow," he roared into Dagr's and Thorulf's minds, but it was too late. They had already shifted and were in pursuit.

"Who is she?" Thorulf asked, his interest more than just mere curiosity. So said the blaze in his dragon's eyes when he caught up with Leviathan. *"She feels...unique... unequaled."*

Leviathan growled before he could stop himself, but his dragon didn't like what Thorulf's beast was putting off. The obvious desire his protégé felt without having even seen her yet.

"She's mine," he bit out, cursing how territorial he sounded. *"Until I say otherwise."*

If he said otherwise.

Which he would. Eventually. Once he knew she meant no harm to his brethren. Or so he kept telling himself as they closed in on the

Realm in record time. He landed and shifted at the mouth of one of the northern seaside caves.

"Do you understand me?" He narrowed his eyes at Dagr and Thorulf when they landed and shifted beside him. "She's off-limits until I determine her purpose here."

"You mean until you've been between her thighs," Thorulf cut back, his disposition off with good reason. She was close. Here somewhere. And there was no missing her sweet feminine scent. She was dragon, and something had her aroused.

Not just aroused, he realized with frustration. She was in *heat*.

Thorulf and Dagr might be large, but they weren't as big as Leviathan. Nor were they half as feared and respected among dragons. He had fought hard to get where he was and wouldn't have his arch-alpha status challenged. Especially not by dragons who'd been alive less than three decades.

So he faced off with Thorulf, glaring at him in a way no dragon could mistake.

"Whether I ride her or set her aside is my business," he ground out, his tone dangerous. "Until then, she belongs to me. Do you understand?" He stepped even closer, his gaze lethal. "Do you, Thorulf?"

Unfortunately, where most would back down in fear, Thorulf was one of Leviathan's own. They might not be blood-related, but he had formed a connection with him and his brethren that went deep. So Thorulf wasn't overly intimidated. He did, however, finally nod, clearly seeing something in Leviathan he'd not seen before.

"I don't know who you think you are," came an all-too-familiar female voice from deeper in the cave. "But I sure as heck don't *belong* to you."

Leviathan forgot to breathe when she emerged out of the darkness with his dagger at the ready.

Or, more appropriately put, her dagger at one time.

"Destiny," he said, his voice hoarser than he would have liked. How was it she'd only grown more beautiful? Her smooth bronzed skin was flawless, and her red curls luxurious and wild. Where he'd thought her turquoise eyes might not be so bright after what she'd been through, they remained large and vibrant. Mesmerizing.

Then there was her body.

Hell and damnation.

Based on the tightly-wound tension of the men on either side of him, they were acutely aware of not just her stunning appearance but her sinful physique. With long, shapely legs that went on forever, she was taller than most women. Her slender curves tempted, and her well-rounded breasts were built to be admired. Lusted after. Stroked and caressed. Add to that the unmistakable scent coming off her, and at long last, his cock stirred to life.

Most women who'd traveled through time and ended up in a dark cave blocked by three large Vikings would show fear, but Destiny did no such thing. Instead, she kept her blade steady, and her gaze narrowed on him. "How do you know my name?" Her eyes narrowed even further. "And how do I know you...because I do, don't I?"

Like Thorulf and Dagr, he could speak English, so conversing with her wasn't an issue.

"We have crossed paths before," he conceded, trying his damndest to lose his untimely erection. Good thing he wore one of his longer leather jerkins.

"Crossed paths?" She shook her head. "You've been haunting my dreams for months now, and..." Her brows pulled together. "We actually met, though, didn't we? Before that...somewhere far away."

"We did." She had dreamt of him as he dreamt of her? Endlessly? Ceaselessly? "My name is Leviathan, and in time, I will explain everything."

"Leviathan," she whispered. Her skin drained of color. "I know that name."

He chilled at the change in her tone. The haunted look that suddenly appeared in her eyes.

"Yes, you know my name," he confirmed but had a bad feeling it wasn't for the right reasons. Something she confirmed soon after.

"I know you because you're supposed to kill me."

Chapter Five

DESTINY MIGHT BE trembling on the inside but showed the monstrous men blocking her way out no fear. Icy wind blew, and angry, churning waves beneath a stormy sky lent a sinister backdrop to her imposing visitors. She kept her blade at the ready as if she knew how to use it and summoned every ounce of courage she could muster.

"What makes you think I intend to kill you?" Leviathan asked, replying to her revelation.

A delicious, all-too-familiar thrill rushed through her at the deep timbre of his voice. It not only brought back more recent dreams about him but ones she had forgotten. Deeply sensual, wild dreams that made it nearly impossible to think straight. She'd never seen him in his entirety, though, and that was probably a good thing.

She would have never left her bed.

Like the other two, he was tall, well-muscled, and broad-shouldered, but that's where the similarities ended. The others were certainly handsome, but he was striking in a way that liquefied her. His features were chiseled and masculine, and his disposition fierce. He had longish black hair with skinny braids interwoven, numerous tattoos, several piercings, and multiple slashes through one eyebrow.

"It came to me in a dream," Destiny managed in answer to Leviathan's question. "You were going to kill me."

"If I intended to kill you," his searing gaze pinned her, "you would already be dead."

"Thor's thunder," one of the men muttered and shook his head. Like Leviathan, his hair was black as night, only he had more facial hair. "Don't mind him, Destiny. Ancients tend to be more direct than most." He smiled and nodded hello, unmistakable interest in his thickly lashed dark chocolate brown eyes. "I am Thorulf Sigdir, Son of Soren, Agatha, and Ava."

He had two mothers? She offered a small nod hello in return, keeping one eye on Leviathan at all times. She might crave him with a ferociousness that left her winded, but that didn't mean she trusted him.

"And I am Dagr Sigdir, Son of Eirik, Kenzie and Goddess Hel." The other man nodded hello and grinned, his blue eyes twinkling with unmistakable wickedness. He had a heavy five-o'clock shadow, and his dark sun-streaked hair was interwoven with braids and pulled back. "It's a pleasure to meet you, Destiny."

What was with these guys having multiple mothers? Must be a Viking thing. And had he said one of them was a *goddess*? Somehow that's what got her in the end. Not the men themselves with their heavy fur cloaks and various weapons, but the pure absurdity of her situation.

She had, without a doubt, traveled back in time.

The daunting part? It didn't bother her in the least. Rather, she felt the same sense of curiosity she'd felt back home. Trying to gather herself, she stepped back. Not to run from them, because where would she go, but a mere stumble as she came to grips with things. As she felt not fright but sinful excitement.

As if something were slowly but surely coming to life inside her.

"Are you well?" Thorulf went to step forward but stopped short when Leviathan issued a deep-chested growl of warning.

Fortunately, his possessive attitude snapped her out of her momentary stupor, and she frowned. Best to make things clear no matter how much he turned her on. "We might share some sort of connection I've yet to understand, Leviathan," she shook her head, "but again, I don't belong to you." She glanced from Dagr to Thorulf. "No man, for that matter."

She might not know much about herself, but she was certain of that. Whoever she was, or had been, she'd been independent. Of her own mind at all times. No man, dragon or otherwise, intimidated her.

"Dragons," she whispered, somehow seeing it clearly now. The added danger around all three men. The primal undercurrent running just beneath the surface. She hadn't seen them when they arrived here but knew they had flown. That they'd just embraced their inner beasts.

In what seemed a direct response to her thought, her vision flared red and vivid. The world appeared crisper. Heat signatures became obvious. She was seeing through her dragon's eyes, wasn't she?

And it didn't faze her in the least.

"No," Leviathan growled under his breath, ceasing both men this time when their dragon eyes erupted in response. Fiery cat-like eyes similar to what she'd seen in her mind when she looked at Maya.

"Put your dragon away, woman," Leviathan bit out. His eyes flickered with fire, his own inner dragon, before he got control, and they returned to normal. His body language, however, was another story. Every muscle strained as if it took a tremendous amount of effort to hold himself back. "They're good men but pups nonetheless. They don't have the willpower to resist the likes of you for long." He shook his head. "Not in your current state."

Dagr and Thorulf muttered something about being able to control themselves just fine, but she wasn't so sure. Not based on how harshly they breathed. How intensely they looked at her. The unmistakable desire and raw lust.

"And what *state* do you think I'm currently in?" Though they could overpower her if they wanted to, she kept her blade at the ready. "What are you talking about?"

"You're in heat," Leviathan stated bluntly. His stern gaze went from man to man. "Go back to the Fortress and let them know the time Níðhöggr spoke of has arrived." He shook his head once. "Don't shift and rile her inner dragon but take one of my boats."

When neither moved, their feral eyes still locked on her, their willpower teetering, Leviathan growled again and unsheathed his blade. That seemed to do the trick because they finally listened, vanishing down a path cut into the rock without a backward glance.

She frowned, not liking the sound of being in *heat* like she was some kind of animal. But then she supposed if she were half dragon, that's exactly what she was. "Is that what I can expect from all men here?"

"Yes, if they are dragons." He sheathed his blade. "Until you learn to stop enticing them so much."

She kept her blade right where it was, somehow more threatened by being alone with him. Her skin burned, and breathing became more difficult. "Why does it sound like you're blaming me? As if I can control whatever the hell this is?"

"Because I am, and you can," he replied, yet again blunt to a fault. "At least somewhat once you have better control of your inner beast." He yanked off his fur cloak as if he were overheated too. "I will help you as much as I can on our return, then leave you to Freya."

How sweet. *Not.* "Return where? And who's Freya?"

"A friend." Leviathan gestured at a nearby rock and proceeded to mortify her. "Sit and focus on the sea until your need for me passes." He tossed her his cloak, raked his gaze over her one last time, then turned away as if that would help. "Once your lust has passed, you will grow cold. Put that on."

"Aren't you a charmer," she muttered, surprised by the weight of the fur. "I don't need to sit, and you aren't all that, sweetheart."

"You will need to sit." His tone turned cold. "And I am not your sweetheart."

"No, you're not," she agreed but heck if he wasn't right when the masculine scent of his fur hit her. An irritating but telling ache sprang to life between her thighs, making her legs so weak she did, in fact, need to sit.

"Why give the thing to me in the first place, then?" she grumbled under her breath before she could stop herself. "Considering the irritating results it might have."

"Because you will get cold," Leviathan reminded. He crossed his arms over his chest and kept his gaze locked firmly on the ocean. "Now do as I said, and it will pass."

"Why?"

"Why what?"

"Why will it pass?"

"Because our dragons are no longer looking at one another," he explained. "Once you embrace your dragon, or even, in your case, accept your dragon, it should become easier."

"Why do I detect a tone?" She tried to keep her gaze on the sea, but it kept drifting back to him. The firm globes of his ass beneath his leather tunic and the cut of his long, muscular legs. "Where did we meet before, Leviathan? Who was I? And why does it sound like I wasn't crazy about being half dragon?"

"We will talk when the time is right," he cut back, curter than ever. "Until then, do as I asked and stop looking at me."

"I'm not looking at you."

"You are."

"How do you know?"

"Because I can feel it," he growled. "Feel *you*." As if catching himself, he shook his head. "I'm an Ancient. We know things Midgard dragons don't. Sense things they do not."

"Just how ancient are you?" she joked, trying to focus on the ocean rather than him.

"Though the Scots and many of my own people think me centuries older, I'm actually far younger," he replied, clearly not pleased with what he considered a short lifespan. "I've only been on Midgard around seventy years."

Again, she wasn't as shocked as she should be despite him looking like he was in his twenties. "Seriously?"

"*Ja.*" He nodded, repeating what he'd said in English. "Yes." He cocked his head a little as if sensing her. "That doesn't surprise you even though it should?"

"No." She frowned. "Any idea why?"

She probably should have toned down the whole I-don't-know-who-I-am-thing from the start, so she didn't seem so vulnerable, but that ship had sailed.

"No, I don't know why my age doesn't shock you," he replied a little too quickly. "See to yourself, woman, so that we might get back to the Keep before it storms."

"Destiny," she warned, never so sure of anything. "Don't call me *woman* again."

"But you are female, are you not?"

"Just don't," she reiterated, finally dragging her eyes away and focusing on the sea. "It makes me feel beneath you, and I'm not."

Not yet anyway, her inner voice taunted. She squeezed her eyes shut then focused on the ocean again before unwanted thoughts bubbled up. Hot erotic ones that had no place in her situation.

Because she *was* in a situation, however undaunted she still felt by it.

"What year is it?" she asked, focusing on getting her bearings instead. "And what part of Scandinavia are we in?"

He shared the year then stated, "Northern Norway, as time travelers call it."

"So time travelers are common here?"

"*Ja.*" He nodded. "More come every twenty-five to thirty years or so."

All, as she soon learned, from the very chalet she'd just left in Maine. Women who had connected with Viking dragons across time and fallen in love.

"And now I'm here," she muttered, cursing under her breath when her vision returned to normal, and a vicious chill did, indeed, whip through her. She finally wrapped his fur around her, grateful for the warmth despite his scent being all over it. "Why am I here, Leviathan? And why do I still get the sense you want to kill me even though you desire me?"

Because as disciplined as he might be, he was just as vulnerable to her as Dagr and Thorulf.

"I don't entirely know." He finally turned and met her eyes before his gaze dropped to her dagger. "Other than to say it likely has to do with that."

He wasn't being entirely truthful, was he? Something bothered him greatly. Something he wasn't sharing. Not yet anyway. Did it have to do with her mother? Why he'd seemed in league with her? Destiny had hoped to discover her at the end of the tunnel, but there was no sign of anyone else. But then, she somehow realized upon exiting the tunnel that it wasn't the same one from her nightmare after all. Nor did she think this was the cave she'd been so desperate to get to.

Yet, in some unknown way, it all tied together because of this blade.

For the first time since she emerged, she really looked at the dagger. It was by no means grand. Aged and weathered, dull and worn, its metal appeared blackened. As though it had suffered the fires of hell itself. She felt the weight of it. The way the hilt seemed to fit perfectly in her palm.

"This is mine," she whispered, never so sure of anything. Her gaze rose to his face. "Isn't it?"

And it was what he'd been trying to give her in her nightmare. What her mother had wanted her to take.

"Yes," he replied gravely. "But it's also mine. Of my people and homeworld."

"Homeworld," she said softly, sensing something. Understanding. "You're not immortal, just age slower."

"*Ja.*" He nodded once. "My parents were born on dragonkind's homeworld, Múspellsheimr, which makes me an Ancient, or first-generation dragon on Midgard."

"Right," she murmured, thinking about that. "One of the Nine Worlds in Norse Mythology." She blinked, never more certain. "They're real...just like the gods...many gods." Her gaze returned to his face. "Dagr wasn't kidding, was he? He really is Goddess Hel's son."

"He is." Leviathan appeared ready to say something but seemed to change his mind. "We must get back." He gestured that she follow him. "For your arrival *does* mark the beginning of something."

"And what is that?"

The answer she got was the last thing she expected.

-Leviathan-

Chapter Six

"WHAT MAKES YOU think my arrival marks the beginning of some foretold Great War?" Destiny asked. "What aren't you telling me, Leviathan?"

Torch in hand, Leviathan led her through the caves leading deeper into the Realm, grateful she followed so peaceably when she might have done otherwise. But then he sensed her unending curiosity. Her quest to figure out who she was. Why she was here.

A godly storm was rolling in, so he refrained from using magic to dress her appropriately. Once they got to the Keep, he'd see her into sturdy boots and suitable clothing. After getting over the initial shock and lust of seeing her, he realized what she wore was half the problem. Not just for functional but physical reasons. While her clothing might be loose on some, it hugged her body in ways that made it hard for men to think. From the way her breasts strained against her top to how her trousers gripped her thighs and hugged her firm, perfectly rounded backside.

The last time he saw her, she hadn't dressed so enticingly. Rather, she wore more conservative clothes that, even then, didn't hide enough of her body to suit him. Or so he tried to convince himself. Better yet, his dragon. If his inner beast had its way, she'd never wear another shred of clothing the rest of her days.

He cursed under his breath and tried to focus on the tunnel ahead rather than the curves of her body. Her fiery sweet scent. The way her breathing hitched every time he stepped too close. How much he liked his fur wrapped around her, held up to allow for their height differences.

"Leviathan?" She stopped short and looked at him, unafraid of being alone with him deep in a Scandinavian cave over a thousand years in her past. Surprising considering what he'd done to her when last they met. Yet, it seemed she had no recollection of that. At least for now. He suspected it was working its way to the surface, though, considering how well she was taking all this. How easily she accepted things that should terrify her.

"*Ja?*" he replied.

"What aren't you telling me?" she repeated, cocking her head. "Why do you think my arrival marks some Great War?"

"Because my seer has seen it." He kept his answer vague for now, no matter how tempted he was to share it all. To tell her about their time in Scotland and Ireland together. How she had once been so much more than she could imagine. Still was, as far as he was concerned. "It was said that a woman fitting your description would travel here from the future and..."

And what? He frowned, not ready to tell her the whole of it. Not when he realized how much he'd wanted her to travel back. To risk her safety just so he could be near her again. He had no right to want such. Not after all she'd sacrificed. Yet he'd still longed for it. Hoped that somehow his seer's ominous narrative would change upon her arrival.

That he would not have to end her life to save his people.

He knew more than most exactly what that would feel like. How excruciating it would be. Only this time would be worse because it would be final.

And that terrified him.

Before meeting her, he'd never felt fear. It wasn't an emotion natural to his species nor one he could afford. Yet she'd invoked it. Forced his inner dragon to feel it. Then ignore it for the greater good. For *her*. He clenched his jaw and denied it even as it simmered to the surface.

What she had asked of him.

What he'd finally done to her.

"And what else did your seer say?" Destiny prompted when he trailed off, in no mood to tell her the entirety of his diviner's prophetic words just yet. That Destiny was absolutely right.

He would be the one to kill her. Had to be.

"Damn it, just answer me already." She frowned, growing more agitated by the moment. "What else did the seer say about me?"

It was on the tip of his tongue to tell her everything, start to finish, if for no other reason than to make her stop looking at him. To turn those almond-shaped eyes in any other direction before they sucked him in.

But he hesitated. Paused. Wasn't ready to turn her gaze away permanently quite yet.

"My seer said you would be needed," he finally relented. "Little more."

"Yet the look on your face makes me wonder." Destiny searched his eyes, not shying away, still so very much *her* under all the forgotten memories. "How is it I'm needed but get the overwhelming sense that beneath your animalistic desire for me, you *will* end me." She kept an ever-handy grip on her dagger. "More so that you'll do it with this blade."

He tensed but kept emotion from his face. She was skirting too close to the truth. One she wasn't ready for. Not just about what he must do but what he'd already done.

"I have no intention of killing you, Destiny." Not yet. "The weather is worsening outside." He continued walking. "We need to press on."

"Why are you so worried about the weather?" She shook her head. "Seems strange for a guy who's half Viking, half dragon."

"It's been more off than usual lately," he muttered. "Far too unnatural."

"Like deadly monsoons and blizzards?"

"Worse." They continued walking. "Not of this world."

"So of another Norse world?"

"In part," he replied. "Other worlds are involved too."

"I don't understand." She considered him. "Like other planets? Ones seen through a telescope?"

"No." He shook his head. "Worlds that people think are mythological."

Startled, she stopped short again and narrowed her eyes in sudden understanding. "You're talking about the Celts, aren't you? Celtic mythology?"

"I am." He wasn't surprised she picked up on it so quickly, considering who she was. "I fear the battle heading our way is a by-product of a much larger war. One between the gods."

"The Norse and the Celts," she murmured as though on the verge of remembering something that might be helpful. As if at one time she might have foreseen or understood what was coming. Lost in thought, she kept walking, muttering to herself. "This must be what Elsie was referring to. What her nieces are readying themselves for. What's their part in it, though? My part? Why was I put in charge of them?"

"What are you talking about?" He scowled and shook his head. "Who's Elsie? What nieces?"

When Destiny kept walking, still lost in thought, he grabbed her wrist only to realize that wasn't the wisest thing to do. Not only because of her wariness of him but because of an ability to fight she'd forgotten but was clearly coming back to her.

She spun fast and nearly had her blade against his neck before he deflected it. He tossed the torch to the ground then dodged right and left when she thrust twice, close to nicking him. When she came at him a third time with even more precision, he decided immobilizing her was best. So he knocked the blade from her grasp and pinned her against the wall.

"What *was* that?" she gasped. "How did I do that?" Before he could respond, Destiny's curiosity morphed back to fierceness. Her dragon eyes flared, her warning ground out through clenched teeth. "Let me go."

"And risk your blade in my throat?" He shook his head. "Not yet. Not until you get your dragon under control and realize I'm not your enemy."

Yet he was, and they both knew it.

He could, *should*, let her go and keep fighting. Battle until the end. See the prophecy through here and now. Protect his people and brethren. Finish her before she bewitched him even more. Before her sweet, permeating scent pushed him too far, and he gave in.

Perhaps that was the way, he reasoned.

Maybe if he finally had what was lost to him before, she would be out of his system. He could take her now. Rip her clothes away, hike her against the cold stone, and lose himself in her hot receptive body. It would be that simple. Soaked and ready, she would have him. Eager in her heated state for all he could give her.

Once he slaked his lust, surely his horrible craving for her would vanish. Then killing her for the greater good would come easier. After all, he was a born fighter. Warrior. An Ancient. Battling and winning was what he did best.

Yet something about taking her now, then ending her didn't feel like winning.

"Will you stand down?" he ground out, painfully aroused, disgusted with himself for not being stronger. "Sheath your blade, and I'll tell you why you know how to fight. Who you once were."

While he wanted to know more about Elsie and her nieces, women he suspected would be traveling back in time, they needed to deal with this first.

Destiny eyed him for a long moment, her internal struggle obvious. The scent of her arousal unmistakable. She wanted to be in control yet still taken. Slake her lust. Experience what he had to offer. Understood on a primal level that he would see her well satisfied. He would, too. Because she'd never been taken by a dragon. She'd loathed their kind.

In the end, however, she showed admirable willpower.

"I'll stand down," she finally conceded. "But you better not touch me again without my permission."

He didn't miss the slightly strangled sound of her voice when she said 'without my permission.' As though she hadn't meant to say it but couldn't help herself. More pointedly, that some part of her *wanted* to give him permission. Arousal aside, her mind craved his touch. A sense of intimacy he was altogether unfamiliar with when it came to women.

Except for when they last met.

When their minds and souls connected in a way he feared there was no turning from.

"Agreed." He stepped back but remained cautious. Not just because her fighting skills were returning but because he suspected they would only grow. Become what they once were. Which meant consulting with his seer was more urgent than ever now. He needed to find out why her powers were growing when he'd been led to believe they were gone.

First, however, he had to tell Destiny what she had forgotten. Who she really was and how very powerful she'd once been.

Chapter Seven

DESTINY FROZE, UNSURE she'd heard Leviathan correctly. "You can't be serious."

Yet she sensed deep down he was.

That she was precisely what he claimed.

"I am serious." He scooped up the torch, his disposition fouler by the moment. "You were once a Celtic demi-god."

"How do you know that?" She pursued when he continued down the tunnel. "What happened to me? Why did I end up in Maine?" She shook her head. "And what do you mean, *once* a demi-god? Why aren't I one now?"

Destiny struggled to remember but kept getting distracted by Leviathan himself, which frustrated her to no end. She wanted her memories back. Not to obsess over the likes of him.

Yet her body and mind thought otherwise. Especially after what he'd just done. What she felt when he slammed her against the wall and subdued her. Came close and threatened her. When she felt the searing heat of his strong body. The thick ridge of his straining arousal.

"I know what you were because we met when you were still a goddess." Leviathan didn't bother slowing. "Then you were not."

If she wasn't mistaken, he tried to flee her. Escape from something he didn't want to face or feel.

"Coward," she muttered under her breath.

"What did you call me?" His thunderous gaze swung back before he grunted something about not being bated and continued on.

She could say it again, challenge him, but sensed he was well trained against letting others get the better of him. So she chose to keep up instead and get to the bottom of things. A task that would undoubtedly be monumental when it came to him.

Best to fish. See what he would let slip.

"Why did I lose my godliness?" she asked again. "Did you have something to do with it? No doubt you did. Why else would you haunt my dreams? Try to give me my dagger? Keep me from the end of the tunnel? From getting to my mother?"

"I know nothing of your mother," he grunted.

Had she detected a strange octave to his voice?

"I think you do." She shook her head when he climbed a ledge then held out his hand in assistance. "What I'm trying to figure out is why you're trying to come between us." She hoisted herself up and narrowed her eyes at him. "Was she dragon or god?"

Though his expression never wavered, she swore she sensed his thoughts. Then, for a flicker of a moment, swore flames curled around them again. Those from her nightmare. The same ones that swept her back in time. Yet it was too quick to be sure.

Best to stay focused on the matter at hand. "And who was my father? Because you knew him, didn't you?"

When Leviathan's pupils flared, and his eyes narrowed on their surroundings, she realized the flames *had* been there. Moreover, that he might have recognized them.

"You saw them too, didn't you?" she asked. "The flames that were just around us?"

"No," he bit out and kept moving. "And get out of my mind, woman."

She'd been in his mind?

"Isn't he feisty," came an unexpected telepathic voice. *"Smokin' hot too."*

Jade? She nearly said her name aloud but decided it best to keep her communications from him for now. Anyone here, for that matter. So she tried speaking within her mind only to realize how easy it was.

"Where's Elsie?" she replied. *"Is she okay? She got cut off earlier."*

"Yeah, everything's fine. It's just a choppy connection thanks to the thousand years or so between us," Jade replied. *"She'll come through when she can. It looks like we all will, considering I just connected with you. Probably because of the sinfully low vibration coming off the guy you're with. He's in a hell of a mood, huh?"*

"Pretty sure it's just his normal disposition," she muttered in return. *"So your vibration thing works across time too?"*

"Seems so," Jade confirmed. *"I imagine Maya will get through when you're around more positive people."* She chuckled. *"Which is just fine with me if I get to tune in around the likes of him. Is that your Viking and—"*

That's all Jade got out before her voice cut off just like Elsie's had earlier. Though she wondered why, what it meant, she was more curious about Leviathan's evasiveness at the moment. He'd said he would tell her what she wanted to know, yet he seemed pretty close-lipped.

"I want answers, Leviathan." She caught up with him, glad to see a glimmer of light ahead. "Who are my parents? Where are they?" When he didn't respond right away, she pressed him. "You told me you'd tell me everything, yet you've barely said a word. Please, I deserve to know. Anyone in my position would."

She frowned when she sensed not only hesitancy but a flash of fear and angst.

"That's coming from you, isn't it?" she whispered before she cleared her throat. "I'm sensing your mind and—"

"You don't belong in it uninvited," he snapped, spinning on her in unexpected anger. "Nobody should be in my mind uninvited, and *nobody* should be able to read my thoughts." His dragon eyes flared. "*Especially* a woman who detests what she is so much."

"You mean being a dragon." Though her back was to the wall again, she wasn't any more intimidated by him this time than she was the last. Likely because she knew he struggled with harming her. The idea of it became harder by the moment.

"Why, though?" She frowned. "Why did I hate being a dragon so much?" Because she had. She was certain of it. "And how do you know that?" She narrowed her eyes and challenged him. "I would think you'd rather tell me than have my dragon pull it from your mind. Because she can, can't she?"

51

She might be new to this, but she had a feeling her dragon was capable. It had some kind of power over him. More specifically, she sensed they'd already merged or were currently merging in a way that both angered and terrified him.

"Perhaps that's the key," he murmured. "Perhaps if I tell you everything, your dragon will leave me be." He shook his head. "Because I will not have this. You and only you. *One* woman." His scowl deepened. "That's not how I work."

"No," she murmured, understanding where at least some of his fear and anger came from. Or should she say her inner dragon understood. "Because you don't do mates."

Interestingly, part of her concurred. Neither did she. Yet another part, namely an inner beast she became more familiar with by the moment, got riled at the thought. She shook her head and frowned at her dragon's defiance. Its stubbornness when it came to him.

"I don't do mates either." She swore the words soured in her mouth even as she muttered them. "And definitely not with you."

"Not with anyone, then," he ground out before he cursed under his breath at his rather possessive sounding declaration. His jaw locked, and his unsettled gaze lingered on her face before, clearly needing some distance between them, he continued walking. "I'll tell you what I know."

Good. Finally. Or so she thought until he shared some hard truths.

It seemed she had forfeited her godliness to save a family lineage in Scotland. If that weren't enough, her mother was a Viking dragon, and her father none other than Donn Fírinne, the Celtic God of Death.

Death? Truly? Yet, once again, she knew Leviathan spoke plainly.

"Though he's still likely licking his wounds, you defeated your father, and all ended well," Leviathan said in conclusion. "Having lost your memory along with your godliness, you were given a new life in Maine to start over."

"Who gave me this new life?" She tried to ignore the irritating hurt blossoming. "Was it you? If so, why?" Her sense of hurt only grew. More so, a feeling of abandonment that had nothing to do with her parents and everything to do with him. "We shared some sort of deep connection, didn't we? Something that terrified you, so you left me behind…let me go?"

"There was no future for us." She swore pain flashed in his eyes before they hardened. "We didn't get along, and that won't change."

"That's not true," she murmured, sensing his thoughts more strongly this time. They might not have gotten along at first, but in the end, something changed. They saw something in each other they understood. That connected them. "What happened to us, Leviathan? Because I know…" Suddenly, a memory slammed into her out of nowhere. She was walking past him in a Stonehenge. Felt a strong sense of familiarity. Asked him if she knew him. "You said we didn't know each other, but we did. We knew each other intimately somehow."

"No," he growled, his mood fouler still as they, at last, exited the cave.

She might want answers but lost her train of thought at the astounding view in front of her.

"Oh, *wow*." Dumbfounded, she looked from the sweeping mountains surrounding several staggered lakes to the monstrous golden ash on the highest peak. From there, her attention went to the stunning gothic-style castle near the tree.

All that wasn't what really got her, though. Not when magnificent winged creatures sailed overhead, their long serpentine bodies carrying them at incredible speeds.

"Dragons," she whispered, taken by the sight. Emotional. How could she *not* want to be one of them? Fly free like that, high above the world?

She blinked, waiting for fear to slam into her, but it never did. Instead, her vision hazed red, and heat flared beneath her skin. In what appeared a direct response, Leviathan eyed the dragons and released a low, threatening sound. They must have caught it, better yet heeded it, because they swung around and flew in the opposite direction.

"I tried to keep them from shifting, boss," came a woman's voice, "but the moment they caught her scent, there was no hope for it." Apparently awaiting their arrival, a beautiful Viking woman with platinum blonde hair appeared and smiled at Destiny. "Hello. I'm Freya, daughter to Davyn and Shea. You must be Destiny."

Ah, just one mother this time.

Freya wore her hair woven into several braids, a simple woolen dress belted at the waist, and a tan fur cloak. Her jewelry was understated, complementing the lovely but dainty dagger sheathed at her waist.

Destiny said hello, and managed a small smile before her gaze returned to the retreating dragons. Meanwhile, scowling away, Leviathan strode into the woodland, muttering something about troublesome female dragons in heat getting his males all riled up.

"Hey, we're not done talking." She started after him only for Freya to fall in beside her, eyeing her over with understanding.

"I see why Thorulf and Dagr were so out of sorts." Clearly chatty by nature, Freya's accent sounded more modern than Destiny would have expected. But then she imagined her mother was from the twenty-first century.

"You really are exceptionally beautiful, so I can only imagine what they're suffering with your dragon in heat," Freya went on, sighing a little. "And now just look at Leviathan." She shook her head. "I suppose I had hoped it wasn't true, but I can see it is."

"Hoped what wasn't true?" She stopped when she realized Freya's hair had black and red highlights that weren't there moments before. "And what happened to your hair?"

"Nothing he's going to like," Freya began only to flinch when Leviathan glanced back and scowled more fiercely. "See."

When Destiny looked from him to Freya in confusion, Freya explained.

"Like my mother, I'm a Cupid dragon, meaning I sense when love's blossoming. My hair reflects that. Who's meant for who." Grinning, Freya fingered her locks and glanced between Leviathan and Destiny. "These colors look familiar?"

Startled, she realized they were the exact shades of her and Leviathan's hair.

Even so.

"Those could be anyone's." She shook her head, only thinking to make her point. "Thorulf's hair was black too."

"Thorulf couldn't handle a woman like you," Leviathan growled into her mind. *"So don't even think it."*

Who the hell did he think he was? She'd made it clear she didn't belong to him the moment she showed up here.

"I can think anything I like," she shot back, irritated by how good his telepathic voice felt. *"Now get out of my head."*

Rather than respond, Leviathan told Freya to see Destiny into appropriate clothing before he vanished down a side path. Just like that, he was gone, and her questions left unanswered.

"Don't worry," Freya assured, clearly a fan of twenty-first-century lingo. "He'll be back soon enough. He just needs time to cool off." She shook her head. "I never thought I'd see the day a woman affected him like this. Made him so territorial and jealous. It's not part of his 'genetic make-up' as mother says." Her brows shot up. "Yet it seems it is after all." She sighed again and offered a forgiving smile as though disappointed but also happy for Destiny. "I didn't think it was possible, but I should've known."

"Why?" She eyed Freya. Maybe she could get some answers out of her instead. "Because of what happened between us the last time we met?"

"So it seems." Freya gave her a look. "Considering how he's been since he got back." She tilted her head in question. "So what *did* happen between you two?" She got a little doe-eyed. "How'd you manage to do what no woman before you has?"

"I'd say it was your inner beauty," came Maya's unexpected voice. *"Because now that I'm in your mind, I can see it all the more clearly."*

"I take it I'm around positive enough energy for us to connect," Destiny replied.

"Yes." There was no mistaking the smile in Maya's voice. *"Freya's pretty upbeat for a dragon."*

Yes, she was.

"I agree it's hard to believe this one brought Leviathan to heel," came a dry voice before another woman melted out of the woodland and fell in beside them. Her flippant, unimpressed gaze raked over Destiny. "But I imagine it will not be for long."

Tall and slender, with striking sultry features and a bold disposition, the newcomer had dark hair with several slender braids and almost metallic silver eyes. She wore leather pants, a rather revealing leather top, and several blades sheathed here and there.

Not surprisingly, with the incoming negativity, Maya vanished from Destiny's mind.

"Destiny, meet Liv," Freya said. "Daughter to Rokar and Tess."

She ignored Liv's hostility and nodded in greeting before focusing on Freya again, determined to put this time to good use. "So you have no idea what happened in Scotland and Ireland? Why Leviathan and I are at such odds?"

"You are at odds because your inner beast means to mate with his," Liv said bluntly. "And that is unnatural for dragons like mine and Leviathan's." She shook her head once sharply. "Connections like that would only weaken us."

"You mean *love.*" Freya grinned, fingering her hair no doubt on purpose, emphasizing words Liv had likely used before in disgust. "That thing *infecting* him as we speak."

"There are several dark-haired men here," Liv replied, echoing Destiny's sentiments. "And red-haired women. So your locks could be reflecting any of theirs, Freya."

"But you know it's not," Freya teased in a sing-song voice. "You more than most considering how hard you've tried to be with Leviathan only to be turned away." She gestured in the direction he had gone. "Then this. He's a changed dragon."

"I will still have him," Liv shot back, unfazed. "When he is ready."

With that, she melted back into the woodland as swiftly as she had appeared.

"Isn't she a pleasure," Destiny muttered. "Looks like I'm making enemies already."

"Just give her time." Freya's eyes drifted a little. "Every female dragon who grows up around Leviathan wants him at some point. Liv just more than most. Now, as you just saw, she remains miffed because he won't have her. Either of us. He swore he would never lay a finger on those born of the last generation, and he hasn't." She shook her head. "Even if he hadn't made that vow, he's known us since we were born, helped raise and mentor us, so he looks at us like kin. Perhaps even children."

"That must be hard on him," she murmured, feeling a sudden kinship with him. Remembering enough to understand. She had suffered that sort of life too, hadn't she? Never able to fall in love with anyone even if she wanted to because she'd watch them grow old and die while she didn't age. "You cared for him too, I take it?"

"Of course, and a part of me still does." Freya's envious but kind gaze returned to Destiny. "Though Uncle Sven is king of my tribe, Leviathan is King of the Dragons. He's," she struggled to find the right words, "I guess you could say his power's intoxicating to females. There's just something about an alpha above all alphas. Especially one who's been able to tame his inner beast enough to set a good example."

Freya shook her head before continuing. "If he hadn't, bringing Ancients and Múspellsheimr dragons together might have gone far differently." She eyed the dragons in the distance. "I hear Múspellsheimr dragons were a fairly untamed lot at the beginning. But then they would be coming from a world of brimstone and fire. War and never-ending strife."

Damn. "There are dragons from another world actually living here?"

"*Ja.*" Freya nodded. "They came here during the last war. Saved by my tribe, Leviathan and his Ancients, who, by the way, can be just as unruly. Just as fierce."

"That's unreal." She looked to the sky again, amazed. "So how many dragons actually live here?"

"Not as many as there once were." Sadness flickered in Freya's eyes. "But then there's a reason for that. One that might have everything to do with why you're here now."

-Leviathan-

Chapter Eight

Y OU'LL TAKE ME to your seer now," Destiny demanded when Leviathan rejoined her later in Freya's lair.

Her glorious eyes were ablaze, and her outfit, much to his dismay, no less enticing than before.

"If your seer needs to meet me to fill in the missing pieces," Destiny went on, "then take me to her so we can figure out how to stop what's been happening here."

He scowled at Freya and shook his head. Not only because of how much she'd revealed but because Destiny's brown leather trousers and tunic didn't hide her curves in the least. Even worse? Seeing her in his people's clothing aroused him all the more. As though his inner dragon liked the idea of her becoming one of them.

Becoming his.

"Don't get upset with Freya for being straightforward when you should've been from the start." Destiny's brows snapped together. "Your dragons have been dying for years because of whatever's going on with the gods? Dying from ailments that normally wouldn't affect them because the gods used their energy to fuel their war?"

Rather than answer, he kept things on his terms.

"We will spend the night at the Keep, then leave on the morn to see my seer." He shook his head. "No sooner. Not until this storm has passed."

Destiny glanced from the raging sea beyond Freya's sizeable cave back to Leviathan, hesitation in her eyes. "Are they that bad then? So bad you would put this off another moment?"

Once again, she was ever the savior, not to mention coming into her own fast by the looks of it. Which told him her personality had always been as much her dragon as her godliness. Then, likely, just the woman she had become over however long she'd existed. He'd asked around about her mother but had no luck. The Sigdirs knew of no woman in their tribe who had lain with a Celtic god of all things.

"Leviathan is right to wait until the storm passes." Freya handed Destiny a fur cloak. "They weaken our dragon magic too much, their lightning strikes even deadly on occasion." She shook her head. "If you were traveling via the Cave Catacombs all the way to Mt. Galdhøpiggen's Peak, that would be one thing, but there are areas out in the open between here and there."

"Mt. Galdhøpiggen's Peak," Destiny murmured, clearly sensing something familiar. "Why do I know that place?" Her gaze flickered to Leviathan. "So you don't know much about my mother despite asking around?"

He cursed how quickly she picked up on his thoughts. No one had ever been able to do that without him letting them in. Even then, it wasn't to this degree. Undoubtedly a result of what had happened between them in Ireland. So said the unnatural fire drawing them closer and closer. Reminding him what they'd shared.

Moreover, trying to remind her.

Her revelations earlier had been troubling. Confusing. Why would he have tried to keep Destiny from her mother when she dreamt of the dagger? If anything, he would have been an ally to her mother if she were still alive. A friend to a fellow Norse dragon.

"We will eat, rest and set out early," he informed Destiny. "As long as you're here in the Realm, especially at the Realm's Keep, you will remain close to Freya and me." Before she could rebuke him, he clarified. "It's for your safety, Destiny. Nothing more." He shook his head. "You are too vulnerable in your current state."

Something he was supposed to have addressed in further detail before they got here. But no, he'd ended up just as distracted by Destiny as the dragons he sought to protect her from. Or should he say *keep* her from? He told himself she needed to better understand her inner dragon before dealing with others but knew better.

He didn't want her with other males.

He wanted her for himself.

Which, he reasoned, made sense. She was stunning, in heat, and he was arch-alpha. The chain of command said he should have her first. Then she could move on to others if she wished. If she didn't, he would turn her away regardless and move on.

That's what he did.

That's what he had done for over seventy years.

"Freya's been helping me deal with...my current feminine issues." Destiny gave Freya a grateful look. "However awkward the topic."

"Being in heat is perfectly natural," Freya replied. "You just have to work on letting your dragon in a little more so you can manage it together. The more you acknowledge your inner beast and what she's going through, the easier it will be. It's not foolproof, but it'll ease the discomfort some." She perked a brow at Leviathan. "Where unnecessary around Sigdirs, you know there's a way to help this situation when it comes to the particular dragons under your rule here."

"No," he grunted. "It's not necessary."

"What?" Destiny looked between them. "If there's something that can help control the in-heat craziness, I'm all for it."

"Great!" Freya flashed a winning smile and pulled something from her pocket. "Then let me add a little jewelry to your attire."

"How did you get that?" he growled, both loathing and relishing the slender leather choke collar Freya snapped around Destiny's neck before she had a chance to say no.

"Nice," Destiny murmured, shocking him. "Suits my outfit." When she ran her finger over its shiny center, it took everything in him not to bend her over and take her right here. "What's this?"

"Gorgeous, isn't it?" Freya kept smiling. "It's a piece of Leviathan's dragon scale." When Destiny's eyes narrowed, Freya kept smoothing the way. "Among the Ancients and Múspellsheimr dragons, that necklace symbolizes a bond of sorts." She shrugged a shoulder. "It makes you untouchable."

It took Destiny no time to translate that.

"You mean it makes me Leviathan's." Her gaze narrowed dangerously on him. "Did you just *collar* me?"

"What would you say if I did?" he replied without thinking. The fresh scent of her arousal was once again unmistakable. Could it be his delicious little goddess enjoyed finally giving up some of her power? Did she like the idea of submitting to him?

"I would say you're out of your fucking mind." Yet when she went to tear it off, she hesitated.

His pulse leapt with excitement. Did she like it there? Understand its possibilities?

As it turned out, her hesitation had more to do with reason and protecting others than anything. She spoke to Freya rather than him, making it clear she was still her own dragon. Or so she thought. "This will keep the riffraff away?" Then she said exactly what she would have said when he first met her. "It'll help keep the peace around here so we can focus on what we need to do?"

"Yes, absolutely," Freya confirmed, not mentioning what else the collar, or specifically, his dragon scale, might do.

To that end, he should make Destiny remove it immediately lest she tempt him even more. Because truly, how strong could he be? She'd pushed him to his limit in the cave. Driven him right to the edge without realizing it. Any other in his position, especially an Ancient, would not have been so strong. Couldn't have been. They ran too primal, acting on animal instincts before reason.

Especially when it came to a dragon in her condition.

A condition he best ignore so he could focus on more important things.

"Before we dine, tell me more about these women you left behind in the twenty-first century." He nodded thanks to Freya when she handed him and Destiny horns of ale. "I've asked Freya to remain here for this so that she might confirm my suspicions."

Destiny glanced between them in confusion before she figured it out. "Ah, you've been speaking telepathically."

"*Ja,*" he confirmed. "I remain in contact with all of my protégés that way. Heeding the Great Serpent's request, I keep tabs on them at all times."

"Liv must love that," Destiny muttered, surprising him. Not because of the feigned amusement in her voice but because of the jealousy he detected underneath. Jealousy his inner dragon enjoyed far too much for his taste.

"Liv understands my vow," he said bluntly, well aware the women had met. Freya had filled him in on everything, including Liv's behavior. "I will never lay with her."

"Do you want to?" Destiny's steady gaze showed nothing of what he'd just sensed. "I don't ask out of jealousy but practicality. Will her attitude toward me cause derision among your people?"

As usual, he appreciated her keeping things in the proper perspective and addressing her concerns head-on rather than letting them simmer. There was no room for that in his world. People and dragons alike must be forthright. Share their issues rather than let them fester.

So he would do the same. Cover everything lest she wonder.

"Liv and Freya are both desirable females." He nodded at Freya, fully aware where she stood. Thankful she understood how things had to be. "But I've never looked at them that way. I claim no woman as my own," not yet, "nor will I ever. Where some dragons mate for life, I do not." He couldn't imagine a worse fate...right? "I prefer variety."

"Good." Destiny nodded, her expression and mind suddenly difficult to decipher. "I imagine that'll make my life easier as we proceed." She took a sip of ale and gave him a look. "Of course, more transparency from you as we go will be helpful too."

He nodded, acknowledging that he'd give her that. At least eventually. Until then, he needed more truths from her first, so he urged her to share more about the women from the future.

"Apparently, they've been at the whims of a prophecy their whole lives," she began before confirming what he'd already suspected.

They were the women the seer had foreseen.

"What do you sense of them, Freya?" He knew she detected their essences off Destiny. Undoubtedly, her bracelet had something to do with that. "Will they be right?"

"Yes," Freya replied without hesitation. Her brow furrowed. "All but the last one...she will be more difficult."

"Right for what?" Destiny looked from him to Freya. "And I take it you're talking about Raven?"

"Yes," Freya said softly, sadness in her eyes. "She is particularly troubled..." Her hair sparkled ever-so-slightly, as though her Cupid magic already struggled beneath the mental weight of this woman. "But all hope is not lost. Someone will help her...love her." She shook her head. "But it will not be easy. Not for either of them."

"Love," Destiny murmured before she figured it out. "So they'll be following the same paths as the twenty-first-century women who came before them. Finding love across time. Fulfilling some great fate. Helping humankind."

"Which would be welcome considering the godly war encroaching on us," Freya said, remaining vague for his sake. Well aware he hadn't told Destiny everything yet. That he had the power to stop what was happening in its tracks. Stop the growing strife before it went any further.

First, though, he must talk to his seer.

Because there could be no doubt Destiny was who he'd suspected she was since he ended her the first time. Since he plunged the dagger into her chest and ripped away life as they both knew it.

Chapter Nine

FOR A FLICKER of a moment, Destiny felt pain in her chest as she looked at Leviathan, but it faded as fast as it came. Yet, she sensed something left behind. Some great emptiness inside her that made no sense.

"We should get to the Keep for dinner," Leviathan stated, almost as if he knew she skirted close to something indefinable. "Then rest."

Thunder rumbled across the sky, ominous and echoing, definitely different somehow. Daunting blue-white lightning zigzagged over the ocean, edging closer as if seeking something. Wanting to take something.

Though she would appreciate Leviathan's promised transparency sooner rather than later, Destiny nodded in agreement at his suggestion. Mainly because she needed to regroup. Sift through her thoughts. Come to terms with her ever-growing suspicion that she and Leviathan's fates were irrevocably intertwined.

She couldn't put her finger on it, but whatever simmered between them was swelling inside her like a tidal wave ready to crest. Pushing them closer. Tightening. And it wasn't just the collar snapped around her neck. While logical to wear it to keep the peace, the truth was her inner dragon reveled in its symbolism. What it truly meant, no matter how much of a farce.

That she belonged to him in some primal, untouchable way.

Back in Maine, living out her mediocre life with no memories, she'd gone to the local bar, even dated a few guys, but knew it wasn't forever. She didn't do forever. Couldn't on some level she didn't understand. Yet when Freya put this necklace—*collar*—on her, she drew a whole lot closer to something she *could* do.

Commitment of the flesh rather than of the heart.

A bond without love and heartache, but a bond nonetheless.

One that would eventually give her all of Leviathan's truths.

When she first learned what the collar was, she'd itched to rip it off until, seconds later, its warmth curled around her, *through* her. It, *he*, his dragon, his very *essence* seeped into her in ways that made her more focused but at the same time immersed in him.

It was impossible to describe her new state of awareness only that she suspected the bit of dragon scale at her throat was responsible. Heat sizzled beneath her skin, unquenchable desire, but somehow it seemed more manageable now.

"It's more focused, yes?" Freya asked softly. They followed Leviathan down a torch-lit tunnel that ran adjacent to the ocean by the sounds of it. "Your dragon is helping you? Perhaps because of the necklace?"

"It's doing *something*," she admitted, realizing it was, in fact, her inner dragon at work. And perhaps even his. "As long as it'll help keep the peace. That's all that matters right now."

"Agreed."

They soon exited the tunnel into a monstrous courtyard protected by a huge clear dome. Crackling lightning and driving rain not only gave it a mystical feel but created an echoing waterfall sound.

"Don't worry," Freya assured. "We're safe from the storm here."

As dumbfounded as she'd been when she saw it from afar, Destiny looked up at the castle towering over her. It wasn't a typical Viking structure but something more sinister yet somehow alluring. Blackened wall walks curved around dozens of towers, and spires shot toward the sky.

"Though he calls it the Realm's, welcome to what everyone calls Leviathan's Keep behind his back," Freya informed. "Because he does so much for us. Gives us safe harbor." She grinned. "He built it to Múspellsheimr standards to make its dragons feel welcome. All dragons, for that matter." She glanced at Leviathan with pride. "It's seen many battles over the years as dragons grew into their own, but in the end, it's always been a place of resolution and accord. A place where dragons can act like themselves among their own kind."

"Impressive." She meant it too. This place was something else.

She eyed people as they made their way toward an ancient-looking grand staircase leading to a behemoth door flagged by massive torches. Though everyone looked normal enough, Viking to the bone, she could feel the fluctuating animalistic energy in the air. Leviathan nodded to many in passing but said little, his expression hard though his eyes were cordial enough.

"It's safe, but he still doesn't want them out here, does he?" she murmured. "He's worried about them."

"Every hour of every day of every year," Freya said softly. "Endlessly." Her knowing gaze slid Destiny's way. "Not many see that so clearly." She considered her. "Or better put, *feel* it."

"My necklace then?" Destiny hadn't missed the shocked glances that went from her face to her collar. Again, she felt the urge to yank it off, declaring her independence, and again, just as swiftly, wanted it right where it was.

"You know better than to ask me that." Freya stuck close, making it clear to all they were allies. Friends despite having just met. "You knew him better than most before I put that necklace on you."

"Perhaps," she murmured, but Freya was right. Whatever had happened between them had bonded them together in a way she knew damn well he struggled with. *She* struggled with.

Yet it had happened.

Was part of them.

And it was locking them together more readily than a collar ever could.

The inside of the castle took her breath away with its stark, towering, regal yet gothic beauty. A massive octagonal great hall led to several long, spiraling staircases going in different directions, rising up so high she wondered if there were an end in sight. Endless cathedral-like stained glass windows depicting sweeping dragons were made more magnificent by the shimmering ash beyond.

"Look at this place," she whispered in awe, not sure what to admire first.

Four behemoth hearths hosted roaring fires, and huge bowls of fire hung like chandeliers as high as the eye could see. The air smelled of smoke, lust, and roasting meat.

"It used to reek of sulfur too," Freya said out of the corner of her mouth, "but Leviathan whipped things into shape and taught this bunch how to get their dragon breath under control."

She bit back a smile. "Glad to hear that."

Everyone might appear Viking with fur cloaks and pagan looks, but there was no mistaking the fire flaring in many a cat-like eye. Dragons peered back at her with such strong curiosity she knew her collar had made a big impact.

Where Leviathan had remained in front of them to this point, now he fell in beside Destiny. Not to introduce her but rather, from what she could tell, to claim his territory. There was no grand introduction that a time traveler had arrived but rather a pointed sweep from his stormy gaze, lingering on a select group of males before he gestured that she follow him.

"Seriously?" she said under her breath to Freya. "Was that Leviathan's way of welcoming me?"

"Yes." Freya chuckled and linked arms with her, again making it clear to all they were friends. "And I've never seen him do it. Not once with anyone." She winked. "Let alone a woman branded by his scale."

"Ah, so that's the official name for wearing this around my neck?" She snorted. "Sounds like ownership if I didn't know better."

"But you *do* know better," Freya reminded. "You know this is all for show because you and Leviathan don't do forever."

"No, we don't," Destiny agreed, noting how streaked with red and black Freya's hair had become. She couldn't help a small smile at her new friend's continued modern-day lingo. "You picked up a lot from your mom, I take it? Have a little thing for the twenty-first century?"

"I do." Freya smiled. "How could I not when so many wonderful people have come from there?"

Though Destiny didn't smile quite so broadly, she agreed and wasn't entirely sure why. Yes, Elsie and her nieces were nice, but she got the feeling she'd known others from there. Cared a great deal for them.

She glanced at Leviathan as he led them into a chamber more primal and impressive than the last. Did he know who she left behind?

Who she might have cared about? Yes, she realized. He absolutely did. He still had so many answers. So much she needed to know. Yet watching him here in his element, surrounded by so many who clearly respected, would even lay down their lives for him, she was okay with waiting to question him more.

With biding her time while she got to know this side of him.

It turned out he wasn't the arrogant beast of a man she was starting to think him. Rather, as they entered a circular room with a bonfire at its center and a huge bowl of fire hovering far above, he seemed quite the opposite. As far as she could tell by the way he paid rapt attention to everyone who spoke to him, be they of importance or a mere child, he was somewhat humble. Attentive. Even, though she'd never say it to him, *caring*.

A true king if she didn't know better.

And a damn good one at that.

So said him building this place for everyone to begin with.

"Come, join me." Freya led her to a slightly raised dais with distinctly different chairs. Though spiked and throne-like, they were by no means opulent or pretentious. Freya sat and gestured at the seat beside her. "Sit, Destiny. Let us drink while we await dinner."

She sat and nodded thanks when she was handed a goblet of what turned out to be very strong red wine. The element in this room was different than the main hall, the atmosphere more intense, the number of towering, fierce-looking men present impossible to ignore.

"They're not just fiercer but higher-ranking dragons," Freya explained.

Was she a mind reader like Elsie or just stating what made sense at the moment? When Destiny looked at her curiously, Freya merely winked.

"No more a mind reader than any dragon eventually." She offered a guilty little shrug. "Sorry, your mind's opened up to me enough that I'm catching quite a bit now." Her brow swept up. "Not just because of what's happening between you and Leviathan but because you genuinely like me, yes?" Before she had a chance to respond, Freya's gaze gentled. "Just say the word, and I'll pull out. Respect your privacy until you're comfortable and want to share more. *If* you want to, of course."

"I appreciate your honesty," she replied, thinking about it.

Did she want such a close ally to Leviathan in her mind? Someone who could tell him things he might not catch himself? Then again, she suspected he was going to have full access soon enough, so why not let an ally in? Someone who understood him better and might be able to buffer a little? And she *did* like Freya.

"So you can sense my thoughts more because I like you?" Destiny asked.

"Yes." Freya rested a reassuring hand over hers on the armrest. "I'm rare, though, Destiny. Even if you like others, they won't get in like I can. My abilities are," her gaze drifted to Leviathan, "selective when in the company of two like you."

Destiny tried not to roll her eyes. "Tell me you're not talking about potential love."

Freya just kept smiling. "I'm not talking about potential love."

She narrowed her eyes. "You're just repeating what I asked, aren't you?"

Freya offered a sparkling wink. "*Ja.*"

"*Ja,*" she echoed and eyed the men across the way, more interested in everyday life for Leviathan than talk of love. She sensed the never-ending play for power fluctuating around her. The truth of things. "They respect Leviathan but constantly challenge him for seniority, don't they?"

"Yes." Freya nodded in approval that Destiny caught on so fast. "Unlike we Sigdir dragons who follow a less intense monarchy, Ancients and Múspellsheimr dragons are in a constant battle to prove themselves. To be head alpha and rule over all."

"That's got to be exhausting for Leviathan."

"Gods, no." Freya shook her head and chuckled. "It's exciting. Entertaining. A true pleasure. Mainly because he does it so well and so differently than they would." She gestured at their surroundings. "He's learned to combine civil with primal. Pushes them to evolve whether they like it or not."

"That sounds like a monumental task," she commented, well aware of the cunning looks from men who thought to challenge him. The way they eyed her as if she might just be a way to achieve their goal. "Like an evolutionary change that needed thousands of years rather than decades."

"Which only proves how suited to the task Leviathan actually is," Freya replied. "When the Múspellsheimr dragons first arrived, things were more difficult, but he's handled it. Made it work." She glanced at Destiny. "The general disposition you're feeling off them tonight is all pomp."

"Are you sure?" She considered them. "Because it feels like competitiveness over me. As though this collar isn't working quite as well as you thought it would."

Not to say it wasn't working in other ways. The strange but welcoming warmth that had been curling through her only grew. As though Leviathan's dragon wrapped around hers and drew her ever closer.

"If you don't think the necklace is working as well as it should, then bring him to you." A strange little light lit Freya's eyes. She pulled something from her pocket and held it out. "Remind them that you're branded by his scale. That he's finally taken the next step in leadership and welcomed a strong woman to his side. A partner."

Welcomed her to his side? *Partner?* That sounded suspiciously permanent.

She peered at the object in Freya's outstretched palm. It looked like a small, ancient-looking coin. "What is that?"

"As if you don't know." Liv, again melting out of nowhere, sat beside Freya. Her slippery gaze went from Destiny's neck to what Freya offered. "That is the key to it all." She gestured flippantly at everything around them before her eyes locked on Leviathan. "The key to him." Her gaze slid back to Destiny, and a sneer curled her lips. "At least for now."

"It's a talisman of some sort," she murmured. Ignoring Liv, she followed the sensations coursing through her. What her inner dragon told her. "One unique to Ancients."

"That's right," Freya replied. "Ancients are given one of these at birth. It's designed to capture the unique essence of their inner dragon as it grows." She shrugged a shoulder. "Essentially, it promotes the best outcome for the race by finding its way to either an Ancient's mate or mates. Or, if they choose not to claim a mate, a female dragon best suited to provide them strong offspring. One who aligns with their particular essence thus producing the best possible results."

"So what, the male gives it to the female?" She frowned. "That sounds more like a personal preference on the male's part to me."

"The talisman is not given but draws the female to it." Liv scowled at Freya. "It's never stolen by another and given to a random female."

"Actually," Freya corrected. "The lore simply states the object finds its way to the correct female." She shook her head. "Never by what means." She arched a brow at Liv. "And you know full well there's no such thing as stealing from Leviathan. It's impossible. So whether he'll admit it or not, on some level, he knows this is no longer in his possession. More importantly, his dragon knows."

Destiny eyed the piece, not so sure about it. Any of this. Yet if she could do more to keep the peace around here until they figured things out, wouldn't it be for the best? "So if I give this to Leviathan, other dragons will be even less inclined to cause problems?"

"If you give it to him and he accepts it, they can be banished or even killed for looking at you the wrong way," Liv muttered. "At least for now."

"Why only for now?"

"Because his dragon could and likely will end up rejecting you to bear its offspring." Liv rolled her eyes and shook her head. "And it would be understandable considering what you are."

Rather than take the bait and get in a tiff over her Celtic lineage, Destiny focused on Freya. "How exactly does this mark him so that others know?"

"The moment he accepts it, it will become obvious." Freya touched the side of her neck. "A tattoo will appear right around here, showing that he's in transition and no longer available to other females."

"At least not right away," Liv reminded. "And even then, it might be a moot point." She shrugged. "It might be before that."

"True." Yet Freya didn't sound convinced. "He could reject the offering. Or, he could accept it only to discover your dragons are too incompatible. The tattoo won't appear in that case."

"Or," Liv continued, clearly anticipating as much, "even if the mark *does* form, his dragon might end up rejecting your dragon anyway. It will depend on how well your inner beasts connect as time goes on. They, or more specifically his dragon, might discover something about your dragon that will keep you from producing the strongest possible offspring."

"Sounds a little too much like being picky about perfect DNA to me," Destiny remarked. "Don't Ancients realize that not being strong isn't necessarily a bad thing? That there are plenty of other admirable traits children can have?"

"They're *Ancients*." Liv looked at her aghast. As though she should know better. "They strive for excellence among their ranks. Strength and perfection. The ability to fight and be the very best." She shook her head. "Anything less is unacceptable."

While she didn't particularly approve, she understood that different cultures had different ways. In this case, it wasn't just cultural but their species. Instincts born of a world so unlike this one.

"I still don't understand how giving Leviathan his own talisman could possibly do all this," Destiny said. "It's his dragon's essence, not mine." She shook her head. "And would a culture that puts so much chalk in perfection and strength really consider their leader claiming a mate that noteworthy?"

Especially one with Celtic blood. Not that she said as much and gave Liv the satisfaction.

"This is a magical talisman unique to dragons," Freya explained. "So the moment you touch it, it becomes yours as well and soaks up your dragon's essence."

Freya's gaze swept over the room before she looked at Destiny and continued.

"Unlike dragons still living on Múspellsheimr, thanks to Leviathan's council, these dragons continue to hold their women in high regard," Freya said with pride. "Treat them as equals." She nodded once with approval. "To that end, especially among the Ancients, a strong female is as revered as a strong male. A strong couple especially revered." Her gaze flickered from Leviathan to Destiny. "If you're a match for Leviathan's dragon, then that means you're every bit as strong as him if not, perhaps, even stronger. And that would only ever be good for these people. This tribe."

"Yet she's Celtic," Liv spat, shaking her head. "So it is impossible."

"How do you know?" Destiny finally spat back, about over her snide comments. Finally baited when she knew better. But she was and couldn't seem to get her suddenly fluctuating emotions under control. Either a result of being in heat or, even worse, her dragon rearing its head against possible competition. "Who knows? It *might* just be my Celtic blood that makes me stronger. That makes me the perfect fit."

Not that she wanted to be. Especially for Leviathan.

Or so she kept telling herself.

"Your Celtic blood stronger than your Norse?" Liv issued a dark chuckle. "Impossible." She gestured at Leviathan. "You with a dragon like that? Even more impossible."

Destiny's vision hazed red. Her blood boiled. "You mean him with a dragon like *me*."

What was she saying? Why was she getting so riled up? This was just bullying at its best.

Yet her anger only grew, filling her with simmering, uncharacteristic rage.

"You will never be strong enough." Liv's dragon eyes flared in challenge. "He will reject you."

"Doubtful," she growled, mortified at her behavior even as she embraced it. Even as her dragon egged her on. Territorial emotions blew through her. Primal and wicked. Wrong, though somehow very, very right.

Freeing even as they tried to bind her to him.

So freeing, in fact, that she abandoned all logic and allowed her ego to take over. Her need to be right. Specifically to let Liv know she wouldn't go down without a fight.

"He will *not* reject me." She clamped her hand around the talisman and shot Liv a triumphant look. "And I'll prove it to you."

Chapter Ten

REALIZING TOO LATE what Freya was up to, Leviathan tensed at the unusual jolt that shot through him. He'd never felt the sensation, but thanks to his dragon, understood moments later when he looked Destiny's way.

She had his talisman.

"Loki's hell, what did you do?" he growled into Freya's mind.

Not surprisingly, she didn't respond. Instead, she glanced Leviathan's way in barely masked amusement and shrugged a little. With any other dragon, he would call them out then and there, but Freya was one of his favorites. And her heart, however misguided by her blasted Cupid magic, knew no better.

As to be expected, the room quieted, and all eyes turned Destiny's way when she headed in his direction. His body, as well as every other male dragon's, locked up at the sight of her in all her blazing glory. It wasn't just in her confident yet sensual swagger either, but her intense dragon eyes. In the palpable aura pulsing around her, unique to her dragon. To the power she carried.

Power making its way to the surface, eager to break free.

She didn't say a word, just stopped in front of him, held out the talisman, and outright challenged him with her gaze alone. Flaming turquoise eyes that pinned him in place. What would he do? Dare he deny her? He wondered if Freya had told her everything about this exchange. The commitment she was making even if he rejected her in the end.

Or she rejects you, whispered through his mind.

If possible, he tensed even more at the taunt from his own inner dragon. At the idea she could turn him away just as easily in the end. That *she* could reject *him.* With any other female, the notion would seem absurd, but with Destiny, he sensed she could. That she possessed the willpower to shun him if he didn't suit her. While that worked out for his human half, it struck his dragon as an outright challenge.

And challenges were never to be refused.

So, in the end, rather than reject it to keep his people safe, he took it out of shallow competitiveness. Out of a need to win and claim her as his and his alone even if he had to finish her in the end. He would have her within this unique, potent bond first. Own her before he let her go. Feel her heated sheath. Hear her cries of pleasure before the silence of her pain. Or so he thought, reveled in, until he took his talisman and felt that same vulnerable fear rear its ugly head again.

Fear directly related to her. *Them.* The fate he must serve her.

Then another acute fear.

Would his dragon accept the talisman from her? *Would* she be able to mark him when none before had been able to? Seconds later, he got his answer when intense heat and desire curled through him before the side of his neck stung with the mental nip of her dragon.

When murmurs of surprise rumbled through the crowd, he knew it was done. Destiny had marked him. But then, the minute he'd plunged the dagger into her in Ireland, he knew this moment was always a distinct possibility.

Perhaps, in a way he was unwilling to admit, he'd even prayed for it.

Despite Destiny's gaze meeting his with equal competitiveness, there was no missing the way the mark affected her when combined with the collar. Blazing challenge turned to obvious lust. Overwhelming desire he knew surprised her no matter how unfazed she seemed. He could feel it spiking through her. Smell it in the sweet scent of her arousal.

A scent that, despite her being in heat, thanks to their new bond, was for him and him alone. Other males no longer got the pleasure of enjoying it. While that was good when it came to keeping the peace, it made focusing all that much harder. His dragon wanted hers with a fierceness now that would be hard, if not impossible, to keep at bay.

In fact, it wanted her so profoundly that when she went to saunter off, he finally did something he'd wanted to do since the moment he met her. He yanked her against him, wrapped his hand into her hair, and closed his mouth over hers. He didn't kiss her gently like some might their first time, but hard and hungry for all to see.

He sensed part of her was tempted to push him away, yet another, far more insistent part craved submitting. To be taken right there, be damned those watching. Many would. Some did. Right here in this very chamber. Some had tossed their fur down and taken their females from behind. Others had done what he envisioned doing to her right now. He'd rip away her clothing. Lift her until she straddled him. Bring her down hard on his eager cock. Let everyone hear her moans of pleasure.

Because she would. Loudly. Ceaselessly. He would accept nothing less.

Undoubtedly catching his thoughts, she groaned and wrapped her fist in his tunic as though trying to pull him closer. *Into* her like the mental images overwhelming his mind. Their minds.

"If you two aren't careful, you might just have the opposite effect on this crowd than what you were going for," Freya said into his mind, amused. *"Between your display and the mental images your dragons are putting off, you're stirring up trouble you were hoping to avoid."*

She was right. This was counterproductive.

Yet hard as hell to pull away from.

Nevertheless, though damn near impossible, he finally dragged his mouth from Destiny's only to discover unnatural flames once again curled around them. Fire no one could see but them. This time, however, the flames were fiercer. Brighter.

Sizzling around them with an intensity he knew all too well.

He should have seen this coming. Knew that their dragons bonding like this would finally reveal the truth. Make her remember.

Destiny frowned in confusion before she grew curious. Even awed.

"I know this fire, don't I?" Her pained gaze drifted from the flames to him. "Our fire...because it *is* ours, isn't it?" Her hand fluttered to her heart, and she flinched. "So much pain...yet relief."

She searched his eyes. "I asked you to do something, didn't I? But you wouldn't do it at first." Her gaze narrowed, and her breathing grew heavier. "My dagger...I needed you to use it on me..."

"Yes," he finally admitted. The flames only grew stronger, the heat building between them tangible. Welcome. *Theirs.* "You asked me to kill you to save a Scottish clan and those you had come to care for."

"And you did...eventually," she murmured, remembering more and more.

He could see it in her mind. Feel it in her soul.

"Yet here I stand, very much alive." She blinked several times. Her voice dropped to a shocked whisper. "Because you didn't do as I asked."

Realizing that seemed to be the revelation her dragon needed because the flames vanished. Her utter shock didn't, though. Rather, things were coming back to her quickly now, which meant he had no choice but to tell her everything.

Not here, though. Not where everyone could see their vulnerability. Because there had been much of it in the moment they shared. A bonding that his people didn't know about. One that might stir up restlessness or uncertainty when they needed to remain patient. Ready. Willing to work together to defeat the enemy when the time came.

"Come." He led her toward his private chamber. Though his lair was at the top of the highest tower, because of dragon magic, they went up but a few sets of stairs before arriving.

He wasn't surprised by the stunned way she looked at everything. Though he preferred his seaside lair, this one was necessary to keep an eye on things. Every corner of the Realm. It's craggy rock walls were made to feel like a cave with open-air exits facing in every direction. A fire burned in the center of room, and his bed rested against one wall flanked by torches.

"It's huge," she murmured.

While she could be talking about the bed because it was large enough for him to enjoy several women at a time, he knew she referred to the chamber itself.

"It's designed to fit my dragon and a few others if need be." And it had several times over the decades, whether he enjoyed females in dragon form or watched others enjoying them.

Though Destiny gave no response, her posture stiffened, and her inner dragon seemed unsettled. Worse yet, so did his at her displeasure. He scowled at the sensation and set it aside. Now wasn't the time to scrutinize his dragon's behavior. Because if he wasn't mistaken, it seemed intent to appease her.

More alarming, devote itself to her and her alone.

"Sit, Destiny." He gestured at a plush seat overlooking Níðhöggr's Ash and the stormy ocean far below. "Sit, and I will tell you everything."

"Now that you have no choice." She shot him a look and accepted a mug of ale. "Because it's starting to come back. I can feel it."

The way she said *it* made him take notice. "You mean something other than your memories?"

"Yes." She looked at him. "Could it be my godliness?"

"I don't think so."

"Think or know?"

"I was told you forfeited it to save everyone."

"By who?"

"A Scottish wizard."

Her brows arched. "I knew a wizard?"

"You knew many who possessed magic," he divulged. "Witches, fairies, druids, modern-day dragons. Likely far more than that in your time."

"How long was my time?" She narrowed her eyes. "How old am I?"

"I don't know." For the first time since meeting her, he didn't want to be *quite* so forthright but knew it was only a matter of time before she remembered. "Long enough to go from being a very dark soul to a very good one."

"Dark," she murmured. Her attention drifted to the sea as the revelation allowed more memories. Ones he recalled right along with her even though they happened before meeting her. How she had once reveled in being Death's daughter. In causing others pain and fear.

"Until I witnessed great love and began to change," she whispered, not cringing in horror at what she'd once been but taking

79

it in stride. But then, he supposed it helped knowing she'd changed. Had ultimately done good.

"Yes," he replied. "Against the odds considering who sired you, you changed…began to care a great deal."

"I did," she agreed softly.

While she didn't recall the details, might very well never when it came to the specifics of helping Clan MacLomain, she sensed what she needed to. Remembered the person she had become.

"Yet I was supposed to die." Her confused gaze returned to his face. "Why didn't I die?"

Because I couldn't let you. Would not allow it. "Because there was another way."

"What way?"

Leviathan sat and gestured at her dagger. "That way." He recalled the first time he held it. How drawn to it he was. "Where a sword forged by Thor in Múspellsheimr's molten core helped the Sigdirs before, your dagger, one forged by Loki for the Ancients in the same fire, will help them again. Help all of us."

"Loki." Her brows shot up. "Isn't he an evil god?"

"No, he's but a cunning trickster who, granted, likes to create chaos and runs darker than most." His gaze returned to her blade. "His greatest magic, felt clearly in that, is fire itself. A unique fire that possesses tremendous power. Untouchable abilities."

"Like keeping me alive," she surmised. "Yet I get the feeling that came at a cost."

"*Ja.*" He kept his gaze with hers and said it plainly. "In our case, it meant we were forged in fire as the Ancients call it."

Then he told her exactly what that meant.

Chapter Eleven

THOUGH DESTINY FELT anger at what Leviathan shared, she also felt strangely electrified. Alive in a whole new way. Granted, some of that might have come from their kiss earlier or even being in his chamber, or *lair* as dragons called it, but mostly it was the bond forming between them.

Not just from his scale or her mark but from being *forged in fire*.

"So you mean to tell me the particular magic you harnessed via the blade when you killed me made us fated mates?" she repeated, making sure she understood correctly. "That we were bonded in a way, according to lore, that connects us so strongly we'll find each other again life after life? That we'll only ever be satisfied when together?"

"That is how it's told." Leviathan took several long swallows from his mug, clearly disgruntled. "There's no way to know if it's true." He shook his head. "Either way, you didn't deserve a final death because it would have been just that. The sacrifice you were willing to make would have destroyed your soul." His jaw clenched. "You would have ceased to exist."

Though that chilled her, she'd been willing to do it. She had cared that much. Though tempted to ask more about it, she knew deep down that part of her life was behind her. The people at the heart of her sacrifice would live on because of her...and Leviathan.

"So you saved my life knowing what it might mean?" That same electrified thrill went through her again. "Knowing we'd be bonded so strongly? You," she glanced at his irritating monster of a bed again, "a dragon who prefers many females to one. Freedom to monogamy." She gestured between her collar and the tattoo on his neck where she'd marked him. "Now these." Her gaze narrowed on the three interlocking triangles engulfed in flames. "What is that anyway?"

"A Valknut," he replied. "To Ancients, specifically our inner dragons, it means coming together in life, death, then back together in life again. Over and over, interlocked like the triangles themselves. I imagine the flames have to do with being forged in fire." He shook his head, frowning. "Ancients usually get Thor's hammer when their mates mark them. A symbol of the extra strength they'll harness coming together."

"Ah," she murmured, understanding why the Valknut might make him uneasy. After all, it symbolized being mates in many lifetimes rather than just one. "So your tat might just validate the lore behind being forged in fire."

She would never forget how she'd felt when he took the talisman. The startling fear that he might not take it to begin with. The race of her heart when he finally did, and nothing happened. Though she'd deny it, she had known at that moment she actually *wanted* to mark him.

Own him.

Claim him.

She knew her dragon was at work because she didn't normally think that way. Humans shouldn't own or claim each other. Yet her inner beast felt otherwise. Possessiveness had clawed its way to the surface. A need to first bite then nuzzle him. Revel in how his dragon could make hers feel.

Because it had been solely their dragons in that moment. Primal. Instinctual.

The same familiar connection she'd felt when he drove the blade into her.

"Where did I get the dagger?" Before he had a chance to reply, she understood. "It could've only come from my mother even though she's not an Ancient."

"Yes," he confirmed, nodding thanks to the woman who set food on the small table between them. Once she left, he continued. "You claimed your mother had given it to you but said little else."

Frustration furrowed his brows. "If we're to learn more about her and this dagger, it will have to come from your own memories because I know nothing else. Nor, as you're aware, was I able to learn much through the Sigdirs."

"Right." Destiny downed several swallows of ale and eyed the lightning zigzagging over the moonlit ash and dark ocean. "Here's hoping I remember then." She frowned, still trying to put the pieces together. "That must've been why I thought you were going to kill me when I first arrived." She watched him closely, hoping she was right. "Because you already had once…or at least I asked you, and you did…at least, possibly, a part of me."

He nodded, his expression impossible to read. "That would make sense."

"You're lying," she murmured, seeing right through him. Feeling his inner angst as though it were her own. "You're *still* supposed to kill me, aren't you? All the way this time?"

Where she thought he might be evasive, it seemed he understood just how much was coming to her and decided to stick to the truth.

"*Ja.*" The corners of his mouth slanted down. He put some meat on a wooden plate and poured himself more ale. "According to my seer, the only way to keep my people on the outskirts of the war between the gods is to end what turned their attention our way in the first place." He slid the plate to her. "By ending your life, I end the threat to everyone here."

"Hell," she whispered, following not just his words but his thoughts. Understanding perfectly. "You, an Ancient, used a blade made by a Norse god to harness Loki's fire and save me. Used a magic so strong in a time technically before this one, in ancient Ireland, on a Celtic demi-god no less, that you put your people on the gods' radar." She shook her head. "And not in a good way."

"No." His gaze went to the sea as if he could see them coming. "If anything, I brought the wrath of the gods down on me and mine and even, likely, all mankind."

Though the situation was dire, and she frowned on him putting so many at risk, her inner dragon reveled in what he'd been willing to do for her. How much he must have cared. And now this. The collar and her mark. Ways to keep her close and protected.

That's when it hit her…Leviathan did *not* want her dead.

More than that, she got the sense he would fight it with everything he had.

While tempted to ask why a dragon who loathed commitment would do such for someone his people considered a half-breed, maybe even an enemy, she refrained. Mainly because she wasn't ready to hear the answer. Wasn't ready to hear him make false promises when she felt his bed burning a hole in her back. A stark reminder of the hundreds, no, thousands, he'd likely bedded on it.

"So if you don't kill me, the gods will cause even more disruptions," she concluded, trying to focus on more pressing things than the damn bed. "They'll continue draining dragon magic to fuel their war."

"Yes." He urged her to eat.

"Not hungry." She frowned at him, seeing everything clearly enough whether she liked it or not. Because he wasn't lying about any of this. She could feel it. Knew it. Which meant there really was only one course of action. "You need to end me, Leviathan. Just like you did before." She did her best to keep her hand steady when she unsheathed the blade and set it on the table between them. "Only this time, it needs to be final."

"I will," he grumbled, downing more ale. "As soon as the seer confirms you're the one."

He was lying. Trying to buy time.

"Of course, I'm the one." She perked a brow. "Unless you've harnessed Loki's fire to save anyone else lately?"

"I cannot risk it." He scowled at the blade and told her to put it away. "Not only that, but I must find out who these women from the future are. If they're connected to you, to what we did, killing you might be pointless or worse yet, it could escalate things."

"I think you're putting off the inevitable." Yet he was right, so she sheathed the blade. "Though I'll admit I wouldn't mind a few more days alive now that I'm getting to know my dragon." And him. "Do you really think Elsie and her nieces will make a difference?"

"I think it's likely." He finally started eating, almost as if her agreeing to put her blade away had revived his appetite. "It makes sense, does it not, considering they've been planning to travel back in time their whole lives? That they think themselves destined to help humanity?"

"It does." She cocked her head. "Care to elaborate on what you and Freya obviously know? What you were talking about back in her lair in regards to the prophecy? How the sisters in the twenty-first century will be *right* for what lies ahead, and how *love* might be involved? Then I'll share what I know."

"You say the word love as if you don't believe in it," he commented.

"I don't when it comes to two people spending a lifetime together." She shook her head. "But then if I was half god and immortal, that'd make sense. Who wants to watch their other half grow old and die while they remain the same age?" She eyed him, wondering if he felt the same. "Right?"

He shrugged as if he hadn't given it much thought though she got the feeling he had.

"I'm an Ancient. Love isn't something I relate to or need to feel." He made a loose gesture at the bed. "I believe in desire and lust. The physical need to satisfy the flesh so I can function at my best." He shook his head. "Nothing more."

"You must function damn well then if the size of that bed's anything to go off of," she nearly muttered but bit her tongue.

She wondered what life as a goddess had been like. If she enjoyed matters of the flesh. If she had ever fallen in love. Ever felt anything like what she'd just experienced downstairs when wrapped in that fire with him.

More specifically, caught in a memory.

She remembered the tortured frustration in his eyes when she urged him to plunge the blade into her. Recalled the connection that had just started forming between them. How she'd wished they had more time. Yet she had to see things through to save everyone, and only he had the power to finish it. But instead, he'd hesitated. Shown her just how much he liked their newfound connection too. That's when she realized he might not have the strength. That he'd encountered an unexpected weakness.

Her.

Thankfully, in the end, he found the strength, but it hadn't been easy. In fact, she sensed it had been brutal. So brutal that he didn't see it through all the way but harnessed Loki's power. A power so great it shrouded most of what really happened on that rock from everyone.

She recalled with vivid clarity Leviathan's dragon eyes locking with hers. How his magnificent wings had wrapped around her. Pulled her closer. Tight against him. He'd been pure granite. Impregnable strength.

Then he had been something else.

Something more tender before he plunged the blade.

She felt the sting of the metal. Cold, then warmth, then searing heat. Her heart struggled around the blade, her life seeping away until something else filled it. Regenerated it.

Made it beat in a whole new way.

Again she went from ice cold to blazing hot, but not before a slow unexplainable warmth curled through her. Much like how she'd felt when Freya put his collar on her, then again when her mark appeared on his neck.

"Tell me about the prophecy in regards to the sisters," she reiterated, determined to keep the focus off her heart. More pointedly, the warmth that seemed to be inching toward it. The change she felt coming over her because of a memory. Because of Leviathan himself. "What does the prophecy say about them? What does it have to do with what happened between you and me in the Stonehenge?" She hadn't picked up on it before, but she did now. "Because it does, doesn't it?"

"Yes, or so we surmise." He poured her more ale when she finished hers. "The prophecy was made by Tor, son of King Sven and Queen Emily, when he was but a child. He claimed he was haunted by a darkness that called to him. A little girl. One born of powerful fire from both the past and future. Fire that riled the gods who then wreaked havoc on their people."

"You think it's one of the sisters." She followed his train of thought, baffled. "That she was somehow created from or influenced by the flames you harnessed to save me?"

"I think it's a distinct possibility," he replied. "The girl, who could very well be a woman now, stopped haunting Tor around the time you and I met. So it's easy to surmise it's related."

"Add to that I've connected with four female dragons who've been planning to time travel and help humanity," she said. "Women connected to unknown locations via ley lines of all things."

"Ley lines you once saw." He looked from the sky to her in question. "But I assume no longer do?"

"No." She frowned. "That must be why they seemed so familiar to me when Elsie mentioned them." She glanced at him. "It's too coincidental to be unrelated, isn't it? Tor's prophecy, the ley lines, sisters, what we did in the flames?"

"I think we'll know more once we talk to my seer."

"There were five distinct flame colors before my blade appeared in the hearth," she murmured, reflecting on every little detail now. Paying attention to what else might prove relevant. "What do you think that means? Because I only saw bright red flames around us."

"I'm not sure," he responded. "Again, if there's something to it, I'm sure the seer will let us know."

She nodded, thinking about it. "So obviously Freya thinks the sisters are meant to travel back, and it sounds like because of Tor's prophecy, the Sigdirs are prepared for this eventuality."

"They are," he confirmed. "What's more, ironically enough, there are four Sigdir men who would be suitable for the task if they must mate."

"Definitely ironic," she agreed. "And telling." She finally ate a few bites of the succulent meat, surprised by how good it tasted. "Should I assume Dagr and Thorulf are two of them?"

"Yes." Clearly glad to see her eating, Leviathan put more meat on her plate. "The third male born to a Sigdir is married, which only leaves two more. Vicar and Tor."

"And how do those chosen feel about their possible fate?"

"All but Tor is open to the idea." Leviathan shook his head. "But then the others don't think they will have to remain as faithful as their parents have been."

"And what do you think?" She chewed and considered him. "Will they have to be as faithful once they're mated? Assuming, of course, they're destined to hook up with the sisters. Or is it like the rules of my collar, and your mark and multiple mates can be taken?"

"About that." His gaze leveled with hers. "How much did Freya tell you about that collar or what it would mean for you to mark me?"

"Very little."

Which, she soon learned, was with good reason.

87

-Leviathan-

Chapter Twelve

LEVIATHAN FIGURED HE would sleep little with Destiny in his bed, and he was right. Especially considering he wasn't there finally sinking his cock into her. Instead, he'd somehow been brought to heel and slept in a chair, tortured by the sweet scent of her arousal lingering in the air. A scent all the stronger as she slept and dreamt of him. Lived out fantasies of what her dragon wanted him to do to her.

So rather than sleep, he suffered a painful erection all night, finally getting it under control shortly before dawn. Now he leaned against the wall with his arms crossed over his chest, waiting for her to wake, which happened just as the sun cracked the horizon.

"What is it?" she murmured, evidently not unsettled by him watching her sleep. If anything, her dragon rather liked it which naturally, aroused his dragon.

"What is what?" he growled, doing his best to embrace a foul mood. Dark thoughts. Whatever kept him from envisioning her in a variety of tempting positions.

She yawned and stretched like a well-satisfied dragon kitten. But then she'd enjoyed a long night of dreamlike sex.

"Why are you standing there watching me?" she asked.

"I was waiting for you to awake so that we could set out."

"You could've just woken me."

He almost groaned at the sight of her sitting up, with her curls frazzled from sleep and her lovely eyes half-mast. She wasn't even nude or rumpled from rough bed play, and she still drove him to distraction.

She gestured at the bed. "Thanks again for this…all things considered."

Those things being what he'd finally divulged last night about what it truly meant not only to wear his collar but to mark him. Then, to be specific, her response to it.

"You've *got* to be kidding me," she'd replied after he told her. "Even if you were inclined to, you couldn't end me until after we slept together?" She had snorted and shook her head. *"Seriously?"*

"That's the way of it for Ancients and those who desire to be with us," he confirmed. "The collar would have made it more difficult, but your marking me will make it next to impossible. My dragon will fight it every bit as much as yours. Fight it until they know if they're meant to mate." He'd shaken his head. "And they won't know that until they've sampled each other."

"Sampled," she had mouthed, imagining right along with him what that meant. Surprisingly eager for it, actually. At least her inner dragon. Her human half was a tad more miffed. "So I can't help your people or save the world until I sleep with you? And if that goes well, maybe not at all because we'll be mated, and our dragons will protect each other at all costs?"

"That's correct." He'd chosen not to tell her he would force himself if necessary. He *would* override his inner dragon if it meant saving his people.

"Then what the hell?" She'd rounded her eyes at him. "Why did Freya want me to wear your scale? And why didn't you say anything before I marked you!"

"As I remember it," he'd inhaled, recalling that her sweet scent had been as strong then as it was now, "you liked my collar around your neck. As to the mark, you wanted that too. So much so that you challenged my dragon." He'd shrugged. "I don't back down from challenges. So it's safe to say if anyone's to blame here, it would be you."

Suffice it to say that hadn't gone over well, and Destiny had ended the night. Despite her dragon craving his, she made it clear she wasn't sleeping with him. He, in turn, made it clear, perhaps not that night but soon enough.

Unfortunately for her, he wouldn't let her leave, claiming she was safest under his watch. She reminded him their whole collar-mark thing was supposed to keep her safe, too, not to mention the godly storm had passed. He then reminded her that he was striving to keep her safe from enemy Vikings and storm or no storm, perhaps even the gods themselves.

In the end, she stayed but only if it was in a chair because she damn well wasn't going near his overused bed and definitely wouldn't be sleeping in it with him. He, after many disgruntled mutterings, finally gave in and used dragon magic to create a new bed but drew the line at replacing furs that had been with him since childhood.

She, not surprisingly, saw right through that and said, 'bull, he just wanted to make things harder for her,' and she was right. If he was going to suffer, so would she. His furs would see to it, his scent arousing her at every opportunity. That, unfortunately, led to his own rotten night of lusting after her. Especially considering he honored her wishes and didn't sleep in the bed.

"Food is already packed, and Freya left more clothing for you." He gestured at said clothing. "We will set out soon, so we don't get caught in the next storm."

"Ha, just look where you ended up!" came an unexpected voice in Destiny's mind. One he heard just as clearly. *"Good girl."*

This had to be one of the sisters from the future. How long had she been speaking telepathically with them?

"It's not what you think, Jade," Destiny muttered, unaware he followed the conversation. *"I'm surprised I didn't hear more from you last night once I was away from Freya."*

He followed Destiny's thoughts as the two conversed. Apparently, she could only talk with certain sisters at certain times because they ran on different vibrational levels. Maya ran on a higher vibration or frequency, so could more easily communicate around Freya. Jade around him because his frequency was lower. No surprise there. Right where an Ancient's should be.

"Well, I'm glad you're back around your brooder." Jade sounded amused. *"Maybe you're increasing his vibration because there was no getting through to you last night. Some kind of disturbance made it impossible to connect."*

He narrowed his eyes, not liking the sound of that.

"What kind of disturbance?" he asked, finally joining their telepathic conversation.

"Damn, your vibration hasn't gone up that much," Jade said with approval. *"Nice to meet you, handsome."*

"What disturbance?" Leviathan persisted, glossing over an introduction when he sensed Destiny's dragon getting agitated. *"What did it feel like?"*

"It didn't feel like anything," Jade replied. *"But it sounded like fire."*

His and Destiny's fire, then? Or something more?

"The storm," he realized, startled, concerned by the revelation. The fact godly storms disrupted their conversations with what sounded like fire only lent credence to the possibility these women were related to him and Destiny being forged in fire.

To appease Destiny's dragon, he pulled out of the telepathic discussion enough to make her think he was no longer there. He suspected, however, even if he wanted to pull out entirely, his dragon would still hover on the outskirts. Always be with her one way or another.

Moments later, sunlight poured into his lair, and Jade vanished from Destiny's mind.

"So the storms can interrupt conversations as easily as you, it seems," she muttered, getting out of bed.

Though tempted to undress her after she fell asleep last night, for comfort if nothing else, he'd refrained. If he had, he might not have been able to control himself. Worse, he might have upset her. Which, naturally, leant to more frustration. Since when did he worry about upsetting a female? Then again, had a woman ever kept her clothes on in his bed?

Never. They were always nude with their thighs spread wide.

After everyone had slaked their lust, they were sent on their way for whoever wanted them next. Preferring to sleep alone, usually in dragon form, he'd never invited a woman to stay. Not once. Yet now he insisted one stay, plus he gave her the damn bed all to herself. What had that fire done to him? Her collar? His mark?

Nothing good.

And nothing he could turn back from.

Yet deep down, something in him reveled in it. Liked that things were changing. That Destiny was by his side. And it wasn't just his dragon liking it either, but, unbelievably enough, his human half.

Destiny picked up the tunic Freya had provided and gave him a look. "Care to turn around?"

"No," he replied bluntly. "I said I would watch you at all times, so I will."

"Don't be ridiculous."

"I'm not." He dared her with his eyes, knowing her dragon would take the bait. "Does changing in front of a man make you uncomfortable?"

"No," she lied. Her dragon eyes flared.

Fresh heat spiked through him at the thought of her finally getting out of her clothes. Removing her tunic. Baring her breasts. Sliding her pants down so he could finally see...

"You could just use dragon magic," remarked another female voice, cutting off his train of thought. *"Unless you would rather play his game."*

Her voice didn't come through as strongly as Jade's, but he could still hear it.

"Maya," Destiny exclaimed telepathically. *"I didn't think you could be around Leviathan."*

"I couldn't initially, but his vibration's definitely gone up," Maya responded. *"Plus, I'm sensing some sunlight."*

Thor's thunder. His vibration went up? *Damn it.*

"Yup, the sun just came out," Destiny confirmed. Assuming he was in the conversation, she introduced the two. Rather than respond, he chose to remain silent for now, just to see what was said. What Destiny might say when she didn't think he was listening.

She deserved it after what she'd put him through last night, he reasoned.

"His vibration's up but not enough to be in a telepathic conversation with me apparently," Maya said when Leviathan gave no response. *"Probably for the best. According to Jade, his dragon doesn't stick around long when you're speaking to other female dragons. Too risky."*

"Why?"

His thoughts exactly.

"*Because his dragon doesn't want to upset yours.*" There was no missing the smile in Maya's voice. "*More to the point, he doesn't want you to shun or reject him out of jealousy.*"

Damnation.

"*Ahh.*" Destiny smirked at him. "*Good.*"

He scowled back but didn't let on why.

"*Is it good?*" Maya's internal smile only grew. "*So you like your Viking then?*"

He ignored his surge of hope. *Did* Destiny like him? He knew she desired him, but as to actually liking him, he couldn't be sure. Was what they'd found just before she lost her memory returning? Because he swore they were actually starting to like each other.

"*I wouldn't go that far,*" Destiny replied to Maya. "*Not yet.*"

It might have been his imagination, but he swore he saw a flicker of the old her when she glanced his way. The Destiny she used to be.

"*Maybe your human half doesn't like him, but your dragon definitely does,*" Maya chided. "*As to using your magic to change clothes, it's easy and will help some when the time comes to fully embrace your inner beast and shift.*"

Though he remained at ease, everything inside him came to attention. The Destiny he used to know wanted nothing to do with her dragon, never mind its magic. So would she now? Because embracing her magic would set her on a whole new path. It might even set them both on one, yanking them closer together or driving them apart.

"*Okay,*" Destiny replied to Maya. "*What do I do?*"

"*Just want it and envision it,*" Maya stated simply. "*Either envision wearing the clothing provided for you or something else if you prefer, and it should happen.*" She paused a moment. "*Go ahead and try. I'll see if my dragon can give yours a little nudge from my end.*"

Destiny nodded and focused, envisioning the clothing Freya had provided. The supple leather material. The way it would feel against her skin. How comfortable she was in it. How much she liked Viking attire when she had once loathed it.

He tensed at her revelation. What would she make of it? Would she remember it all now? How much she despised her mother? Her Norse heritage?

94

In the end, she had little time to ponder because her inner beast, along with a nudge from Maya's overly loving dragon, got things done. Her dragon eyes flared, and her magic ignited.

"Loki's *hel*," he growled under his breath when her clothing changed in a split second. Yet it had been a split second too long, teasing him with all she had to offer. From the flash of her full, rounded breasts to her small waist and flared hips to the bare, smooth flesh of her long slender legs.

He took two steps forward before he clenched his fists and forced himself to stop. Not just his cold-blooded dragon but the hot-blooded man in him wanted to bend her over his bed and be done with it. Nudge her legs apart, wrap his hands in her hair and take her as roughly as she could handle it.

"That is *not* how you dress," he managed, painfully aroused. *Again.* "Not how you used to dress."

She wasn't in the clothing Freya had provided but supple curve-hugging black leather from head to toe. Knee-high fur-trim boots hugged her shapely calves, and just enough tantalizing cleavage peeked over her tunic. As a whole, no matter how dangerous to his manhood, the outfit *was* good for fighting. Nothing would snag on blades or slow agility. Weapons were sheathed and strapped to logical easy-to-grab locations.

"Maybe it's not how I *used* to dress," Destiny grinned at her attire, "but it is now." She smoothed her hands over her tunic, nodding with approval at the various blades her dragon had evidently decided she knew how to use. "I might not be evil anymore, but I'm feeling the black."

He wondered at that. The Destiny he knew before had rejected darkness and embraced the light. Her wardrobe had reflected that with lighter colors. But then that version of her had rejected her dragon where this one seemed to be embracing it. That alone could change her perspective. Morph her to what she was always meant to be.

Leviathan was about to reply when a heavy, insistent knock came at the door. He'd been so wrapped up in Destiny, kin had approached without him sensing them. Not good. He would need to be more careful in the future. Remember that she made him susceptible to weakness.

He opened the door to Dagr and Thorulf, who were equally disgruntled. By the way Thorulf's gaze locked on Destiny, his frustration was solely due to her collar.

Dagr, however, was upset for another reason altogether.

Chapter Thirteen

"WHERE IS SHE?" Dagr ground out. His gaze swept over Leviathan's lair. "Where is the dragon that was just here?"

"There was no dragon here," Destiny replied before Leviathan had a chance. "It's just us."

"You lie." Dagr started to stride in but stopped short at Leviathan's growl of warning.

"Nobody, even you, steps foot into my lair without permission." Leviathan's gaze flared with his inner dragon, his tone dangerous. "And you will *never* talk to my woman like that again, or I'll gut you where you stand."

Though her dragon preened at his possessive behavior, Destiny kept her expression blank, understanding this wasn't something she should react to. It was between Leviathan and his protégé. Yet, it wasn't easy. Not when Dagr's eyes turned black in defiance, and Leviathan had him against the wall with a blade to his neck in the blink of an eye. Her dragon might have been impressed, but her human side tensed.

Not because of Leviathan's actions either but because of Dagr's terrifying gaze.

Caught off guard, she realized she feared for Leviathan rather than the other way around. But then it wasn't every day a girl saw death in a guy's eyes. Or was it? She shivered at the sensation, the absolute certainty, that she *had* looked into death's eyes a great deal. Celtic death. Her father.

And she hadn't feared it in the least. Any more than Leviathan seemed to fear Norse death.

"*Never* direct Helheim's power at Destiny or me," Leviathan ground out, nose to nose with Dagr. "Do you hear me, dragon? Put it away. Save it for your enemies."

Meanwhile, Thorulf made no sudden movements. Rather, his attention seemed torn between her collar and the mark on Leviathan's neck.

"Listen to him, cousin," Thorulf warned. "She's marked him, so don't test this. He will not be so lenient this time."

She vaguely wondered how often Leviathan was lenient. He didn't seem the sort. But then he didn't seem the type to create a whole new bed and let her sleep in it alone either. Not to say he hadn't made it difficult when he insisted his furs remain. She knew why he'd done it, just not how excruciating it would prove to be. How his scent would wrap around her and entice her to no end. How he would come to her in dreams and tempt her so strongly. Urge her to take him into her. Force her to ride him with rough, reckless abandon.

When he growled into her mind to stop thinking such thoughts so he could focus, she realized just how important it was he hold his ground with Dagr. That his protégé see only strength, not weakness. That he respect and heed Leviathan at all times, so he learned to control his powers well rather than get too cocky or arrogant and wield them poorly. After all, he was born to Hel, so a demi-god by right.

And even half-gods, she realized, no, *remembered*, were not easy to humble.

Moreover, a demi-god dragon who had undoubtedly locked onto Maya or Jade's essence.

Fortunately, though Leviathan and Dagr remained nose to nose for another too-long moment, Dagr finally backed down, and his eyes returned to normal. While clearly tempted to mention the female dragon he'd sensed, Dagr dutifully focused on why he and Thorulf were there instead.

"We need to leave soon if you hope to make Mt. Galdhøpiggen before the next storm." Dagr removed his hand from the hilt of his sheathed weapon when Leviathan put his blade away. "It comes faster than usual, and there's rumor of trouble between here and there."

Leviathan's eyes narrowed. "King Ødger's men?"

"*Ja.*" Though Thorulf's gaze remained on Leviathan, she got the overwhelming sense he'd rather look her way. "If we didn't know better, we'd say he's aware you need to get to your seer and has purposefully put men in your way."

"Men we can handle." Leviathan pulled various blades off the wall and strapped them on. "Is Vicar here?"

"Yes," Dagr confirmed. "And Tor remains at the Fortress."

"Good." Leviathan's gaze swept over Destiny's weapons before he gestured at the wide variety he had to offer. "If you want more, take them. It's time to go."

"Naw, I'm good." She rested her hand on the dagger sheathed at her waist like she knew what she was doing. "If everything else I have doesn't work, I'm sure Loki's dagger will do the trick."

"We'll be downstairs shortly." Leviathan shot Dagr and Thorulf a stern look, evidently a cue to leave immediately, because they left without a backward glance.

She tensed when he turned his attention her way and stepped close. Intimidated her as only his dragon could. "Do not boast about that dagger." He shook his head, frustrated. "Not until we know more about it." His gaze raked over her and his brows furrowed. "And *never* imply you have fighting skills until you actually have them. Not among the Ancients and Múspellsheimr dragons and *especially* not among your enemy."

"I can fight," she defended. "You saw that firsthand."

"I also saw how quickly you were subdued." His gaze narrowed, and his tone turned mildly threatening. Just enough to get his point across. "Whatever happens as we go forward, know that I'll end you quickly if you put my people at risk." His gaze narrowed further still. "And I'll do it even if our dragons mate."

"And here I thought that would be next to impossible," she ground out. "Yet you make it sound easy enough."

Rather than back down, she felt a familiar sense of defiance. As though she might have argued with him before in a life slowly but surely coming back to her.

Unafraid of him, or death for that matter, she grabbed his wrist and slammed the hilt of Loki's dagger, as she called it, into his open palm. "Do it then," she taunted, coming as nose to nose with him as she was capable of at her height. "Finish it now because I won't be threatened, and I sure as shit won't be brought to heel."

"Are you sure, little dragon?" he replied softly. *Too* softly. His pupils flared. "Because I think you will be," he taunted, switching gears, "and it won't be by my blade."

Changing his game, coming at her in a way that weakened her defenses, the corner of his mouth curled up ever-so-slightly, as he took the dagger. Slow, like a lion stalking its prey, he slid the blade back into its sheath, wrapped his hand into her hair, and walked her back until she hit the wall.

"This is what you want, is it not?" He came close, so close she could feel his heat. The burn of his rock-hard shaft against her belly. "Not death, not yet, but…"

Her dragon melted, liquefied, drowned in his gaze, tempted beyond reason, but her human half wasn't ready for him to have his way quite yet. To give him all the control. Because she would eventually. She'd relinquish every last bit when the time was right.

Until then, she'd hold her ground.

So she came up hard and swift with her knee. He chuckled and deflected before he had her against the wall, her back to his front.

"I think I'll enjoy your internal struggle," he murmured in her ear. His hot breath fanned her neck. "You feel it, yes? How what's left of your former dominant goddess craves to submit? To revel in the freedom I can give her from all the obligations she once carried?" When he nipped her earlobe, she swore she purred. "I'll show you just how free you can be, Destiny. Just how much you can finally let go."

She stilled at his dangerous promise. How it made her feel. Something deep down inside thrilled at the idea. Welcomed it where she never could before. She wanted to lose herself in the escape he offered. The wicked, sinful delights she'd never indulged in.

When his hand inched along her thigh toward the throbbing flesh between her legs, she nearly gave in. Let him show her what it could be like. *Would* be like. Because he was fully capable. Eager. Designed to pleasure her. Make her scream. Dominate her until she lost all sense of the mental weight she'd carried.

But not yet.

Not until they figured out how to save his people.

"We need to go."

Though damn hard, she sidled free of his grasp and, much to her pleasure, managed to manifest a black fur cloak that fit her perfectly. She headed for the door rather than look into his alluring eyes again and risk what little willpower she had left.

There was no need to look back to know he followed nor that he both approved and disapproved of her actions. Approved because she put his people first. Disapproved because he wanted to be between her thighs as much as she wanted him there.

No doubt the time would come too. She'd resolved herself to that much. Knew her dragon had to have his before everything was said and done. Which, based on her ever-growing need, would be sooner rather than later.

"What's Vicar's mood?" Leviathan asked when they joined Thorulf and Dagr at the bottom of the stairs. Fewer people roamed the great hall than the night before, most going about day-to-day business rather than socializing.

"It's damn dark," Liv groused, joining them. She shot Destiny a look. "But that's where we want him so we can get the princess to her perch on the mountain, *ja*?"

"Go, Liv." Leviathan gestured at the door, paying her no mind. "Start scouting. We'll join you soon." He looked at Dagr. "Go with her. Keep Helheim at the ready."

Dagr nodded and strode after Liv.

So the Viking who liked her least was coming? Wonderful.

"What's going on with Vicar?" she asked, pursuing Leviathan when he strode toward the chamber they were in the night before.

"My younger brother is in one of his more unusual moods," Thorulf explained, falling in beside her. "His inner Múspellsheimr dragon has emerged so that he might lead Leviathan's people well in his absence." He flinched. "Or should I say better than most as long as we're not gone too long."

When she frowned in confusion, he only shook his head. "You'll see soon enough."

She did too when they rounded the corner into the adjacent chamber with its roaring fire and plethora of intimidating dragons. It felt darker somehow in the light of day. More sinister and domineering. But then she imagined the man sitting on the throne-looking chair had something to do with that.

Like his Sigdir brethren, Vicar was broad-shouldered and handsome as sin. His dark hair was unbound, and his sizzling gold dragon eyes feral and dangerous. Tempting in a way that had several females simpering at his feet, clearly willing to service him. He wore nothing but leather pants, heavy boots, and a fur cloak over his muscular torso, allowing all to see the triangular tattoo covering his chest and bottom half of his neck. His long legs were stretched out casually, and his demeanor that of a man who belonged on a throne whether it was his or not.

"Wow," she muttered under her breath, glancing at Thorulf. "What's up with Conan the Barbarian?"

When Thorulf looked at her in confusion, she shook her head and mouthed, "Never mind."

Vicar and Leviathan never exchanged words, but she knew they spoke telepathically when their eyes connected. Leviathan was making sure he was fit to rule. That he would keep the peace. All the while, those present looked back and forth between them as though waiting for a possible confrontation that never came. Instead, Vicar merely nodded once in response.

Leviathan nodded once as well and addressed the room. In fact, she suspected he used dragon magic to address the whole Realm.

"Vicar will lead you in my absence." His fierce gaze swept over the chamber, locking on several of the larger males. "Defy him once, and you will deal with me."

When all nodded, their respect obvious, Leviathan spun back only to slow at her side and meet her eyes. Understanding, willing to be what he needed to keep up appearances, she fell in beside him and left. Not behind him as his slave, but beside him as his equal.

As his possible mate.

She remained between Leviathan and Thorulf as they headed through the crowd that had formed outside. Many stopped and nodded in goodwill to Leviathan, where others, mostly men, had their weapons at the ready, hoping they could join them. Fight with him.

"I'm going to see my seer to find out what comes next," he announced. "To find out if the time has come to make a stance."

Although Leviathan spoke loud enough for everyone to hear, she sensed he didn't need to. That his magic carried his words. His gaze went from person to person as they slowed, stopped, watched him.

Waited for him to make things right. To fix the long plights they'd suffered because of the gods.

"We will be free of this soon enough," he promised, looking from man to woman to child. "You have my word. My vow."

She knew that hadn't been easy for him to say when there was no way to know how true it was. If he could put an end to what had been happening. Yet it had to be said. These people, *dragons*, needed hope. It was clear in too many eyes.

Many nodded, some made what appeared religious symbols in the air, where others yelled out their approval. Some even cursed the gods before Leviathan shook his head sharply, his dragon eyes blazing.

"Though difficult, we must not curse the gods until we know if any stand with us," he counseled, finally introducing Destiny. Sort of. "My potential mate's arrival marks change. A chance in this war. With any luck, my seer will know what that is. How we move forward."

Leviathan again met many an eye before he continued, hinting at unrest in the Realm. Division. But then she'd just glimpsed such when some prayed to the gods and others cursed them.

"Until I've spoken to my seer, we must all play our part," Leviathan said. "Support each other. Stand as *one*." He shook his head. "*Never* divided. For that is how the greatest empires fall. The greatest people." Leviathan's gaze swept over the lot of them. "Be better. Wiser. *Stronger*."

With that, he continued moving, and she fell in beside him again, pleased to see not two but three horses awaiting them at the gates. Leviathan took the reins of the smaller black one and stepped close, his gaze on her face, his voice within her mind. *"Do you remember how to ride?"*

"Because I knew how to before I take it?" She ran her hand along the horse's nose, liking the feel of it...remembering it.

"Yes, you knew how to ride." His eyes never left her. *"Though it would be best if you rode out of here on your own horse to show strength, my people will understand if you don't."* He paused, his momentary silence more telling than words. *"You are from a time where horses are not ridden as often. Not for transportation."*

What he didn't say, but she could see in his eyes, feel in his dragon, was that his people knew she might be more. Someone greater than a time traveler. Greater, even, than his mate.

"And what do they think of that?" she wondered. *"I assume they don't know I might be at the root of their troubles, but what do they know about who I once was?"* She cocked her head. *"Or do they even know I was once among those they call their enemy?"*

"No, not yet," he replied. *"But remember, the Norse gods are just as much at fault for draining our energy as the Celts."* He glanced from Thorulf back to her. *"Not just that but Thorulf and Vicar have Celtic godliness too."*

"Ah." Now it made sense. *"That's why Thorulf seems,"* how to say it? *"particularly drawn to me?"* She narrowed her eyes. *"Yet Vicar doesn't?"*

"When in his current personality, Vicar shuns his Celtic blood so he wouldn't be drawn to you," he explained. *"Thorulf has no such issue."* Though Leviathan cast a frustrated glance at Thorulf, no doubt because he desired Destiny, he defended him. *"He's never met an unrelated dragon with Celtic blood, so it's to be expected. He is strong, though, so you need not worry."*

"I wasn't." Destiny swung onto the horse like it was the most natural thing in the world. *"But it's good to know."* She considered what he'd said. The thoughts flickering through his mind. *"It's not just my lineage he's drawn to, though, is it, but maybe more?"* The same sensation she'd had the night before washed over her. A sense of power that was unrelated to her dragon. *"Could it be my godliness? Something I'm not supposed to have anymore?"*

"Perhaps." He swung onto his horse as well and steered it alongside hers. *"I feel it in you too, but I can't be entirely sure it's your godliness. When we first met, we weren't bonded, so I wouldn't necessarily recognize the feel of it."* He glanced from Thorulf to her. *"I imagine, however, he will if it's truly returning."*

While it ground a little on her dragon that another male might understand something about her before the male she'd marked, her human half was fine with it. If anything, she was grateful she wasn't alone when it came to possible Celtic godliness.

She glanced from Leviathan's monstrous horse to Thorulf's when he pulled up on her other side. "Impressive."

"Beasts born and bred to suit our size and species." Dragon eyes flaring, Leviathan nodded to his people that they stand strong, then the three of them exited beneath the vicious-looking portcullises and left his Keep behind.

She frowned. "Isn't Freya coming?"

"No, she will stay to help balance Vicar," Leviathan replied.

"She sends her regards and wishes you well," Thorulf added. "She would have spoken to you telepathically or came to send you off but best that she remain undisturbed right now. She must gather her strength until she's needed."

"Needed?" She frowned between them. "What does that mean exactly?"

"It means her positive influence will keep Vicar from going too far," Leviathan said.

"And what's too far?"

His response shocked her.

Better yet, made her wonder why he would leave the whole of his kingdom in Vicar's care.

-Leviathan-

Chapter Fourteen

"**H**OW CAN YOU be so sure he won't turn on your people?" Destiny finally asked after Leviathan explained why Freya needed to assist Vicar. After she learned the truth about who he was.

Better yet, who he had been.

"Seems pretty risky leaving him in charge," she commented. "Too risky."

They had been riding for hours, all of which she'd silently brooded because he'd requested everyone remain silent, both aloud and telepathically, as they passed through a particular area.

"Freya will keep Vicar level," Leviathan reiterated. "Outside of Tor, she's the only one who can."

"For a time," Destiny replied. "Or so it sounds." She glanced between Thorulf and Leviathan. "Has he really been like this since he was a child? Straddling two worlds? One foot here half the time and the other in Múspellsheimr?"

"It's been staggered." Thorulf sighed. "But yes, from a young age, Vicar has battled with who he was in his former life. His previous incarnation."

"An incarnation that led dragons here who wanted to escape that awful world," Destiny confirmed. "Who was, in another life, one of the most powerful dragons to ever live. One who risked everything to see his people safely to Midgard. A world where they could cherish their females rather than enslave them. Brutalize them." Her pained gaze went between them again. "Now, despite all that, he suffers what we'd call in the twenty-first century a split personality disorder? Worse yet, it sounds like he's a smidge rougher around the edges this time."

Leviathan appreciated her angst, that she felt so strongly, because he did too. Always had. But that didn't change Vicar's plight any more than it did each of his protégés. They all faced struggles, and he helped them the best he could. Tried to lift them up even as he pushed them over the edge and forced them to try harder. Be stronger than all the rest. Prepared for what was coming.

Little did he know that he might have been the key that unleashed that very 'coming.'

Either way, Vicar had displayed two very prominent personalities since childhood. One, a Sigdir dragon. More kind-hearted, friendly, a devoted family member. The other, very much a Múspellsheimr dragon only tempered by the fact he'd been born on Midgard this time. With a knack for leading, he was driven and primal, embracing all the traits of their homeworld. Ancient and Múspellsheimr females alike flocked to him, and he welcomed all, only endearing himself more to the males of Leviathan's tribe.

So it only made sense as the years wore on that Leviathan trained him to be his second-in-command. To lead in his absence. Which, interestingly enough, worked whether Vicar was Sigdir or Múspellsheimr dragon at the time. The personality that embraced his homeworld, however, was always preferred, as seen clearly earlier.

"I wouldn't say Vicar's rougher in this life," Leviathan replied. "Just more heavily influenced by the fluctuating temperaments of our dragons lately. He's eager to fight. Lash out and defend our people. Likely because his former dragon felt responsible for them."

He shook his head before continuing. "That's not the way to go yet, though. Not until we know exactly who our enemy is. Otherwise, we could bring the wrath of the gods down on us rather than remain on the outskirts of their war." He sighed. "Even then, knowing which gods are the enemy, how do we wage war on them? Must we travel to their worlds? Engage them in their natural habitat where they're stronger?"

There was no right answer. Not yet. But there would be. Had to be.

"Hopefully, my arrival will mean your seer has the answers you're looking for," Destiny replied, still concerned about Vicar. "What do his parents think of his plight?" Her worried gaze went to Thorulf. "Your parents?"

"My stepmother Ava, Vicar's blood mother, frets over him," Thorulf admitted. "But our father Soren keeps things level. Makes it work somehow." He shook his head. "So it's not all that bad."

Likely because of their Celt lineage, she sensed things he didn't say. Realized he was next in line to his own throne.

"That must be tricky even if your father's king of his own realm." Destiny peered at Thorulf, just as concerned about him as she'd been about Vicar. "And what about you? This can't be easy."

"It is not," Thorulf conceded, enjoying her attention more than Leviathan would like, but there was no hope for it. He had to accept they would bond on some level. If her godliness was, in fact, returning, then Thorulf could more readily aid her in how to navigate it. Not just that, but they were fellow Sigdirs. Her people, whether she remembered them or not.

"I help Vicar when I can," Thorulf said. "When and if I'm able."

"Right...because of Tor," she murmured, obviously sensing the connection. "A brother to Vicar even though he's really a cousin."

Leviathan nodded. "Tor inherited much from his father, Sven. Not just an ability to heal but his father's gift of foresight and a wisdom and levelness that few humans possess. He's always stabilized Vicar well, grounding him better than most."

"You make Tor sound like the strongest of your protégés," she remarked, picking up on quite a bit, "even though he's the only one who doesn't possess godliness."

"Because he is as long as the war between the gods rages," Dagr replied. He and Liv rode behind them. "The gods' mayhem is affecting those of us with godliness."

"Dagr and Vicar especially," Thorulf clarified. "Likely because I have the least amount of godliness."

"I would think no matter how much you all possess, one way or another, your godliness will end up helping somehow." Destiny gave Leviathan an odd look. "Because it seems like it should, shouldn't it?" Before he had a chance to ask her why she felt that way, her gaze drifted to the forest ahead of them. "What is this place anyway? It feels…"

"Familiar to you," he murmured, sensing her thoughts, the conflicting emotions tied in with them.

"Yes." Her eyes narrowed in confusion, her question out of the blue. "Why didn't I ask you about her sooner, Leviathan?"

"Who?"

"My mother?" Her gaze shot to him. "I spoke to you about her when we first met, didn't I?" Before he could answer, she figured things out. "I despised her…hated her for shunning me."

"Yes," he confirmed, unsure why she remembered just now. Perhaps because she was embracing her inner dragon? Had used her dragon magic for the first time? All he knew was the idea of disliking her mother bothered her a great deal. He felt it in her troubled thoughts. Saw it in her eyes. In the pain she tried to hide.

He made to respond, to ease her distress, but didn't have a chance before they were attacked from all angles.

"Fight the ones coming in from the right," Leviathan roared into everyone's minds. *"They're Ødger's men."* It was better to battle on foot with this many coming at them, so he swung down from his mount and pulled Destiny after him. *"The ones on the left are part of a memory."*

"Part of a memory?" Destiny frowned at the very real-looking men on their left. *"I don't understand."*

While Liv and Dagr attacked the incoming warriors head-on, he and Thorulf took up position beside Destiny until they knew how well she could wield her blades.

"This place is called the Forest of Memories." Leviathan whipped a dagger into the throat of an incoming warrior then side-kicked another. *"It replays random memories. Usually, ones related to whoever's passing through."*

"Whose memory is that?" She gestured at the warriors, who appeared to be taking a stance against something coming. *"They almost look like they're protecting…me."* Despite keeping an eye on the memory warriors, she still managed to whip an axe and down one of Ødger's men. *"In fact, they are. I can feel it."*

Leviathan and Thorulf perked their brows at how well she'd felled the enemy and kept fighting. He ran his blade across the midsection of one man, then banged the heads of two more together.

"They are protecting you." Dagr's eyes turned black and narrowed on the woodland while he fought. *"They protect you against the other side...the darkness."*

"Darkness," Destiny whispered. Her blade suddenly dropped from a lifeless hand, and her gaze drifted to the same area. "He's coming for me."

"Hell," Leviathan muttered, having no choice but to fight on. "She's caught in the memory now."

The moment he said it, everything shifted. Grew brighter. Sharper. More vivid. Most of all, though, his surroundings became more revealing. The battling still raged, but now he could see spirits rising out of those who just died.

Destiny had vanished. Instead, a woman with similar features stood where she once had.

"We've shifted to the other side," Dagr said, the only other one who could see what Leviathan saw. "Because I'm here, we see it as Helheim, but that's not what it was. How it really looked."

"No, it was dark and sinister." He saw it out of the corner of his eye. Sensed its familiar evil. "Though we stand in Hel's realm, the land of the dead, Celtic death has come for her."

Unsettled by his surroundings, Celt and Norse alike, Leviathan scowled and whipped his axe into a man rushing him. This was how Dagr saw things more often than not lately. Spirits that others couldn't. Honestly, it was a wonder he kept his humor.

"I still sense Destiny, but I can't see her." Leviathan suddenly understood when he glanced at the woman's swollen stomach. "She's in there. Yet to be born."

"Ja." Like the men defending her, Dagr's attention remained fixated on the woodland. "They won't be able to protect her from what comes. He's far too powerful." Dagr sneered. "He's not welcome here. This is *not* his land."

"No," Leviathan growled, sensing the intruder as well. One he had dealt with before. "It's her father."

"Get me out of here," Destiny roared from what sounded like a great distance away.

Unfamiliar panic blew through him at her distress. What should he do? How could he help her? Thankfully, moments later, sunlight burst through the forest and burned away the memory before it had a chance to continue.

The woman vanished, and Destiny returned.

Everyone formed a protective circle around her and kept fighting when she dropped to her knees and hung her head. Leviathan punched a warrior so hard he fell flat on his back, then shot Liv a nod of thanks when she blocked an incoming arrow before it hit Destiny.

"Are you well, Destiny?" He felt her overwhelming fear. "What just happened?"

He wanted to go to her, comfort her, but had to keep fighting. End this lot. So he fought harder, faster, felling three, sometimes four warriors at once before Thorulf took down the last of them, and it was finally over.

"Destiny." He crouched and tilted her chin up, surprised to find tears rolling down her cheeks. Pained by it, actually. "Are you all right?"

"Yeah," she whispered, still trying to gather herself. Her fear had vanished, only to be replaced with something else. "I just...she was...not what I expected."

"No," Dagr agreed, crouching beside them. Interestingly, his eyes had returned to normal in record time. "Who was she? I sensed her in Leviathan's lair earlier too."

Destiny blinked in confusion before she seemed to realize.

"That was Maya who drove the memory away." She kept her answer simple for now. "She's a friend."

"A powerful one at that," Dagr praised, impressed, and most definitely interested.

"That's not who you were talking about, though," Leviathan surmised, disgruntled that he was tempted to wipe away her tears. When had he ever wanted to do that? Never. Tears weren't something he dealt with nor typically had any use for. Yet seeing hers, feeling what had caused them, touched something in him he didn't know was there. Compassion he had no idea he possessed.

"No, I wasn't talking about Maya," Destiny murmured. "I was talking about my mother." Emotion flickered in her gaze. "She loved me, Leviathan. A great deal...and I think I loved her too...I think we must've had time together before my father took me." She narrowed her eyes. "Because he *did* take me in the end. Stole me away and turned me against her."

Remembering her mother when she did made sense now. Somehow her mother's dragon was reaching out to Destiny's. Making sure she knew the truth. And what better place to do that than in the Forest of Memories?

"If you had time with your mother, then your father didn't succeed in taking you during that memory." He helped her up. "Something powerful must have come to your mother's aid. Something we might have witnessed had the memory not vanished."

"True, but I couldn't be more grateful to Maya for getting rid of it." She glanced at Dagr. "Usually, she can't be around that low of a vibration, but because of my mother..." Her gaze returned to Leviathan, and she brushed away tears. "She was exceptionally good. Very kind."

He believed it, considering Destiny herself. Not just the woman she had been when they first met but who she was becoming again.

"I'm glad you learned as much." Though not one to be tender, he couldn't help but cup her cheek, touch her in comfort. "Are you truly okay, Destiny? That was...a lot. Your father is a monster, and you just remembered that, yes? Felt it?"

"Yes." A shiver went through her. "Knowing he was coming was terrifying. If Maya hadn't pulled me free," she swallowed hard, "let's just say it felt so damn real. As though he were really here, not in a memory. As though he were seeking me out, determined to end me rather than steal me."

He didn't like the sound of that but kept it from his face and thoughts the best he could. She'd sent her father back to the dredges from which he arose, but he would always exist. So *could* he be coming for her? Might he have better access because of this war?

Yet another question for his seer.

"I'm all right now, Leviathan." She gave him a grateful look. "And glad you were there. That I wasn't alone." She looked at Dagr. "You were there too, weren't you? Caught in that weird sub-dimension? Oddly, though I couldn't see it, I felt it." Another shiver went through her. "It was both beautiful and horrifying at the same time."

"As death can be," Dagr murmured. "Yes, I was there because I was partially raised in Helheim." He wiped the blood from his blade and kept his gaze from the bodies at his feet. A courtesy to the spirits departing them that they might move on in peace. "It can be very uncomfortable for those not used to it." He nodded once in approval. "You did well keeping fear at bay as long as you did. Not easy for such a young one."

Though Destiny's brows perked in surprise, not just at what he'd said but because of what she sensed through Leviathan, she merely nodded in thanks.

"That's got to be disconcerting," she said into Leviathan's mind, confirming she'd picked up on what Dagr was capable of. *"To send people to their death only to see their spirits when they're gone. To confront the soul you just ended."*

"The spirit never ends but continues on." Convinced she was okay, he gathered their weapons. *"Vikings take great pride in dying during battle, eager to take their place by Odin's side in Valhalla,"* or so he hoped nowadays, *"so Dagr did them a favor."* He wiped and sheathed his blade. *"We do not mourn death but celebrate it."*

At least that had been the case until he'd plunged his blade into her in Ireland. Until he felt the intense fear that came with ending her. The sadness that followed in its wake.

"We need to continue on," he said when thunder rumbled in the distance. "The next storm approaches."

Everyone nodded in agreement and continued gathering their weapons. By the time they made their way through the woodland, the sky was darkening. Fortunately, they came across no more sinister memories and made it to the Cave Catacombs before lightning spiked across the sky.

"So we travel underground from here on out?" Destiny eyed the endless dark tunnel ahead as they dismounted and led the horses to a stream. "What about the horses?"

"Men will come for them after the storm passes." Thorulf pulled blankets out of a chest they had tucked away. "They'll be well protected inside the cave until then."

She nodded and patted hers while it drank. "Good."

"You like her then?" Leviathan asked, putting blankets over their beasts.

"I do." She smiled when her horse's ear twitched in pleasure. "I get the sense I shouldn't, nor that she should like me, but I still do…and she still does."

"Then she's yours." Anything she wanted was. "Even if they hadn't been bred to allow dragons near them, I sensed your horse would like you. That she understands what's at the heart of you."

That earned him a look of amusement from Thorulf and Dagr, who had never heard him talk like this. Normally, he'd be bothered by that, too, but he wasn't. Which *should* alarm him. But it didn't. Instead, a strange sense of acceptance was coming over him. A bizarre transformation.

That's when he realized…he was changing.

She was changing him.

And he had no one to blame but himself.

He had chosen this path, knowing deep down she wouldn't be easy to walk away from. More than that, there was a good chance had she not traveled back in time, he might have sought her out. Might have suffered the garb of a twenty-first-century man just to knock on her door and talk to her one last time.

"I'll hunt then catch up with you," Dagr said, pulling him from his thoughts when he vanished into the woodland.

"We have enough food on us." Liv scowled at the sky. "He pushes it."

"You mean tempts it." Thorulf scowled at the sky as well. "I'll go after him."

"You'll stay with us," Leviathan corrected. "I won't have two of you caught in the storm." He gestured that they get the horses settled and frowned into the woodland after Dagr. "You cannot stop a man with a mission."

When Destiny looked at him in question, he explained. "He hasn't seen his birth mother in some time and worries over her welfare."

"Understandable." She glanced in the direction Dagr had gone. "Does he think he'll come across Hel in one of these storms?"

"So it seems." He sighed. "And now that he shifted into Helheim in that memory, he thinks it even more likely. That she might be trying to reach out to him somehow."

"Maybe she is," Destiny murmured, her gaze suddenly fixed on a nearby location. "If that's anything to go off of."

Chapter Fifteen

DESTINY FELT THE black mass before she saw it. Sensed *him* before she saw him. Not her father but something...*someone* else. Based on the way Leviathan and the others tensed and slowly drew their blades, whoever it was had them on high alert.

Almost as if it warned them what was coming, thunder cracked directly overhead, and lightning flashed brightly.

"Thor's thunder," Thorulf murmured into their minds. He and Leviathan shifted closer to her in protection. *"The gods take notice. Thor takes notice."*

"Of what, though?" Leviathan narrowed his eyes on the shifting darkness that flickered in and out of the darkening woodland. *"There is great power in it."*

"It's familiar," she whispered, trying to lock onto it. See it more clearly. It had a form. Maybe even a human shape.

A blink later, it was directly in front of her.

Leviathan yanked her against him and held his blade at the ready as the foggy mass twisted and morphed until it seeped into the ground, leaving a man behind.

As tall, broad, and intimidating as Leviathan, he was clad from head to toe in black leather with long, flowing ebony hair and sharp, striking features. Fiercely handsome and dripping with arrogance, his magnetic gaze never left her face. He seemed to cherish her appearance. First, in a way a man might admire a woman, then with a different sort of tenderness. One she couldn't quite place.

"Praise the gods," Thorulf whispered. He and Liv dropped to a knee and lowered their heads.

"Praise Loki." Liv made some sort of Norse symbol in the air without looking up.

Destiny forgot to breathe. *Loki?* As in the actual god? But then Leviathan *had* harnessed his power to save her life. She sensed Leviathan was tempted to fall to a knee, too, but remained where he was, unwilling to let her go.

Loki remained perfectly silent, eerily quiet, studying her face until his gaze slowly fell to the dagger at her waist. *His* dagger. His hand flexed as though he intended to take it, but he didn't. Instead, his dark gaze slid to Leviathan and held for several long moments, almost as though he sized him up. Then, half a breath later, he vanished not within the shifting darkness but a whoosh of all-too-familiar flames.

Liv cursed and looked at Leviathan as she and Thorulf rose. "Has Loki ever appeared to any of us? To any dragon?"

Leviathan shook his head. "Not that I know of." Rather than let Destiny go, he kept her close, his strong body still tight. Tense. Ready to fight and protect her. "If he has, he probably looked different, and we never knew."

Right, because Loki could shapeshift.

"That was him, though," she said softly, never so sure of anything. "That form was his real one. At least when he visits Midgard and becomes human."

Lightning flashed more vividly, as if angry this time, reminding them a war raged overhead. A dangerous battle between powerful entities.

When Thorulf looked at Leviathan in renewed concern about Dagr, Leviathan finally relented.

"Go get him," he agreed. "But make it fast." His arm tightened around her reflexively, as if he didn't want to let her go but had no choice, before he stepped away. "We'll await you at the first waterfall."

Not needing to be told twice, Thorulf was gone.

"The two of them are close, I take it?" she concluded. They left the horses safely at the mouth of the cave and headed in.

"Yes, since they were boys," Leviathan replied. "Though everyone gets along, some are closer than others. Tor and Vicar. Thorulf and Dagr."

She glanced at Liv, wondering who she was close with, figuring it out quickly enough based on her and Leviathan's easy comradery. The way she tracked him everywhere he went. Which made her wonder. Despite his vow to never lay with her, how close *was* Leviathan to Liv?

"Close enough," he replied into her mind. He removed several wall torches, lit them, and handed one to Liv. *"But not for the reasons you think."*

When Destiny glanced at him in confusion, he explained. *"Liv, or better yet, her dragon, is drawn to me because she's drawn to my younger brother without realizing it."*

"How can she not realize it?"

"Because they barely know each other," he replied. *"Torc prefers a small sub-group of dragons who keep to themselves. They pay homage to our main tribe and recognize me as their leader but prefer their own community. He's wanted Liv since she was young but had to wait for her to grow up."*

"Meanwhile, her dragon will settle for you because, what, you share similar DNA?" she guessed.

"Exactly." He glanced at her with approval. *"You're thinking more and more like a dragon."*

Her inner beast preened a little at the compliment, but she made no comment.

"So when will Torc approach her?" And get her attention off Leviathan. *"Make his intentions known?"*

"Soon, I imagine," he replied. *"His offspring have been meandering around the Realm more often lately. No doubt, getting a sense of her dragon. What they can expect."*

"So you have nieces and nephews?"

She wondered if he had any children of his own but couldn't seem to ask, mainly, she realized, because it discomforted her dragon. Honestly, though, what did she care if he had kids? He'd been around a while, so it made sense. Yet her inner beast only grew more disgruntled at the thought. The idea that he might share that kind of bond with another female dragon.

"Yes, I have nieces and nephews." He shook his head. *"As to your dragon's other concern, no, I don't have any offspring."* His voice sounded a little gruff, as though he wasn't entirely truthful. *"It was not something I ever desired."*

"You're lying," she murmured before she could stop herself. But he was, and her dragon wanted to understand why. *"What held you back?"*

He didn't respond right away, likely weighing how transparent he wanted to be before he decided to come clean.

"I'd prefer to tell you my dragon didn't find a suitable enough female to sire its offspring, but that wouldn't be the whole truth." The corners of his mouth tugged down. *"Every generation of Ancients live shorter and shorter amounts of time, adjusting to the lifespan of those here on Midgard...or Earth as you call it..."*

When he trailed off, she caught his apprehension and understood. *"You don't want to outlive your children."*

"No," he admitted. *"I've watched it happen enough to fellow Ancients, and it's not good."* He shook his head. *"Though such devastates humans, it's far worse for dragons. We connect on a different level with our offspring. It is..."*

When he struggled to find the right words, she understood because her dragon made it clear. The unthinkable horror of it. *"Unbearable."*

"Yes," he confirmed. *"I've seen dragons die from losing their offspring. The pain's too great. Too difficult to process."* His brows furrowed. *"Now, with what the gods are doing and having watched many die, Sigdir and Ancient alike, I'm even less inclined. Though they weren't mine, the children the next generation of Sigdirs lost was...very difficult."*

"How many?" she asked softly.

"Two so far. Liv's brother, and Dagr's sister."

"I'm so sorry." And she really was. How awful for them.

"So you see why I choose not to sire any?"

"I do." Yet, it troubled her on a primal level. Upset her dragon. Though she shouldn't ask, she couldn't help it. She wanted to know where he would stand if things were different. If he would, as it sounded, enjoy having children. *"So if there wasn't a war and your children didn't outlive you, would you want to have them?"*

She did her damndest to keep her dragon's distress repressed but had a feeling he sensed it. Knew it struggled with never creating offspring with its potential mate. But then, in her defense, she was in heat. The dragon equivalent of ovulating.

"Likely not," he murmured, yet she sensed his interest, the churn of his thoughts. *"Why do you ask?"*

Because I might be your damn mate, she thought. A dragon who deserves children if I want them. If he didn't sense that, she certainly wasn't going to tell him.

She shrugged. *"Just curious, I suppose."*

Though she suspected he knew it was more than that, he returned to talk of Liv. Not just to take her mind off procreating but to eliminate some of her dragon's anxiety on the competition front. Or so she assumed.

"Whether Liv knows it or not, even as she seems to desire me, she subconsciously pushes me away because of Torc," Leviathan went on. *"That's why she incited you to mark me last night. She had to know her taunting would make your dragon act."*

Destiny had wondered about that because, in the end, it had been Liv, not Freya, who pushed her over the edge. Liv, who ensured Leviathan would be lost to her. At least for a little while as she put it.

The day wore on without them conversing much more, but that was okay. She needed time to think. To soak up all she'd witnessed today between her mother, father, Loki, and now learning that Leviathan didn't want children. Or so he'd led her to believe.

She wondered if she'd ever had any of her own.

"No," she whispered, almost certain of it.

When Leviathan glanced at her oddly, she realized he'd followed her thoughts. Wondered why. But it was clear soon enough as those particular memories returned. Her plight had been similar to his. Once she began to move beyond the darkness of her father, a time when she had no use for offspring, she saw the flaw in producing children.

They would grow old and die while she remained young.

"Aforementioned reasons aside, is that why you never took a mate?" She knew she should leave it alone, but her dragon remained curious. *"Because you didn't want offspring?"*

After all, Ancients and Múspellsheimr dragons likely lived as long as him, so it wasn't a matter of them aging while he didn't.

"In part," he replied. *"But mostly because I prefer...diversity."*

Was it her imagination, or had he sounded hesitant? As though perhaps he wasn't completely sure about that anymore? If so, she understood because she felt the same. Wondered. Collar and mark aside, *was* there something more between them? Potential for fidelity? Perhaps even something akin to love?

Yes, her inner voice said without hesitation. *Yes,* to remaining by his side.

But most of all, unfortunately, *yes* to having children.

She tried to keep the avalanche of thoughts tumbling through her mind private but knew he sensed them. Moreover, she felt his human half pull back instinctually while his dragon remained intrigued. At attention. Drawn to her inner musings.

So much so that she said the last thing she intended.

Chapter Sixteen

"SO SHOULD I listen to my dragon?" Destiny said. "Or should I listen to the demi-god I once was?"

"*Always* listen to your dragon," Liv muttered. They had just made it to the waterfall Leviathan told Dagr and Thorulf to meet them at, so they stopped. Highlighted by lightning flashes overhead, water poured down from a massive crack in the ceiling and vanished into several more cracks far below.

Liv frowned at Destiny. "Why, what is your dragon telling you?"

"Just things I'm not used to," Destiny replied.

Leviathan knew she pondered a great deal. Thoughts she had stopped entertaining in her old life. Namely taking a mate, or falling in love as she would have called it then, and having children.

While he could claim he was averse to the concept, he'd be lying. Destiny might be his weakness, possibly affecting his ability to rule well, but the idea of her being his and his alone had begun to sit far too well. Worse yet, and far more daunting, the idea of belonging to her and her alone. Yet he knew by the way envisioning his offspring swelling in her belly made him feel he was in trouble.

He'd never met a female who tempted him so much in that regard. Who made him imagine what it might be like pushing past his fears. Letting his seed take root. Sharing such an intimate connection. What would it feel like to make a little one with her? A dragon he would cherish…then eventually lose one way or another.

"Would you, though?" Dagr asked, catching his thoughts, drawing closer, much to his relief. *"Perhaps it will be different with you and Destiny because she's coming back into her godliness."*

He narrowed his eyes at the insinuation. At the certainty in Dagr's internal voice.

Then he realized. *"Loki's appearance made you stronger somehow."*

"It did," Dagr confirmed aloud when he and Thorulf appeared. He tossed down several hares in front of the fire and grinned. "And I've never felt anything quite like it."

Liv glanced from Leviathan to Dagr. "Like what?"

"I was back there, cousin." Dagr clasped Liv's shoulder and grinned. "I was fully immersed in Helheim again. Not in a memory this time but as I was before all this started." He shook his head. "I didn't see Hel, but I did see another. *Loki*. A great warrior made of fire, who spoke of his dagger winning this war. He claimed only a great goddess torn between two worlds and the man who ended her could lead us." He looked at Destiny. "Is that not you?" Then Leviathan. "And are you not the man who ended her? Or was supposed to?"

He'd shared everything with his protégés since Destiny's arrival, so Dagr knew she was. Knew she was likely part of their future. Possibly a crucial part of the coming war.

"Yes, I was, *am*, the goddess Loki spoke of," Destiny said softly, her gaze a tad different. "And he was right..." She closed her eyes, feeling something Leviathan couldn't quite define. "Because my godliness isn't gone just...out of reach." She opened her eyes to Leviathan, wondrous. "Can you sense it? The power inside me trying to make its way to the surface? Because it's not my inner dragon."

"No," he agreed, sensing the power she referred to.

Was it her inner goddess? Could it be? If so, what would that mean? Would the connection they had before resume? Or would she shun all of this? Her inner dragon and where she'd ended up?

Loki's appearance had been harder than he was willing to admit, once again igniting that same irritating fear. Only this time, he feared he wouldn't be able to keep Destiny safe if the god wanted her. Took her. There was no way to stop him.

"Gods aside, I think the bigger question is this, Destiny." Liv murmured a chant, flicked her wrist, and a skinned hare roasted over the fire. "Despite what Dagr just shared, where do you think your loyalties will stand if you become a Celtic demi-god again?" Her eyes narrowed, and she gestured upward. "Because as far as I can tell, it's the Celts against the Norse up there, so one way or another, you'll have to choose sides." She shook her head. "Not Loki but *you*. Because as he said himself, you're torn between two worlds."

While tempted to intercept and defend Destiny, he knew better. It was best she answered. Show his protégés who she really was, goddess or no. Take her stand here and now if she so chose.

Which, as they all learned quickly enough, she did.

"Exactly, Liv." Destiny's gaze leveled with Liv. "And it would make sense I'm torn between two worlds because I'm *of* two worlds." She paused, contemplating that for a moment. Truly *feeling* it. Understanding it. So said the determination on her face. "And that's what'll make all the difference as we move forward. Understanding both the Norse and Celtic gods. Why they war. Why they're willing to drain their own people to accomplish their goals. The very people who in turn fuel their strength by worshiping them, right?"

Destiny shook her head, looking from person to person with an inner strength he knew all too well before her determined, strong gaze returned to Liv. "I don't have to choose a side, but I need to understand them both. Understand what makes them tick so we can figure out how to keep your people safe." She perked a brow. "Not just them but the Celts, *humanity,* because they're just as much at risk. Just as much innocent bystanders as you and yours."

The fire crackled, and the waterfall roared as Liv eyed her and contemplated that. She liked what Destiny had said but was by no means ready to admit it.

"And what about the dragon who should be your first priority?" Liv gestured to Leviathan, testing Destiny yet again. "Will you stand by the Ancient you marked if he wishes it?" She cocked her head, a challenging glint in her eyes. "Will you choose him over all others no matter what?"

"I'll choose who my *dragon* chooses in the end," Destiny said without hesitation. "Because I trust Leviathan's process. The Ancients' process." She gestured from her collar to his mark. "More than that, and you have my word, no matter how much I might have shunned and rejected her before, I accept and trust my dragon's decision." Her gaze met his with conviction. "I know she won't steer me wrong."

There was no mistaking the pleasure his dragon found in that. How much pleasure *he* found in it. Because she meant every word. She was finally embracing her dragon. Yet what she'd said before impressed him even more. Her willingness, despite having only started remembering who she was yesterday, to take on so much. Not just that, but to do it with wisdom and compassion, seeing the harm caused to people on both sides of the war.

"I wouldn't think you'd admire compassion," she remarked later that day as they traveled. The sun was setting beyond the thick rock, and they had just started making their way up into the belly of Mt. Galdhøpiggen. "It seems off somehow when it comes to the strength-is-the-master-gene-mentality your kind so favors."

"You're not wrong," he conceded. They walked behind the others, affording them privacy. "When I was younger, Ancients had little use for compassion, but I've since tried to instill some in them as well as the Múspellsheimr dragons." He shook his head. "It hasn't been easy and still not where it could be."

"And by *could be* I assume you mean like the Sigdir dragons?"

He nodded. "Granted, they're generations of Midgard-born dragons, so they have the advantage. It will take time, but I'll get my dragons there. It's the only way they'll be able to keep on living here for longer than a few more centuries. They must adapt. Evolve. Become something that can survive on this world indefinitely."

"And they will," she assured, having no real way of knowing that but supporting his agenda regardless. "How could they not with you leading them? With influences like the Sigdirs?"

"I will not live forever, though." He frowned and bit back a sigh. "What of them then?"

"At that point, they'll have the knowledge and know-how to carry on well," she replied. "I don't doubt for a moment they'll be everything you hoped."

Destiny stopped and looked at him with both pride and concern, sensing more than most. Sensing things he kept to himself for fear of appearing weak. "You can only do so much, Leviathan. Only get them

126

so far before they've got to manage on their own." She placed a supportive hand on his forearm, her gaze strong yet empathetic. "Just like your protégés, they've got to find their way and will because you've set them on the right path. Surely you see that? Saw that in your people when they bid us farewell this morning?"

Unused to being counseled or made to *feel better*, he merely nodded, appreciating it when she continued walking and offered a firm, "I thought so. How could you not?"

He smiled to himself and followed, appreciating her support. Moreover, that she understood he wasn't used to this sort of conversation. Having someone to talk to. The dragon he once was would have shunned such a thing. He didn't take advice or lean on others but made his own decisions whether people liked them or not. It had been his way or no way.

"But you're not that dragon anymore," Destiny said. "You're the dragon Níðhöggr tasked with mentoring the next generation of Sigdirs. The dragon who brought primitive warring dragons together and taught them how to co-exist in peace. How to flourish in a world so unlike their own."

Though he gave no response, she knew he appreciated her vote of confidence as they continued down the long, winding tunnel. One that would have discomforted humans greatly but made their dragons feel perfectly at home.

"It does too," she murmured, running her hand along the craggy rock wall. "More so by the moment." Her dragon eyes flared at the torch. "I almost wonder if we need that." Her gaze narrowed ahead. "I'm starting to get the feeling I'd see better without it. That my eyes are built for this."

"They are." Pleasure shot through him at her admission. At how she embraced her dragon more and more. He could only imagine what it would look like when she shifted for the first time. How stunning she would be. "Most dragons are nocturnal by nature. Our eyesight is at its sharpest in absolute darkness." He leapt up a steep incline and held his hand down to her. "Once we settle for the night, I'll show you the darkness your dragon craves. Show you how very…bright it can be."

"I'd like that." She allowed him to pull her up, not moving away when the momentum brought her close. Rather her eyes met his in the flickering torchlight and lingered. Tempted. Told him all he needed to know.

She didn't just want to see the dark for the first time but something else entirely.

Something he knew full well he should not give in to until they saw the seer.

Chapter Seventeen

THE TIMING MIGHT be bad, but her dragon was in such a state of need, Destiny made it clear to Leviathan where she stood. The question was, would he see it through? They'd stopped to rest for the night, and everyone had gone their separate ways to bathe. Leviathan had said little to her over the past few hours, but then he'd been consumed with his own inner battle.

Namely, how wise it was to give in to her before seeing the seer.

Something she grappled with as well as they continued on. Was it worth the risk? He seemed convinced he'd be able to end her no matter what, but he'd never mated, so how could he be sure? Suffice it to say, by the time they made their way into an intimate little cave with a large enough pool to bathe, her good sense was battling with her dragonly needs.

On the one hand, she wanted him so bad it hurt, and now that she'd marked him, they had to get the deed out of the way regardless. On the other hand, the seer might tell them something they needed to know beforehand. Something crucial that might be affected by them giving in to desire too soon. Then there was the obvious concern.

What if she conceived considering she was in heat?

"I can prevent it," Leviathan muttered under his breath, not surprisingly following her every thought. Especially when it came to this. "Where Midgard dragons can control impregnating females any time except when they're in heat, Ancients can do it all the time."

"Good to know." She eyed the steaming pool, heated from hot springs deep beneath the mountain. A shimmering wall of water poured down the rock beside and behind it. "But unfortunately, that doesn't eliminate the other concern."

"No," he murmured. His steady gaze never left her as he debated. Fought his baser instincts.

She braced her hand against the wall, liking the way the warm water contrasted with the cool rock. Just like it had felt when she and Leviathan were forged in fire. The stone's chill at her back. His heat all around her. His dragon eyes watching her. For a split second, the world had looked different. Magnificent and changed.

"You saw how a dragon sees within flames," Leviathan said softly. "Not all that unlike how it sees in the dark."

With that, he doused the torch and thrust them into darkness.

At least at first.

She couldn't help a small, wondrous smile when the cave slowly resurfaced. It seemed a living, breathing thing in all its splendor. The walls glowed. Water sparkled. Everything was clearer. Brighter.

"It's stunning," she whispered, caught by the sight of him when he joined her. His dragon eyes were afire, and his skin had a dark sheen, shadowing the scales of his inner dragon. Something about it, *him*, made her need almost unbearable, but she couldn't look away.

"*Ja,* stunning," he murmured, caught by the sight of her as well. Fascinated, he brushed the pad of his weapon roughed thumb over her cheek. "Your dragon isn't the color of your eyes or hair but of your godliness. Your inner glow."

She glanced down at her hand only to discover her skin sheened the same color as her bracelet. A shimmering pearl.

"Your eyes, though..." He dusted his finger over her temple, and she shivered with awareness. "The same brilliant turquoise."

She couldn't move, let alone breathe under the magnetizing, lustful weight of his gaze. He'd never looked at her quite like this. As though he saw something in her no one else did.

Something his and his alone.

A delicious warmth curled through her when he trailed his thumb along her jawbone, over her lips, then down her neck until he looped a finger around her collar and reeled her closer. He was by no means rough, not yet, but possessive in a way that made her toes curl in anticipation. She might not have all her memories back yet, but she knew she'd never lain with a dragon.

Especially one like him.

He wrapped a strong hand around the back of her neck, and his gaze continued roaming her face with appreciation. He trailed his fingers over her shoulder, arm, the side of her waist before he clamped his hand over her ass and yanked her lower half against him.

Let her feel just how much he wanted her.

Her pulse skittered through her veins, followed by a swift flood of fire and molten heat that pooled below. She'd never been so eager. Ready. Her core throbbed painfully. Her body trembled.

There was no missing the rampant lust in his eyes or his quickly fading ability to slow this down. Step away. Their desire burned too strongly. Consumed all willpower until he cursed under his breath then closed his mouth over hers.

Their first kiss had been intense and revealing, but this one was untouchable. Their dragons synced up instantly, understanding exactly what the other needed when, where, and how. As if they had kissed and touched a thousand times before. Their tongues swirled, danced, and lapped, ravenous to taste more, devour everything the other had to offer.

She barely felt the water when he walked her back against the wall. When he dug his hands into her hair, groaned into her mouth, and kissed her harder still. Desperate and untamable, her inner beast took matters into her own hands. Wanted this too much. Needed it. So she used dragon magic to remove her clothing, leaving her nude and vulnerable against him.

More specifically, making it impossible for him to turn away.

A tremble rippled through his strong body, and he hesitated, fought it, only to inevitably give in.

His hands wandered, touching and exploring as his mouth continued its knee-weakening assault. Eventually, he traveled lower, licking, tasting, sometimes nipping various things before he fell to his knees, and his hungry gaze ate her alive. Where some might be intimidated by the fierce, near-violent way he looked at her, she reveled in it. Came alive. Wanted his eyes on her always, fueling the sumptuous creature she became for him.

He seemed fascinated by every little part of her, eager to explore and learn. Map her out. Make her his. Claim every inch of flesh until she didn't know where she ended, and he began. It was slow torture. Deliciously erotic. But she needed more. An escape from the building pressure between her thighs. While she liked his attentiveness, her inner dragon was nearing its breaking point, and he knew it.

Played with it.

Ruthlessly teased her.

Especially when he did away with his own clothing and finally let her see him. The muscles roping over his strong body. The scope of his tattoos and battle scars. The cut ridges of his abs. The 'V' leading to his long, thick rock-hard arousal. She only had a second to feast her eyes on it before he hoisted her against the wall, wrapped her legs over his shoulders, and took her with his mouth.

"*Hell,*" she groaned. Gripping the rock at her side, her eyes rolled back in her head, and she lost herself in pure, shameless pleasure. He, in turn, seemed equally pleased, his tongue and teeth doing wicked things, pushing her to the edge time and time again. Forcing her to feel so much, she nearly wept.

Then he did the unthinkable.

He told her she couldn't let go.

Not yet.

Not until he gave her permission.

Interestingly she not only listened, but his order aroused her all that much more. Made her whimper with the cruel yet sinful pain-pleasure of it. Despite needing to release, she couldn't. Wouldn't. And he took full advantage, driving her up and up, only to keep her hovering, suspended, unable to find the fulfillment she so desperately craved.

In fact, he pushed her so high that her body shook by the time he wrapped his arms beneath her knees and stood, holding her prone against the wall. Trapped in sensual agony, growling in her ear that she *still* wasn't allowed to let go.

Even when he finally lowered her onto his shaft.

Their eyes connected as he stretched and filled her, finally giving her dragon what it wanted. Needed. Not only the feel of him but the satisfaction of watching his own features contort in ecstasy. Pure primal pleasure.

Steam poured off their skin they were so heated, so aroused. So ravenous to finally take each other. His thrusts were slow and steady at first, drawing out the exquisite sensation, yet soon enough, that changed. Morphed. His movements became more intense. Driven. Wild. Matching his thrusts, she wrapped her arms around him, dug her heels into his ass, and raked her fingernails down his back.

"Leviathan," she groaned hoarsely, desperate and frustrated. "Let me..."

Though she sensed a flash of hesitancy in his mind, he was too far gone to fight it.

The moment he gave her free rein and told her to let go, everything went supernova. She hurdled over the edge, slamming into so much torturous pleasure she cried out. Growling with approval, he thrust hard one last time, locked up inside her, and roared with release.

They stayed that way for a time, him buried deep inside her, immersed in pleasure, gone in the way they'd made each other feel before he finally lowered her. While it seemed for a moment, he wanted to cup her cheek tenderly, perhaps even kiss her again, a disgruntled look came over his face, and he shifted away.

"I should not have allowed that yet," he grumbled darkly. "Not until we talked to my seer."

While she understood his reasoning, his concerns, it still stung. More than that, her dragon felt not only insulted but rejected. Lying with her should have left him feeling pleased. Well satisfied. Yet he was upset, and her inner beast felt conflicted. Even crestfallen. Rather than let him see it, she tried to remain unaffected and flippant. "Either way, it had to happen, so best we got it out of the way."

He didn't respond, but he didn't need to. If his sour disposition wasn't enough, his thoughts were. How vulnerable she made him. Downright weak. How he couldn't think clearly or act sensibly around her. A liability that could very well affect his ability to lead.

"Well, then you should've damn well not let Freya collar me to begin with," she finally shot back as they bathed, doing their best not to stare at each other. It was difficult, though. He was made too well, his body appealing to both the dragon and woman in her.

And now that she'd had a taste of how he could make her feel, forget it.

"A collar I'm sure will come off soon," he shot back, yet she caught the hesitation in his inner dragon. The defiance in her own dragon at the idea. She also caught a flicker of something else in his mind. A concern he buried so deep she couldn't see it quite yet but knew she would eventually.

"Maybe my collar will come off, but your mark looks pretty permanent," she remarked, only to stop short and narrow her eyes at it. "Why has it changed?"

The Valknut was now colored the pearly sheen of her inner dragon.

He stilled and touched it only for his dragon eyes to flare. At first, his inner beast was defiant, arrogant, feeling out the change, exploring it, before at last, it succumbed with an internal roar of approval.

"Way to dial up the notch of his inner vibration," Maya said into her mind out of nowhere, the smile in her voice obvious. *"Whatever you did, whatever that tat is, it's lifted him up some."*

She got the sense where Jade would be gawking at him in all his nude splendor, Maya politely looked away. When Leviathan's gaze grew more turbulent, dropping his vibration again, her speculations proved true.

"Good God, are they all made that way?" Jade applauded, undoubtedly licking her lips. *"I hope to hell you rode that—"*

For the first time since arriving, Destiny booted someone from her mind, sending Jade on her way before her own inner dragon got jealous. Something, despite his darkening mood, Leviathan took note of.

"Your dragon's powers are growing fast." He finished bathing and dressed himself. "Blocking other dragons from your mind usually takes more time."

"Is that why your mark changed? Because of the change in my powers?"

"No." Leviathan relit the torch, likely determined to remove them from their magical oasis. "It changed because it became permanent. My dragon accepts yours as its mate." He shrugged as if he hadn't just said something so profound. "Not that we'll suffer the bond long if I have to end you."

That's it. He'd gone one step too far.

"Suffer?" Both her human and dragon were offended. Why had he reverted back to being a dick? "Is that how what we just shared felt to you? Painful?"

"We shared lust, woman," he grunted. "Nothing more."

"You're right," she agreed, dressing herself, frustrated. No, more than that, actually. Angry as sin. So angry she swore darkness skirted the edge of her vision. "It *was* lust and nothing more." She shook her head. "And it'll *never* happen again."

With that, she did something totally out of character.

Something neither saw coming.

-Leviathan-

Chapter Eighteen

LEVIATHAN SNAGGED LOKI'S dagger moments before Destiny ran it across her throat in defiant anger.

"Thor's balls," he growled, alarmed by what had just happened.

Not just to her but him.

Before she could deny him, he tossed her over his shoulder and telepathically urged the others to gather right away. Trouble was afoot.

"Put me down, asshole," Destiny growled, her voice off. Not quite hers. "And give me back my dagger so I can free myself from this blasted place. From *you.*"

"Not until we see my seer." He'd never felt so disquieted. Disgruntled and sickened by the all-too-familiar darkness that had just washed over him. "Then and only then, if the lore is right, I and I alone must end you once and for all."

He couldn't imagine it, dreaded it, but knew he must.

"What is it?" Thorulf asked as the other three joined him in a larger chamber.

"I felt death." Dagr frowned at Leviathan. "Celtic death."

"It was Destiny's father again." Leviathan set Destiny down. "Or at least he had his hand in it somehow."

He should step away from Destiny. Put some much-needed distance between them while one of the others saw to her. But he just couldn't. It felt too much like abandoning her. So he chanted away her weapons, anything she could harm herself with, and kept her pinned against him.

"She's not herself right now." He sensed someone else in her mind other than the darkness that had seeped into them. "There's another dragon..."

"Raven," Destiny whispered, trembling. "She's helping..."

Seconds later, whatever had gripped them fled, and she slumped against him. Just like that, the darkness was gone. Yet again, he should hand her off to another but would not. Instead, he scooped her up and sat. When her head lolled against his shoulder, and she dozed off, he rested her cheek against his chest and comforted her the best he could.

"What happened?" Liv looked at him in alarm. Her sharp gaze didn't miss the change in his tattoo. "Because it happened to you too, *ja*?"

"Yes," he confirmed. "While it had her father's essence, there was more to it. Another Celt, or minion, who locked onto Destiny at the Forest of Memories." He scowled. "It got to me through her mark. In turn, I riled her enough to end herself." He shook his head. "She wasn't doing it for any noble cause, though, just simple vengeance..." He narrowed his eyes, sensing something he hadn't before. "Had she been successful, it would have changed everything. Tipped the scales somehow."

"We're lucky Raven helped, then, yes? Another woman from the future?" Thorulf tilted his head in question. "Because she drove away the darkness much like Maya did?"

"Yes," Leviathan confirmed. "Only this was much worse. Not just a memory but more than one dark deity."

"Then Raven is very powerful," Dagr praised.

"Or very, very dark," Thorulf murmured.

"Can the two not go hand in hand?"

"They can." Liv scowled, clearly not concerned about another woman from the future. "So these Celtic deities can possess? Get inside Norse minds?" She shook her head, flicked her wrist, and started a fire. "That cannot be good."

"Nothing about this is," he muttered, nodding thanks to Dagr when he handed over a skin of mead. "Though I would rather set out now so we can get much-needed answers, we must rest first. Each of us in shifts lest Destiny tries something again."

Dagr nodded in agreement. "I'll take first watch."

Grateful, Leviathan leaned his head back against the wall and closed his eyes. He wouldn't let the others see it, but whatever got to him and Destiny had drained his energy considerably. A fate he'd managed to avoid thus far with the gods, but alas, if something happened to her now, it happened to him too.

Though he'd suspected it the moment he took Destiny's life the first time, when he saw her earlier, by the light of utter darkness, there was no longer any doubt. His dragon wanted hers in a way that would be eternal. Forever bonding. How else could it be considering what he'd felt looking into her dragon eyes? Normally, dragons experienced an intense, profound connection when they locked eyes for the first time in dragon form, but for him, it had been then.

When her glorious gaze had met his in the darkness.

When she finally embraced a whole new part of her and her skin sheened for the first time.

He'd never seen anything so beautiful or tempting. His dragon had been thoroughly beguiled, its need to claim her overwhelming. He'd meant to wait just one more day until they'd seen his seer, but his resolve was too weakened. His inner beast too susceptible.

Especially when her dragon set to seducing him and did away with her clothing.

Exposing her luscious body had been a failsafe trap on her dragon's part. There would be no turning away. No stopping. He would sample every part of her. Feel everything she had to offer. Yet when he tasted her sweet juices and lost himself in her, he realized his dragon was diving in headfirst.

It was losing control.

He had enjoyed countless women over the years, especially dragons, but he'd always remained in control. In charge. Dominating as befitted his breed. Destiny had changed that, though. Took control before he could. Lured him into a web of lust he hadn't experienced before. Granted, it didn't last nearly as long as he would have liked, days if he had his way, but it was long enough.

Her dragon had owned his completely.

Sure, he'd played with her, teased her to the edge and back several times, but there had been no caution on his end. Only a driving force to experience all of her. To finally bury his cock deep and lose himself completely. To throw consequences to the wind.

Which meant his seed wasn't controlled by magic but free to do as it would.

Though he intended to keep this from her for now, as he wrapped a fur over her, he couldn't help but wonder. Was his seed taking root even now? If so, had the darkness harmed it somehow? Could the gods have destroyed his offspring before it even had a chance?

The thought angered him almost as much as it terrified him.

He touched the mark on his neck, understanding how the darkness got in. The weakness it had sensed. *His* weakness. Vulnerability born of the defiance and anger he'd felt when she officially claimed him. When his dragon accepted her as its mate and learned the cold hard truth.

Destiny was stronger than him.

She always had been.

Though brief, for a flicker of a moment, his Ancient blood had taken over. Blood straight from his homeworld where females being stronger than males simply didn't happen. If it did, the female was enslaved or killed because males dominated.

And that mentality was all the darkness needed.

However fleeting his primitive thinking, it opened him up to what possessed them. Ashamed by his momentary lapse, he tightened his arms around Destiny, grateful she was okay. Relieved that she hadn't been quicker with her blade.

He figured he wouldn't be able to sleep, but between recovering from the draining energy and having her in his arms, rest came quickly and deeply. So deeply, he didn't stir until she did. Until she yawned and cuddled closer to him.

He cracked his eyes open to find everyone sitting around a fire, roasting some sort of stew.

"You didn't wake me for my watch," he said into their minds, startled that for the first time in his long existence, he'd slept right through it.

"You needed the rest." Dagr's amused gaze swept over him and Destiny. *"You both did."*

While not pleased with seeming weak, he could admit he felt better.

"What happened?" Destiny murmured, waking in that way he so enjoyed. Her drowsy sensual half-mast eyes met his. "Where are we?"

He reminded her where they were, what had happened, and where they were heading.

"I'm sorry," she whispered, surprising him with the sentiment. She touched his tattoo. Her mark. "About all of it."

He frowned, not pleased that she felt the need to apologize. But then, in his ever-darkening state the night before, he'd made it clear he wasn't thrilled they were mated. While he wanted to tell her that wasn't true, now wasn't the time.

Not with his protégés watching him so closely.

Best they only see strength, not emotion. Hard determination, not softness.

"Apology accepted." He stood and set her aside, keeping his eyes averted. Focusing on what lay ahead. "Best we eat and set out."

He ignored the way his dragon bristled at his dismissive behavior and set to eating. As it happened, her account of what had happened wasn't that much different than his. Her father had been in the essence of what influenced them as well as something else. Something just as sinister.

"It wasn't just the Ancient in you that opened her to the darkness," Thorulf said into his mind later that day as they neared the summit, *"but her own godliness. It's definitely in there, small but growing, struggling to the surface."*

"Are you sure?"

"Yes." Thorulf hesitated before continuing. *"And I think you know that. I think you saw it when she claimed you physically, then felt it in your mark when your dragon accepted hers."*

"Perhaps I did." He left it at that rather than let his protégé know just how much his revelation both pleased and upset him. He wanted Destiny to regain her powers, they were part of her, but at the same time, he feared they might rip her away from him. Because all aside, would they not make her immortal again?

That's when he realized what was truly at the heart of his fear.

If she were immortal, how could they possibly be fated mates? He would, in time, grow old, die and be reborn but not her. A couple he'd come across in Scotland shared a similar heartwrenching tale, and he wanted none of it. Not for her or him.

"Are you sure we'll reach the summit today?" Destiny asked, interrupting his thoughts. "We might've been traveling straight up for what feels like eons, but even then, Mt. Galdhøpiggen is huge. Shouldn't it take days?"

"Normally, yes," Thorulf replied. "But nothing about this mountain is normal. It's home to the seers, so it functions on a different level."

"Here's hoping you mean the same magical function as the stairs in Leviathan's Keep." Destiny stared up at the monstrous cave they'd just entered. "That would mean we really are getting close."

"We are," Liv muttered. "And would have been there already had you embraced your dragon."

He bit back a sigh, looking forward to the day Torc pursued Liv before she became more difficult. Especially now with what she considered competition.

"I didn't know we could embrace our dragons in here." Destiny frowned at him. "Why didn't you tell me?"

"Because there was no point." He shook his head. "You were not ready."

"No, she was not," came a familiar voice that made Destiny stop short in shock. "But she is now...she is ready for so very much."

Chapter Nineteen

DESTINY WAS RIVETED by the couple who had appeared out of thin air. Though considerably older, they were mesmerizing, beautiful in a way she suspected the demi-god she once was would have appreciated. Beautiful because they straddled both sides of the spectrum, light and dark, high vibration and low.

"You must be Destiny," the woman said. With long flowing white-streaked black hair, her movements were fluid and sensual. "We have been waiting for you. *She* has been waiting." She gestured at herself. "I am Vigdis." Then at the man beside her with his fiery eyes and pulsing black aura. "This is my husband, Magnus. A fire demon." Her affectionate gaze drifted upward. "She who awaits you is head seer, our daughter, Revna."

Having envisioned Leviathan's seer as old and wise, that surprised her more than she let on, and she wasn't sure why. Maybe because of his advanced age or perhaps because of the way he spoke of her.

Vigdis walked around Destiny, eyeing her up and down in a way that should have made her uncomfortable, but it didn't. Instead, she felt at ease, confident, and knew it had everything to do with claiming Leviathan. With letting her inner dragon surface more and more.

Magnus said little, but then he didn't need to. His sheer presence and the steady way he looked at her said more than words ever could. He would let her see his daughter, but she best do so with caution and respect, or he'd bring his demon wrath down on her.

"Fear naught, husband," Vigdis murmured, her eyes not quite right when they connected with Destiny's. "She will do well in our daughter's presence." Her gaze lingered on Destiny's face for another moment before drifting to Leviathan. A small, womanly smile curled her lips. "Her mind is much too preoccupied to cause trouble."

Damn straight it was. Since the moment she cracked her eyes open this morning and inhaled his delicious scent to this very moment. It had been one thing waking up in his bed, another thing altogether waking on his lap, immersed in his heat. She'd wanted to straddle him, take him into her, ride him until the end of time.

Right up until he shunned her. *Again.*

It was different this time, though. Easier to navigate. In fact, her sense of rejection faded quickly when her dragon saw the truth of things. He wasn't really shunning her but determined to appear a certain way to his protégés. While it frustrated her, she didn't let it get the better of her. Like accepting his culture, she would accept how he went about things. Did it hurt? Of course. But she was strong and growing stronger by the moment.

Something she saw reflected clearly in Vigdis' eyes.

"Carry on just as you are," the seer urged. Though she spoke to all of them, Destiny knew the words were for her. "And all will be as it should." Her gaze returned to Leviathan. "Revna will find you when she's ready."

With that, Vigdis and Magnus vanished as swiftly as they had arrived.

"I like them," she murmured, meaning it.

"Good," Leviathan replied as they continued walking. "Because not many do."

"Why, because they're so different?"

"Because they are half evil," Liv corrected. "So trusting them does not always come easily."

"Maybe evil to you," she countered, feeling the same way about them that she'd felt about Raven, "but not to all."

Though Leviathan made no comment, she felt his approval, which, despite her best effort not to, lightened her step. He'd been distant and quiet most of the day, and it was getting to her. Granted, the sex had been amazing, downright astounding, but she'd liked the comradery they'd begun forming before that. Seeing past his alpha moodiness to the dragon underneath. It wasn't much and not for long, but it had felt good. Natural. Like something she could get used to.

Like something she might have sensed before in another time and place.

Which made her realize.

"It's all because I went from evil to good, isn't it?" She glanced back at Leviathan before they started up a steep, winding path through the rock. "That's why I feel protective of the sisters with their varying vibrations? Vigdis and Magnus with theirs?"

"Yes," he said without hesitation, almost as if he understood before she did. "I think your particular life journey allows you to relate more than most."

She wanted to continue their talk telepathically, find their way back from the darkness that had consumed them the night before, but he returned to being closed off as they continued upward.

Why was he so distant when he knew the truth? When he knew her father and another Celtic god had come between them and caused strife? Yet, it didn't seem to matter. He remained closed off. She still sensed things, however. One thought, in particular, struggled to come through to her dragon, but she couldn't quite lock onto it. Whatever it was, he worked hard to keep it from her.

Something that would be impossible soon enough.

Their dragons desired each other too much for it to be any other way. Had connected to a degree that would prevent them from keeping anything from each other.

"Yes, they have," whispered in her ear before a thin trail of fire sizzled along the stone to her left. "But will it be that way forever?" A trail of fire sizzled on her right, following the indentations in the craggy rock. "*Should* it be forever?"

She tried to follow the feminine voice, see what she sensed was right in front of her, all around her, but had no luck.

"Revna," she whispered. As though in a daydream, she ran her finger along the trail of fire. Breathed in the smoke left in its wake. "Where are you?"

The moment the words left her mouth, her surroundings morphed, and she stood in a cave partially immersed in dark storm clouds. Everyone had vanished, and a stunning woman with flames curling ever-so-slightly over her flawless skin leaned against the cave entrance. Wearing a long, black flowing dress and a hooded silken cloak, she ran a hand nonchalantly through a particularly sinister cloud crackling with lightning.

Revna said nothing at first, only watched the moisture around her before her gaze finally rose to Destiny and took her in. *Drank* her in. As though not just seeing her but sensing everything about her. Things even she didn't know.

"Welcome back amongst the clouds, goddess." She cocked her head, and the smoky aura around her fluctuated. "Though this does not feel like home anymore, does it?" A blink later, moving much like Loki, Revna stood in front of Destiny. She tilted her head this way and that, studying her, considering her. "No, you have found another home, haven't you?"

"Yes," she replied. "In the twenty-first century."

"Are you so sure?" Revna peered closer, and Destiny swore she saw familiar flames in her eyes. Fire she knew all too well. "Or might your home have been born in fire…" The flames curling over her skin intensified, giving off palpable heat now. "After you were conceived in darkness."

She might be coming into her own and open to everything being thrown at her lately, but Revna caught her off guard. Made her take a step back. Open her eyes in a whole new way. Truly *see*.

"There are more memories to be found," Destiny murmured. "Memories I need to remember…"

"Yes." Revna's voice echoed all around them, within the clouds then beyond. "Such memories at that." Her gaze fell to Destiny's collar. "But memories nevertheless."

What did that mean? Because it meant something profound. Something just beyond her reach.

"How do I remember them?" she managed, her voice hoarse, her emotions high. "Where do I find them?"

Did she need to return to the Forest of Memories?

"They will come." Revna's gaze drifted to Loki's dagger sheathed at Destiny's waist. "And they will come quickly once you make it back to the Sigdirs." Her words turned ominous. "Once you end where you began." The moment stretched before Revna's demon eyes rose to Destiny's face. "Until then," she made a flourish with her hand only to reveal the others sitting by a fire that hadn't been there moments before, "we must talk about this thing you and Leviathan did with Loki's fire."

While Leviathan's expression seemed unchanged, Destiny didn't miss his relief at seeing her again. Clearly not as comfortable in the seer's presence as their mentor, Dagr, Thorulf, and Liv watched everything with a cautious eye.

Though she should ignore Leviathan's response to her returning unharmed, Destiny was curious. Would he admit he cared?

"Why would you worry about me with your seer?" she said into his mind. *"Don't you trust Revna?"*

"Yes," he replied. *"But that doesn't change my dragon's response to its mate vanishing into thin air."*

Outside of initially stating they were mated when it happened, this was the first time he'd mentioned it again. Acknowledged the intense connection they'd made. One that would, one way or another, last at least this lifetime, however short that might be. Something they would find out soon enough, she imagined.

"Not find out soon," Revna whispered, yet her voice carried, wrapping around all, "but already know." Her gaze returned to Destiny's dagger. "Thrust the blade into the fire, and I will see what you already know. See what your soul cannot."

Destiny went to pull the blade free but stopped and looked at Leviathan first. Was he ready for this? Would his dragon be strong enough to do what it must if they had no choice? She knew it wouldn't be easy for him. That he'd likely kept her at a distance today for this very reason, but still. She needed to know.

His gaze lingered on her face before he finally nodded, showing her the strength she needed to see. The strength that enabled her to free the blade, crouch in front of the fire, only to hesitate with the blade halfway to the flames.

What if this showed her something she didn't want to remember?

If it took her further down the dark rabbit hole that was her father's legacy?

"Then we will go down it together," Leviathan murmured, crouching beside her. He met her eyes and put his hand over hers on the hilt. His dragon eyes flared, and he promised more than she expected. "You will not be alone, mate." He shook his head once. "Any more than you were alone the first time we faced the flames."

She held his gaze for a long moment, letting it renew her strength before she inhaled deeply and turned her attention to the fire. Time to do this. Face the truth. So, holding fast to the hilt, they immersed the entire dagger in the flames.

Just like when he thrust the blade into her in Ireland, she didn't feel the searing heat. Her skin didn't burn. Instead, she felt all the same sensations she'd experienced when his kiss reminded her what it was to be forged in fire.

Fiery heat against soothing cool.

Brilliant new life against agonizing death.

"There it is," Revna murmured, reverence in her gaze when she crouched on the opposite side of the fire. She tilted her head and narrowed her eyes on the blade. "Do you see it? Do you see *you*?"

For a split second, Destiny swore she saw herself laying on a rock with Leviathan over her, their dagger at the ready. Her pleading. Him denying. Then him giving in. More fire. Blazing flames.

Then dead silence.

"There it is." Revna shook what sounded like dice but turned out to be runes. "The beginning..." Her gaze rose to them. "Or the end."

Chapter Twenty

LEVIATHAN HAD SEEN Revna act strange over the years, but never quite like this. Never so ominous. Normally, some humor or even lust would have come to her eyes by now, but her gaze remained glossed over, seeing something only she could see and not liking it.

"Kill death." Revna's lips pulled back in a snarl, her voice not right. "Kill her Leviathan and stop what happens. What comes. At least for now." Her daunting eyes drifted to Thorulf and Dagr before landing on the flames. "Or let her live and make it ten. You and Destiny plus eight others. Forged in fire. *Four* men. *Four* women. Locked in a fate they never chose. Battling a war they might never win."

"Destiny is no longer death," he ground out, angered by Revna's horrible ultimatum. "She is my *mate.*"

"A mate you knew you had to end," Destiny reminded softly. Her eyes met his. "We both knew this was coming. And we knew we might only make it worse with this collar and mark." She wrapped her hands around his on the hilt and brought the flaming blade's point to her chest just as she had that fateful day. "You need to finish what you started, Leviathan."

He knew. Understood. But that didn't make this any easier.

"Will we see each other again, Revna?" he ground out, trying to find strength wherever he could. Hope. "If I end Destiny, will the power of being forged in fire still hold true? Will we be fated mates?"

When Revna hesitated, he glanced her way. *"Will* we?"

"No," she finally replied, her voice still different. "Ending Destiny with that blade will end the magic of the forge."

He hung his head a moment, trying to come to grips with that. Accept it. But it seemed an impossible task.

"You ask my mentor to kill his mate, yet offer no peace of mind." Liv narrowed her eyes. "What do you mean ending Destiny will only stop what comes for now? That sounds like it will still come eventually."

"What comes via Celtic death has too strong a foothold," Revna responded. "It has aided in the unrest between the gods and…" Black suddenly churned in her eyes as she studied the runes. Flames rolled over her skin more intensely. "Her name is *Mórrígan*," she hissed. "Sometimes a triple goddess, sometimes not. Phantom queen. Banshee. Crow. Goddess of war, fate, and even sexuality…very, very powerful." Her gaze narrowed on Destiny. "And it all started here. With you."

"At the Sigdir's?" Destiny said.

"Because of a Sigdir." Revna's unnatural gaze slid to Leviathan. "Ending Destiny will banish Mórrígan from the land of the Norse and seal the gateway between the gods, but it might not be enough. Her foothold has been here too long, her influence strong. Not just that, but it's possible she's already let Goddess Carman in. So you must choose." She looked at the lot of them. "Harness the power of Loki's forge and grow stronger. Or end Destiny now in hopes Carman isn't already here, and the gateway remains firmly shut." She shook her head. "Neither choice will be easy. And neither will guarantee victory."

Revna's gaze returned to the two of them. "Know this, though, if you choose the forge, Mórrígan will come for you sooner rather than later. She will try to finish you both and take the dagger to extinguish any more threats."

"To be expected," Destiny murmured. "Who's Goddess Carman? How worried about her should we be?"

"She's the Celtic goddess of evil magic," Thorulf replied, troubled. "She tends to roam and leave destruction in her wake thanks to her three evil sons, Dub, Dother, and Dain. Or in English, Darkness, Evil and Violence."

"Super," Destiny muttered. "So we should be damn worried then." She glanced at Revna, obviously trying to make sense of everything. "How did I have Loki's dagger in the first place?" She shook her head. "I know it came from my mother, but I can't imagine my father letting me keep it. Not a blade forged by a Norse god."

"I have no answer to that." Revna resumed studying the stones. "I only know what I have told you."

"So, is Destiny's father coming for her or not?" Leviathan asked. "Because I've sensed him twice now."

Revna studied one rune in particular before she shook her head. "I think him too weakened." Her eyes rose to Destiny. "But not Mórrígan. Not nearly. And she can influence many things." Her gaze turned sensual as it drifted over the men. "She has great power over the opposite sex and uses that to her advantage." She traced her finger over another rune seductively. A warrior rune. "Perhaps you saw such in King Ødger's men recently?"

"Hell," Leviathan cursed, recalling how Ødger's warriors seemed to know where they were headed. "Mórrígan was behind that?"

"I would say it likely." Revna swirled a thin trail of blackened cloud around her runes absently. "If they were but mortal men, they would have been helpless against her allure, doing her bidding whatever it may be."

"Are dragons as susceptible?" Destiny asked.

"It would depend on the dragon," she replied vaguely. "I'd think those mated would be less vulnerable."

"So the more mated dragons, the better." Destiny frowned at Revna. "You foresaw the sisters in Maine coming. What happens if Leviathan ends me now and they don't? Because it sounds like they might be connected to this place via ley lines." She got an odd look in her eyes. "Like cutting those lines might prove harmful to them."

"That is beyond what I can see at this time." Revna looked from Destiny to Leviathan. "It could just as easily free them if you end this here and now."

All fell silent for a moment, digesting everything Revna had shared.

Eventually, Thorulf spoke. "I don't see that there's much of a choice."

"Nor I," Dagr agreed.

"You will not see me end Destiny," Leviathan murmured, following their thoughts.

"We will not," the men said simultaneously.

"There remains too much risk if you do," Thorulf went on, trying to embrace logic when it was clear he simply liked Destiny and didn't want her gone. "If the gateway doesn't remain closed or if Goddess Carman is already here, we'll be in more trouble than we already are. Not only will we have lost the chance to gain the power of the forge, but we'll have lost Destiny, a demi-god dragon who grows fiercer by the moment." He gave Leviathan a knowing look. "Not only that, but we stand to lose you."

Leviathan frowned. "Me?"

"Yes." Dagr glanced from Destiny to Leviathan. "You might not like to hear it, mentor, but your dragon will not perform at its best if she's gone."

"As much as I hate to say it, he's right," Liv grumbled. "There is new strength in you, Leviathan. A change in your dragon. We all sense it."

He was surprised by that, considering he'd felt weaker since Destiny arrived. Vulnerable. So how was it they sensed the opposite?

"Because you are thinking with your human half," Revna murmured, running her fingers over the runes, "not your dragon half." Her gaze rose to him. "Once you shift, you will understand."

"We must also remember what Loki said," Dagr contributed. "That this war could be won with his dagger." He glanced at Leviathan and Destiny. "That only a great goddess torn between two worlds and the man who ended her could lead us."

"Which could just as easily mean Leviathan ending me now," Destiny pointed out, not allowing Leviathan to pull the blade away yet. Despite how much it clearly pained her, she was as stubborn with determination now as she'd been the first time.

"And it does pain me," she admitted into his mind. *"More than I could've imagined considering the short time we've known each other."*

"Ah, yes, I see him now," Revna whispered, her gaze on the runes again. "Loki and his tricks, his meddling ways..." Her gaze flickered to the blade in interest. "Very tricky indeed, but how exactly..." Her eyes narrowed before they widened and glazed, her seer magic strong.

Sensing something. Her random, likely prophetic words, daunting. "Just grab it, Leviathan! Give it to her...she still has a chance! Hope!"

There was no need to ask her what she meant because those words weren't part of the here and now. They *did* seem familiar in their own way, though. "That's what I felt when I first went to Scotland," he realized, looking at Destiny. "That all hope wasn't lost for you."

He'd thought at the time it had to do with everything going on there but realized now it could be related to what was happening here. Because something hovered just beyond his reach. Something he had forgotten. He was sure of it.

"But it's getting closer," Destiny murmured, following his thoughts. "You'll remember soon...*we'll* remember."

"We need to get to the Sigdir's Fortress." He was certain that was the right course of action. "We must get our answers before I consider ending you."

"Agreed," everyone but Revna and Destiny said. When he looked at the seer, she merely nodded. "You've heard all I have to offer this day. The decision must be yours in the end, dragon." Her gaze went to Destiny. "Both of yours."

"I'm torn," Destiny admitted. "I feel like there's more to get to the bottom of, but I also fear the longer we put this off, the harder it'll be."

Destiny considered Revna for a moment before continuing. "Setting aside my own quest for answers, I'm still curious about Tor's prophecy. How he was haunted by a darkness that called to him. A little girl. One born of powerful fire from both the past and future. Fire that riled the gods who would then wreak havoc on their people." Her brows shot up. "Then, once again, there's the sisters following their own prophecy. Four women, coincidentally, who knew they would be traveling through time to help humanity."

"It could all mean something," Revna granted. "Or it could be the dagger's residue leaving a path open in case Leviathan doesn't end you."

"Like some grand magical dagger-induced backup plan?" Destiny's brows pulled together. "Doesn't that seem a little far-fetched?"

"There are no limitations on what the gods can do." Revna shook her head. "Especially when you harness their magic." Her gaze returned to the blade. "And of all the gods, Loki's."

"A god who appeared to us and seemed to recognize you," Leviathan reminded Destiny, about done keeping this blade poised against her chest. "We need to understand why before we do anything else with this dagger. Wouldn't you agree?"

Their gazes lingered a moment as Destiny debated before finally, *thankfully*, she agreed. In turn, almost as if they'd chosen the right course of action, the flames on the blade died, and the dagger returned to normal.

He was never so relieved when she sheathed it, and the threat had passed.

"Thank you for your help, Revna." He nodded at her once. "As always, true and wise."

Revna nodded in return. Though her expression was impossible to read, giving them no hint as to whether she approved of their decision or not, he swore he spied a little light in her eyes that hadn't been there before.

"You must go now so I can rest," Revna said softly, but not before she drifted to Destiny and took her wrist. She traced a finger over Destiny's bracelet, leaving flecks of ebony mixed with the pearl. "Now, not only will I be able to converse with you, but the bracelet's creator will be able to communicate more effectively." She touched Destiny's temple. "Never let too many into your mind at once, though, dragon. Especially with their vibrational levels so varied." She shook her head. "It could weaken you."

"Noted," Destiny replied. "Thank you, Revna. I hope to meet again someday."

Revna gave no answer but simply vanished. When she did, their surroundings changed.

They were no longer on Mt. Galdhøpiggen's Peak but somewhere else altogether.

"Impressive as always transporting us like this." Liv shook her head and eyed the area. "Are we sure Revna's not a god too?"

"Where are we?" Destiny's gaze locked on the boats moored nearby. One vessel in particular. "I know that ship. I've seen it before."

"We're in a harbor on the outer edge of the Realm." Leviathan glanced from the boat to her. "And that is my ship."

"I saw it on the horizon in Maine just before the dagger appeared," she murmured. Her interest only grew as they headed that way. "Yet now I feel like I saw it before that..."

"It was built by my father," Leviathan said. "And has been with my kin since before I was born."

"I don't understand," she murmured, slowing, clearly sensing something. "This makes no sense. How could I have..."

That's all she got out before she stopped short, her eyes glazed over, and she vanished from his mind.

-Leviathan-

Chapter Twenty-One

ONE SECOND DESTINY stood on the dock, looking at the ship moored in the harbor, the next, she stood at the mouth of a cave somewhere else watching it bob on the water a ways out. Moments later, a little black dragon popped its face over the edge, then sank down again, as though playing hide and go seek with her.

"Leviathan?" she whispered, both shocked and charmed. Positive it was him though she'd never seen him shift.

The dragon popped its head up again and spoke telepathically. *"How do you know my name?"*

How *did* she know his name, she wondered vaguely, suddenly not quite herself. Or should she say herself but much smaller. She looked down only to realize she was a *child*.

Clearly too curious for his own good, determined to come investigate, Leviathan's dragon leapt onto the edge of the ship, puffed his chest, then jumped again, only to flail wildly and splash down into the water. She giggled and flinched when he splashed around a few times, then managed to half fly, half tread water all the way from the ship to the land before rolling onto the shore.

She put a hand over her mouth, trying to staunch more giggles when he stood up proudly, released a mighty but very small roar, then trounced her way.

"How do you know my name?" He looked her up and down with curiosity. "And what are you doing in this lair? This is for Ancients, not Sigdirs."

"I don't know," she whispered, suddenly frightened for no reason. "I'm scared."

"Scared," he exclaimed, perplexed. "Dragons do not get scared." He cocked his head. "Embrace your beast, and you will see."

"I don't know how to," she whimpered. "And I don't think I'm allowed to anyway."

Before he could respond, Destiny was whipped out of wherever she'd been and onto Leviathan's ship at sea. More specifically, she sat on his lap yet again. Confused, she blinked and looked around. His little dragon was gone, and things had returned to normal. Well, as normal as being on dry land one moment, then a stormy ocean the next could be. "What happened?"

"I don't know." He shook his head, disgruntled, pulling her hood up against the rain. "Seeing the ship triggered something, and you went into a trance. I couldn't follow where your mind went." He cupped her cheek. "Are you all right because I need to help the others sail. The weather shifts quickly, and we must make the Sigdir Fortress before the next godly storm."

"Yeah, I'm okay." The ship lurched heavily. "Go help."

He eyed her with concern for another moment before he nodded and strapped a cord around her and the bench. "Best to strap down for this." A flicker of excitement lit his eyes. The corner of his mouth twitched. "At least the first time."

He wasn't kidding. Soon enough, she got a first-hand taste of just how crazy Vikings could be. The seas grew rougher by the moment and the waves higher and higher. Unfazed, laughing at the elements, Leviathan and his kin navigated the ship with ease.

"We'll keep the sails up to make good time," Leviathan said into her mind because the driving rain and howling wind had become too loud. *"But they'll make the ride more treacherous."*

"Dear God," she whispered when the ship climbed an especially high wave.

"Ohh, what an adventure you're on," came an unexpected voice in her mind. *"How thrilling!"*

"Elsie, is that you?"

"But of course. Finally!" Elsie's presence was, as always, soothing. *"But then it looks like you could use a bit of company right now."* She paused as if sensing something. *"Your bracelet has*

changed. Someone's manipulated it...made it easier for me to navigate all the vibrational turbulence."

"Yes." She told Elsie about Revna. "So glad she did too. It's good to hear your voice. Especially, like you said, right now."

"Glad I could be here, dear." Her presence was calming despite her excitement. "This really is wild, isn't it?"

"It is." Fortunately, Destiny was easing into the ride better than expected, almost as if she'd been born to the sea. "How are things back in the twenty-first century? Have Trinity and Raven arrived?"

"Yes, all are here." Concern plagued her internal voice. "It's been a bit of a struggle for everyone but mostly Maya at the moment. Whatever's happening there is definitely influencing her."

"I can imagine." She held on tight when the great sails filled with wind and the ship lurched dangerously to the right. Waves crashed over the side, drenching her even more. "Why is Maya struggling the most, though?"

"I'm not sure," Elsie replied. "She's been subjected to two of the darker Norse and Celtic worlds, and it's throwing her off-balance."

"It must've happened when she helped me in the Forest of Memories." She frowned, thinking about it. "My father was coming for me, so she definitely felt the Celtic underworld. Dagr was there too, so Helheim as well."

"Helheim," Elsie echoed. "That sounds rather sinister."

"From what I hear, not nearly as sinister as the Celtic underworld," she replied. "But, for obvious reasons, considering it's the land of the dead, its vibrational level is much lower."

"I would think," Elsie replied. "Who's Dagr?"

Destiny held on tight as the boat lurched and explained who Dagr and his kin were the best she could. How they might tie in with the sisters' prophecy. A fate that some might say they were already actively participating in.

"Please thank both Maya and Raven for what they did," Destiny said. "I really appreciated it."

"I know Maya helped." There was a frown in Elsie's voice. "But I was unaware Raven did as well. That's...alarming." She hesitated, likely following Destiny's thoughts. "No wonder she's so tired. She drove away great evil...or redirected it."

Before Destiny had a chance to ask her what she meant, she vanished, almost, interestingly enough, at the same time the water calmed some. Rain still fell, but the wind had lessened, and the seas weren't as rough.

"That's worth noting," Leviathan said into her mind, having evidently followed the conversation while manning the ship. *"It almost seemed like her comment about Raven redirected this ship out of immediate danger."* He glanced back at the horizon. *"The godly storm still comes, though, so we must make haste."*

"We wouldn't survive it out here, would we?"

"No." The lightning at their back became more vivid. Different. *"Considering how strong this outer storm is, it will be especially bad."*

"Almost as though it knows I'm nearing the Sigdirs," she murmured aloud.

He didn't respond to that, but she knew he agreed. Could it be Mórrígan again? Could she be hindering them to keep Destiny from the truth?

"What happened when you were in the trance?" Leviathan asked. His turbulent gaze told her his concern had waned very little.

"You happened." She was still trying to understand what she'd seen. Better yet, *how* she had seen it. "I was a child and saw you as a young dragon on this ship. I stood in a cave you claimed was for Ancients only." She couldn't help a small smile. "I might not understand why I witnessed it, but one thing's for sure. You were trying to cheer me up. I'd never shifted before, wasn't allowed to, but you were having none of it. You insisted shifting was for the best."

"While I can't imagine wanting to cheer anyone up at that age, insisting you shift sounds right," he replied. "It would've made no sense to me that you hadn't yet." He glanced her way, confused. "That memory has to be false, though. I never came across you when I was young."

What neither said but both found interesting was the idea of them being children at the same time.

"Could it have happened, though?" she pondered. "Could it be we're the same age? That we knew each other as kids but don't remember?"

"Having seen what I've seen, I'd say anything's possible." He shook his head, frustrated. "That would mean both of our minds were manipulated."

"Which means it was likely by a Norse god," she concluded. "Because a Celtic god wouldn't have been able to influence you."

"No." He frowned, clearly disgruntled. "Unless it was Mórrígan." His gaze flickered to the sky. "We'll talk more once we're safely in the village. Perhaps one of the elders will be able to help. They were connecting with their fated mates across time around then."

She nodded in agreement, eyeing the incoming storm with its monstrous black-bellied clouds. Thankfully, Leviathan's ship was swift and closed in on the shore quickly. Not only that, but they were on the outskirts of the storm enough that it had stopped raining. Fortunately, that meant nice dry clothes with a flick of Leviathan's wrist.

Though uptight about the weather, a strange sense of warmth or homecoming washed over her as they drew closer to the walled Viking fortress back-dropped by towering mountains. Endless rows of docks housed ships of all sizes, and the numerous people pushing carts in before the storm bespoke a thriving community.

A striking middle-aged couple wearing fur cloaks awaited them at the end of a dock. After they pulled the ship in, the other three used magic to batten down the hatches while Leviathan made introductions.

"Destiny, meet King Sven and Queen Emily."

Sven offered a kind smile and nodded hello, where Emily squeezed Destiny's hand and offered a warm, friendly smile. "Welcome. We've been looking forward to meeting you." Amusement lit her eyes. "A true pleasure to meet Leviathan's mate." She shot Leviathan a teasing grin. "We didn't think it would ever happen."

Where she thought Leviathan would issue his usual grumbling alpha brush-off, he surprised her when he remained halfway civil. "Yet it has, and she is."

Emily's brows swept up in surprise. It seemed she knew Leviathan well. "So she is, and you're not grumbling about it." She winked at Destiny. "That says something."

Emily linked arms with her and started up the dock, clearly comfortable with time travelers. But then she was one herself, wasn't she? "How are you adjusting to everything, sweetie?" She cringed a little. "Especially considering you were thrust back in time not only in heat but into the Realm with a bunch of Ancients and Múspellsheimr dragons. That'd be daunting for any twenty-first-century woman." She gave Destiny a telling look. "But then you're not any average woman, nor are you truly from the twenty-first century."

"No." She shrugged. "Though it certainly felt like it for a while."

"But not anymore," Emily surmised. "Because your memory's coming back." Her astute gaze remained on Destiny as they left the dock behind. "You are remembering your origins. Your people."

"I think I am," she said softly. They passed through the gates and continued down a dirt road running between thatch-covered houses with roofs nearly touching the ground. She stopped and spun, taking it all in, blinking back tears at how wonderfully familiar it felt. "My mother was carrying me, chatting with others in this very spot. I remember an older, intimidating, but kind man. A man amongst men." She blinked again before she remembered him clearly. "King Naðr Véurr."

"He wasn't just a man amongst men but a dragon amongst dragons," Emily murmured.

"Who feasts in Valhalla now with Queen Megan." Sven eyed the sky with frustration. "Might his dining go undisturbed by the warring gods."

"No doubt it does." A young replica of Sven with a tall broad-shoulder build and handsome features joined them. He issued her a dashing smile. "Welcome, Destiny. I'm Tor, Son of Sven and Emily."

She nodded hello, at ease with him right away. How could she not be considering his natural charm? It wasn't just that, though, was it? She sensed the level nature Leviathan had spoken about. The calm wisdom. It was hard to believe he'd been haunted by darkness because he seemed so well-rounded. In control of himself where Thorulf, Dagr, and most certainly Vicar, had to work harder at it.

"Only because their inner godliness is wreaking havoc," Tor said into her mind, surprising her with how clearly he came through. *"Just as yours is in its own way, yes?"*

"Yes," she said aloud, preferring to keep their conversation where Leviathan could hear it. Yet another sign of how close their dragons had become. She considered Tor's question, more so the man himself. "You can sense my godliness more than most, can't you? Which is strange considering you have no godliness in you."

"No, but like my mother, I'm a medium," he replied as they continued walking. "That gives me the benefit of seeing all that's in someone, whether they're possessed or otherwise." He shrugged a shoulder. "I've also spent ample time helping Vicar navigate what haunts him, so it's helped sharpen my gift."

"Ah." She nodded. "Makes sense." As much as it was going to at this point. "So you definitely sense my inner goddess? She's still there?"

"Without a doubt." Tor eyed the tumbling black clouds heading their way. "And she is attracting much attention."

"Yes," Sven agreed. "The Fortress as a whole is safe, but we should seek shelter soon."

"We should," Destiny murmured, slowing when she spied the huge building ahead. "I remember that," she whispered and glanced at Leviathan, shocked. "It's where we met as children the second time."

-Leviathan-

Chapter Twenty-Two

"I WAS STANDING right there holding my mother's hand when you came in with your parents." Destiny pointed to a spot off to their right when they entered the main lodge. "I'm not sure how I knew it was you, considering I'd only met your dragon, but I did." She narrowed her eyes and smiled a little, clearly following the memory. "You were my new friend."

"But that never happened." Leviathan shook his head. "I would not have forgotten you." He fingered one of her curls and met her small smile. "This hair."

The moment stretched, and their gazes lingered on each other. He liked the idea that he might have known her as a child. However, he strongly disliked that someone might have stolen his memories of her.

"Let us talk to Heidrek." He led her to a trestle table where Thorulf and Vicar's grandfather, Heidrek sat with their grandmother Cybil and introductions were made. Because of their telepathic connection, all were caught up on everything that had happened since Destiny's arrival. The only part they didn't know was what just took place, so they sat down and caught them up.

"Do you know of a Sigdir who had a babe with a Celtic god?" he asked. "Do you remember Destiny being here as a child?"

Though Heidrek and Cybil were in their late seventies, they remained sharp and still very much in love. So said the way they held hands and sat close.

"No." Heidrek shook his head. "I would have remembered." He gestured that drinks be served to all. "Unless the gods were involved, and Loki was meddling. In that case, anything is possible."

"That means he would've had to wipe out everyone's memories of me and possibly my mother," Destiny pointed out. "Does he have that kind of power?"

"Absolutely," Cybil replied. "In fact, if any god's capable of such deception, it's most certainly Loki." She considered Destiny. "Back in those days, Ancients rarely visited this place. Especially families. Do you recall what sort of event it was?"

"No." Destiny shook her head. "I don't get the sense it was a celebration but maybe some sort of meeting." She seemed to search for the right words to describe it. "Like a court process, I guess."

"They must have been attending a Thing," Sven concluded. "It's when Viking tribes come together to hear grievances, try a criminal or discuss land and economic happenings."

"Back then, it would have been to establish land and lair boundaries," Heidrek said as drinks were served. "Especially for the Ancients."

"Why would my mother and I have been at one of those?" Destiny wondered, sipping her ale.

"It would have been a strange place for you to be," Thorulf agreed. "Especially considering your Celtic blood. Ancients back then would have been far more prejudiced against it."

"Assuming they knew about it." Leviathan gave it some thought. "Then again, if Loki were involved..." He narrowed his eyes when something occurred to him. "What if Loki wasn't just playing tricks but somehow directly involved and the Ancients knew it? That would have made Destiny's Celtic lineage more tolerable." He glanced at her. "Much more, in fact."

"Right," she murmured, seeming to sense something in that. Or, more to the point, remember something crucial. "I recall you looking at me across the room a certain way. Sort of smug." She smirked. "And most definitely arrogant. As though you were doing me a great favor." Her eyes softened. "But you were also...protective. Sad for me, I think. Wanting to make me...less sad."

"I can't imagine thinking that way at that age," he replied honestly. He wanted this to be true but struggled with it.

"You didn't think that way at that age, but you did eventually." Emily perked a brow at him. "If I remember correctly, you were the first of your kind to start acting differently. Who evolved into an Ancient better suited to Midgard. You brought the Múspellsheimr dragons and Ancients together and taught them how to adapt and evolve too. How to work together. Protect not just their mates but each other." Her brow shot up higher. "What if all that was possible because of a connection you made with Destiny, however lost to your mind she is at the moment?"

"That makes good sense, wife." Sven nodded. "It sounds like whatever transpired, Destiny brought out the protector in Leviathan. A trait common to Midgard dragons but almost nonexistent in Ancients at one time. They might have protected their females, but that was about it."

"No doubt." Heidrek mulled it over and shook his head. "Truth told, Destiny and Leviathan connecting like that certainly sounds like something that might have happened around here. Because the gods know, truly strange things have happened over the years."

Everyone raised their mugs to that and drank.

"Destiny is a very good fit for you," Tor said into Leviathan's mind. *"I'm glad you chose not to end her yet."*

"Good to hear you feel that way." And it was. He might have known where Dagr and Thorulf stood, but it had been impossible to reach out to Tor and Vicar from Mt. Galdhøpiggen's Peak. Revna tended to put off her own disruptive vibration or frequency when divining.

"Revna handled it well." Tor's inner voice shifted ever-so-slightly. *"She might have simply told you to end Destiny without recourse."*

Having clearly caught that, Destiny's startled glance shot to Tor. It took her no time to put the pieces together. *"Because of you…"*

After all, if Leviathan had ended Destiny, chances were good Tor wouldn't be meant for one of the sisters. He would remain available.

"Ja." Tor left it at that and pulled out of the mental conversation, likely to prevent getting too upset.

"Tor and Revna are in love?" Destiny exclaimed, looking at Leviathan. *"Are you serious?"*

"Sometimes they are, sometimes not," Leviathan replied. *"Only when Revna allows it."*

"Allows it?"

"It depends on her mood," he explained. *"Sometimes, she reciprocates Tor's feelings. Other times, not."*

"Well, doesn't that just throw a monkey wrench in everything." Her eyes rounded at him. *"How's he ever going to relent to 'forging in fire' with one of the sisters if he's smitten with another?"*

"As he made clear when he said he approved of my decision not to end you," he replied, *"Tor, like all of us, will do what he must to keep his people safe. Of that, I have no doubt."*

Though she offered no comeback, he felt her continued unease as the storm rolled in and they ate. Like his people, the Sigdirs had learned to deal with the unnatural weather. While wary of it, they didn't let it ruin a good time. Life had to go on. Yes, it was daunting, a rhetorical shadow hanging over everyone's heads, but there was little to be done about it.

Or at least that had been the case before.

Now he could tell by the way people glanced at him and Destiny as day turned into eve that they grew hopeful. They might finally have a say in all this. A means to get out from under the gods' influence. End the storms, the general restlessness on Midgard, and most importantly, dragon deaths.

Too many had been lost over the years. Especially children.

He eyed Destiny as she chatted with the others and got to know her tribe. Could she imagine raising her own children here? Or would she prefer raising them at the Realm's Keep? To that end, did one grow in her belly even now?

Though he'd managed to keep it from her, the possibility had weighed on his mind all day. His dragon seemed surprisingly eager. As if waiting with bated breath. He hadn't detected anything yet, but sometimes it didn't happen right away. Sometimes it took a little longer. On rare occasion, dragon embryos even chose to hide themselves from detection.

"So that's what you've been hiding from me today!" Destiny exclaimed into his mind, frowning in his direction, her gaze alarmed. *"I thought you could control pregnancy even when I'm in heat?"*

"Hell," he muttered.

It seemed the time for keeping anything from her dragon had passed.

He didn't want to talk about this here and said as much telepathically. They would bid everyone goodnight and talk once alone.

"We should get some rest, Destiny," he said aloud. The weather had stabilized, the storm no longer godly. "Tomorrow, I'll take you to the Sigdir's lair to see if it invokes more memories."

She nodded and joined him, her frustration only growing as they made their way to a sizeable lodge closer to the mountains. It had been given to him when he first started mentoring his protégés. Food and drink were waiting, and a fire crackled on the hearth.

"Good to see this one's a tad smaller," she muttered, eyeing his bed. "But I imagine just as overused."

"Not nearly as much as the other." He sat in front of the fire and pulled her onto his lap before she got into an even bigger snit. "Typically, Sigdir dragons aren't to my taste."

"Could've fooled me." She frowned at him. "Why aren't we to your taste?"

"Because Ancients tend to like particularly rough bed sport." He wrapped a finger around her collar. "We also tend to dominate all the time where Sigdirs accept it both ways." He wrapped his finger a little tighter and gave her the truth. "You're the first female I've ever let take control...and it might have cost me."

"Cost you?" Her gaze lingered on his face a moment before she understood, and her dragon eyes flared. "You lost control...in the cave last night."

"I did," he relented. His vision hazed red as he envisioned all the things he wanted to do to her even now. How much he wanted to lose control again. Lose himself in her. Still dominate but be free of the magic that held him back. "And I can't guarantee it won't happen again." One by one, he untied the strings holding together the top of her tunic. His arousal strained against her ass. "There's nothing quite like filling you with my seed. Of making you mine like that. Claiming you in a way no other can mistake."

"But I thought you didn't want children?" she replied hoarsely, her frustration quickly turning to desire. "That you didn't want to outlive them or risk their lives in this war?"

"I don't…" He trailed his fingers over the voluptuous mounds of her cleavage, pleased by the way her breathing switched. How the scent of her arousal grew. "But I do." He struggled to say what he meant. "I don't want to suffer what others have, but it no longer matters as much as it once did. I would rather make offspring with you and risk the heartache than never make one to begin with."

"But you don't know me," she said softly, her voice hoarser still with emotion.

"Yes, I do." He fondled her breast, then trailed his knuckles up the side of her neck before digging his hand into her lush curls. "Somehow, I know you better than anyone, and I cannot say why."

"Because we knew each other as children," she replied. "Must have."

Whether they had or not, he still felt the same. As though they were becoming one. She was his other half. The perfect fit for him.

"Will you let me take you again?" he murmured, wrapping his hand more firmly into her hair. His cock throbbed, and his vision flared deep red, his dragon eager for her response. "Will you have me again knowing I can't control if you conceive?"

"You ask when you could just take." She ran her finger over his tattoo, her mark. "My dragon appreciates that."

His body tightened at her delicate touch. A teasing touch that drove his inner beast wild.

"What about your human half?" he asked. "What do *you* think?"

Rather than respond aloud, she gave him her answer when she flicked her clothes away and straddled him. When she did the same to his clothing and ground her wet center back and forth on his arousal.

He'd never seen anything more arousing than the sheen of her skin in the firelight. The way she devoured him with her eyes. Her liquid gaze took him in as though she couldn't get enough. Feel enough. Touch enough. Her hands began a slow wander as she rocked her hips, testing his resolve. How long he could hold back before taking matters into his own hands.

As it happened, not long.

Growling with need, he clamped his hands down hard on her hips and steered her onto his shaft before she could tease him anymore. Drove up into her so hard, she cried out. Her dragon eyes flared brighter, and a shiver rippled through her. While clearly startled at first by his hard intrusion, it wasn't long before fresh desire lit her gaze, and her lips fell open.

Though it took a great deal of effort to remain still, he kept her locked in place, his arousal buried deep inside her, and trailed a finger over her full lips. Envisioned them glistening and straining around his cock. He pressed two fingers into her mouth, liking the feel of her soft tongue. The way she sucked and hollowed her cheeks, showing him just what he wanted.

Feeding his imagination.

Pushed to his breaking point in record time, he released a deep-chested growl of approval, clasped her other hip again, held her up just enough, and slammed into her. Again and again, loving the way her eyes drifted, and she dug her nails into his shoulders, drawing blood.

In fact, the scent of her arousal combined with the sting of her touch pushed him over the edge. Better yet, it brought them to the bed, where he finally showed her exactly what she could expect from his kind.

-Leviathan-

Chapter Twenty-Three

DESTINY BARELY HAD a chance to catch her breath when Leviathan tossed her on the bed, then whipped her onto her belly before she could stop him. But then, deep down, she didn't really want to, did she? Not when the flash of fear she felt at his hard, ruthless gaze turned to all-consuming lust, and she knew she'd let him do anything to her.

Anything at all.

She'd snapped the tether between his human and animalistic side. Between the civil dragon he'd become and the wild, primal beast of their homeworld. She saw it in his eyes. A whole new inner beast had taken over.

"On your hands and knees," he growled. *"Now."*

While part of her was tempted to say 'no' just to see what he would do, another, far more rational part knew now wasn't the time to test him. To push the limits of something she barely understood. So she did as asked and waited.

And waited.

She felt the weight of him on the bed. The heaviness of his stare. His raw admiration. How pleased and aroused he was by what she presented. It turned her on to no end. Built a sweet, near painful ache in her core. Made her sensitive flesh pulse with anticipation.

What would he do to her?

How far would he take things?

She finally went to look back, only for him to order her to stay right where she was. She would move her head when and if he gave her permission. No sooner.

"But—" She flinched in painful pleasure when he came behind her fast, twisted his hand in her hair roughly, and pulled her head back.

"But nothing," he growled in her ear. "You do nothing without my permission."

Where she thought fear or even anger would flare, she felt no such thing. Only excitement that he had full control over her. That she had no choice here. No responsibility.

It felt almost as good as the arousal itself.

As if he sensed her giving into his will, he grunted with approval and grabbed the back of her collar instead. She flailed at the sensation, but he stilled her with a firm hand on her hip and a warning in her ear. "Your dragon will always be harder to tame than your human."

She released a low, throaty growl and tried to buck her hips, but he didn't budge. His hold on her was too strong, her inner beast all but bridled. He was the master, and she would be ridden. She grappled with that until he wedged her thighs apart with his legs and manipulated the flesh between her thighs with his too-talented fingers.

Just like that, all defiance fled, and she downright melted.

"I don't know what I like better." Holding the collar firmly in place, he nibbled the side of her neck. "When you fight me or purr for me."

She trembled and arched back against him as he drove her up and up only to keep her on the edge with a single order.

No.

Time and time again.

No.

Even when he curled first one, then two fingers up into her, she still wasn't allowed to let go.

"Bastard," she part whimpered, part sobbed, squirming against him in agony, trying to will her body to let go.

But her inner beast simply wouldn't do it.

Not until he said so.

"Shh, little dragon," he whispered against the flesh of her shoulder. "Almost."

His tongue flicked over her sweat-slicked skin before he tilted her chin and closed his mouth over hers, his kiss as excruciating as his touch. Hard, hot, and hungry. Eventually, he traced the tip of his tongue over the seam of her lips and nudged her hips forward just enough that his cock replaced his fingers.

"Don't let go, Destiny," he warned against her lips. "Not until you have permission."

He wrapped his fingers more firmly around her collar. Not enough to choke her but enough to let her know he meant business. Then he thrust so slowly she started whimpering again.

How was she going to survive this? Hold on? It was pure torture.

Not lovemaking by any means but cruel punishment.

Yet, it made her come alive in a whole new way.

Her blood pumped faster. Her dragon squirmed with delight. Rampant lust. Delicious, brutal need. His fingers worked the flesh between her thighs, and his thrusting intensified, his hips rolling just enough to drive her insane. Through the roof.

"I can't wait," she groaned, teetering on the edge. "I just can't."

"You can and will," he growled. He released the collar and pushed her down to her elbows, gripped her hips, and slammed into her. His movements were savage, and it set her on fire. She wanted more.

Harder.

Faster.

She clenched the furs until it hurt and moaned at his untamed power. His sheer force as he drove into her. He pushed her body down with the weight of him, his front nearly flush with her back. Their bodies slickened all the more. Hearts pounded. Breathing grew harsh. Passion drove him deeper still. He hit every little part of her. Made her groan then cry. Maybe even wail.

He ground out something about never lasting long enough with her before he moaned, "Let go," in her ear, released a strangled roar, and locked up inside her.

Just like before, her body obediently let go when she felt the pulse of his cock, and the pressure of his hot seed. She screamed over the edge into blazing ecstasy and clamped down hard on him. Moments later, her body released completely, and bright fiery colors exploded around her.

Not just any fire, though. And not just any colors.

Loki's fire. Loki's colors.

Then, just like that, everything went black, and Leviathan vanished.

She got the sense she'd passed out but wasn't entirely sure. Caught in a strange limbo, she hovered somewhere between coming down from her orgasm and trying not to panic. She strained to see. To understand what the hell was going on. Where was she? Because it felt eerily like the nightmare she'd had before traveling back in time.

Seconds later, she heard the ocean. Felt the damp, cold rock around her. When her eyes adjusted, her suspicions were confirmed.

She was, in fact, back in the tunnel she'd dreamt about.

Though she called out to Leviathan telepathically, he didn't respond, so she edged forward, careful to remain quiet.

"Do you like it?" came a familiar voice from up ahead. "I did it just for you."

It was her and Leviathan as children again.

She made her way along until she spied them sitting alone in human form on the same shore where they'd first met. Torches crackled, and waves crashed, drowning out the sounds of other dragons in the distance.

"It's all right," her little self consented, clearly sad as she eyed the spacious lair. "But I will miss everyone." She sighed. "My tribe."

"But you still have me and your kin." His brows drew together in confusion when her shoulders remained slumped, and she hung her head. "I thought this was what you wanted? That things were going to get difficult within your tribe? That's why I asked my parents to do this when I found out your mother had been here seeking shelter for you. Somewhere safe to live before too many people realized. Before things became bad."

What things? What were they talking about?

"I just don't understand what I did wrong." Her little self sighed again. "All I know is that I did something or will." A tear slipped down her cheek. "I'm a bad dragon." She shook her head. "And nobody will accept me in the end."

"I will," he declared, crossing his arms over his scrawny chest. "I will collar you and make you mine, so nobody dares harm you." He gestured at the monstrous cave. "This will become my lair. *Our* lair. And you will always be safe here."

Her lower lip wobbled, and more tears fell. "But I don't *want* to be collared."

Not then, she thought. *But you don't mind it so much now.*

She went to touch hers only to realize it was gone.

"Where is it?" she exclaimed with alarm, only for one reality to snap shut and another to open. She was wrapped in Leviathan's arms under a warm fur. Dim daylight seeped through the window, and rain pounded on the ceiling. She sat up and looked around. "Where's my collar?"

"Here," he murmured drowsily, offering a very un-Leviathan-like smirk when he gave it to her. "Glad to see you missed it so soon."

She frowned. "Why is it off me?"

"Now that we're mated, you need not wear it all the time, Destiny. It was just a means to help our dragons determine if they were meant for each other." The corner of his mouth curled up, and a naughty twinkle lit his eyes. "And for other things, of course."

"Nevertheless." She snatched it from him and snapped it on. "I prefer to wear it for now."

Leviathan eyed her for a moment before he sat up and frowned with concern. "Are you okay?" He brushed a curl from her cheek. "As far as I knew, you passed out last night and slept soundly yet…" His mouth slanted down. "Something happened, didn't it?"

"Yeah." She looked at him in question. "Have you had the same lair since you were born? Or did you get another in childhood?"

"I insisted on my own lair at seven." His brows pulled together. "Why?"

"Is that a normal age to have your own lair?"

"Yes." He thought about it. "Though it's safe to say most young dragons don't request lairs that big nor keep it into adulthood."

"So you still have the same one?" A strange feeling washed over her. "After all these years?"

"I do." He narrowed his eyes, more concerned by the moment. "Why?"

She shared what she'd just dreamt. The memory she witnessed. "I think you requested that lair because of me, Leviathan."

His frown deepened, and he shook his head. "No, I just wanted it because it was the largest, and I was determined to be arch-alpha someday."

"That would make sense, but I think it was more than that." Though her dragon liked the idea of crawling back under the blankets with him and picking up where they left off, she got out of bed. "I don't think we need to go to the Sigdir's lair but yours." She chanted herself into clothes. "And sooner rather than later."

He scowled, clearly not liking her dressed again. "Are you sure?"

"Positive." She sheathed her dagger. "That's where we'll find the answers we're looking for." Her eyes met his. "That's where we'll learn what happened to me in the end... or should I say the beginning."

Chapter Twenty-Four

WHEN THUNDER RUMBLED, Leviathan shook his head. "Another storm approaches. It's unwise to leave."

"Yet we must." Destiny glanced out the window. "How far is your lair from here?"

"Too far."

She frowned, reading his thoughts all too well now. "There's another way, though, isn't there? A way to get there as fast as Revna got us down the mountain and somewhere else altogether?"

"Yes." He sighed. "Sage or her son Ulrik could get us there with their fiery gateway tunnel."

"Sounds right up our alley." Destiny added a few blades from his wall to her ever-growing collection. "Where do we find them?"

"Sage and Håkon are visiting another tribe," he grumbled, chanting himself into clothes when he would much rather be inside her. Owning her.

Loving her.

Damnation. That word wasn't for him. Didn't belong in his realm, lair, or bed. Yet it had slammed into his mind hard enough to know his dragon approved. Wholeheartedly agreed.

"Ulrik and his wife are here," he said, sending a telepathic message to his protégé to come join them.

Though Destiny said nothing, he knew she caught his errant far too sappy thought about love. One that didn't belong anywhere in his mind, let alone his heart. Yet he feared, despite trying not to feel it, the foreign emotion was worming its way in.

"We need to go see Ulrik and his wife, then," she replied, glossing over anything she might have caught. "This is important."

And urgent by the looks of it. "Why must we get there so quickly?"

"Because I'm desperate," she replied, clearly frustrated. Even a touch sad. "I want to know what happened to my mother. Why no one's heard of us." She swallowed hard and met his eyes. "Why your people gave her and I shelter from my own tribe in the end..." She ground her jaw, gathering her emotions. "Because they did. I saw it. My people were going to fear me, so your people took me in. Were willing to keep me hidden..."

He frowned, suddenly unable to follow her thoughts. "Hidden from what?"

"My father," she whispered. "I'm sure of it."

"So he conceived you, tried to take you when you were still in the womb as witnessed in the Forest of Memories, then came back years later when he failed the first time?"

"I think so." Destiny nodded. "Or at least it seems that way." She narrowed her eyes. "The only thing that doesn't make sense was why he waited so long to return...and why it almost sounds like I didn't come into my deathly godliness right away. Because that *had* to be why my mother left the Sigdirs."

"That would make sense." He strapped on several weapons and shouldered into his black fur cloak. "And you wouldn't be the first to come into your powers, be they dragon or godly, later than most. It happens."

Destiny was about to reply when a rap came at the door, and Ulrik ducked in, followed by his wife, Frida. A lovely, soft-spoken dragon, Frida claimed Ulrik would be her mate when they were mere children, and she was right. They married when they came of age. Ulrik was the first Sigdir male in generations who hadn't married a woman from the future, but all accepted it. How could they not when Frida protected Ulrik's unique gifts in ways no other could?

Leviathan introduced them and explained how Frida would clear a path for Ulrik's magic through the turbulent godly storm. No easy task.

"I'm sorry, I had no idea." Destiny frowned at Ulrik and Frida. "It sounds like I'm putting you in harm's way..."

When she trailed off, Frida nodded kindly. "It's all right." Her gaze flickered from Leviathan back to Destiny. "You two play an important role in all this, so if you need to get somewhere quickly, Ulrik and I will see you there." She glanced out the window at the driving rain. "But we should do so soon."

Destiny nodded. "Thank you."

Though tempted to argue that this could wait, Leviathan knew it couldn't. Destiny was desperate. Determined and willing to take the risk. So he pulled her against his side and nodded to Ulrik that they were ready.

"You'll want to keep her closer, mentor," Ulrik warned. "Traveling through my fire is becoming more and more unstable." He gave them an apologetic look. "This might be uncomfortable."

Leviathan looked at Destiny. "You're sure then?"

"I am."

"Then we will." He wrapped her in his arms and braced his legs for impact. "We're ready, Ulrik."

Ulrik and Frida said nothing more but closed their eyes, raised their hands, and chanted. Moments later, a fiery tunnel whipped up and sucked Leviathan and Destiny forward through a jarring blustery heat. Despite their ability to breathe oxygen-deprived air, it grew difficult for a stretch before they dropped several feet sharply and hit cold hard rock, nearly buckling them at the knees.

"Damn," Destiny gasped. Eyes closed, she rested her forehead against his chest for a moment and gathered herself. "Hope we don't have to travel like that too often."

"Agreed." He kept her against him and inhaled the sweet scent of her hair, more aware of her than usual if that were possible.

But then this was his spot.

His favored lair.

"Yet you never brought a female here," she whispered. "Why is that?" She finally opened her eyes to his dominion. "Why..." Her voice trailed off as she took in her surroundings. "This is it." She clenched his tunic. "This is it, Leviathan. This is where we met as children. The lair you got for me."

She shook her head and kept looking around. "And though I never actually laid eyes on it in my nightmare, this is the cave from my dream. The one at the end of the tunnel. I couldn't tell when I witnessed our younger selves together, but now that I'm actually here, I can." Her eyes met his. "Almost as if I needed to step foot in it again with you." She swallowed hard. Her gaze returned to his lair. "This is where I was trying to get to time and time again when I slept…my mother was at the end of the tunnel…"

How could that be? He had no recollection of it. Her. *Them*. None whatsoever.

Yet something occurred to him. Something he should have noted long before now.

"No, I never brought a female here," he murmured, startled by that given Destiny's recollection of him as a child. That he'd wanted her as his mate even then. That this would have been their lair. "I always thought my dragon wanted a place all his own, untouched by any, but that was never it." He might not remember her but knew she was the sole reason. "Somehow, on some repressed level, my dragon knew…but I forgot."

"What did you forget, though?" Destiny started into his lair, looking around as if she might find the answers hidden in a corner. "What did *we* forget?" Her all-knowing gaze lingered on the bed in approval, her voice soft. "There really have been no others here." She glanced back at him. "You kept it all ours even though I suspect I was gone at a very young age."

He was about to respond when he felt a nip, then a slight burn on his tattoo. Her mark.

"She's trying to remind me of something," he murmured. "Now that your dragon's here, she's trying to make me remember." He joined Destiny and blinked at his lair as though suddenly seeing it through younger eyes. "She's here…you're here…" Suddenly, the lair flickered then seemed to roll back in time. "We're both here."

Destiny blinked, seeing the same thing as him.

A glimpse into the past.

The child she once was appeared on a rock at the shore, with him sitting beside her. And it *was* him. *With* her. His inner dragon growled in distress at the sight. Growled at the memories that had been so ruthlessly stolen from him.

Because as the two children laughed and chatted, he began to remember.

Began to recall the little dragon he had once so adored.

"Who did this?" he cursed. "Who took you from me? Who ripped away all we might have had together?"

"I don't know." She wiped away a tear when his younger self held out a hand to the child she once was.

"Just take my hand and try shifting," little Leviathan pleaded. "You say you're not allowed, but I'm sure once you do, everything will be different. Your people will welcome you back because they'll know what I know." He shook his head. "You are not evil but a powerful dragon who will keep them safe alongside me." A crooked grin curled his mouth. "Because surely that's what we will do someday."

Leviathan couldn't help but smile as well. How ironic and prophetic.

"I want to," little Destiny replied. Her wild red curls blew every which way in the wind. "But I was told I cannot. That it's too risky." She shook her head and looked at him forlornly, like a child being denied her favorite candy. "So I must not."

"No, you must not, daughter," a woman reiterated, appearing from one of the side tunnels with an all-too-familiar man. "And you must heed us always."

When little Destiny raced to them, they embraced her, their affection for her undeniable.

"What the..." Destiny whispered. "My mother and...*father*?"

Leviathan couldn't find the words. *Loki?* He narrowed his eyes and shook his head. "It can't be for you *are* Celt. It's in your blood."

Almost as if his words triggered it, everyone faded, only for another scene to appear.

"I think we've traveled further back in time," Destiny said softly. Her mother leaned against a wall at the mouth of the cave weeping.

Loki manifested out of thin air and went to her. "What is it, love?"

Her teary gaze went to his face, and she rested her hand on her womb. "It was not without consequences."

"I will destroy him for this," Loki ground out. He pulled her into his arms and rested her cheek against his chest. "Mark my words. Somehow, some way, I will have my vengeance."

"You cannot." She held on tight as if unwilling to let him go. "I was tricked, and there's no hope for it. My child…" she rested her hand on her womb again, "my *daughter* should not have to suffer for what Donn Fírinne did. She shouldn't have to suffer because I thought I was lying with you instead of him."

"Oh, God." Destiny put a hand over her mouth in shock. "I should have known."

She *had* been conceived by the Celtic God of Death. And such ruthless trickery certainly made sense of her birth father. Few were darker.

This, though, witnessing Loki being affectionate, *loving*, was unexpected.

"Your daughter, *our* daughter, will not suffer." Loki tilted her mother's chin up until she looked at him. "I will raise her like my own. She will have my protection."

Destiny blinked, stunned, as if his words rang true. "He would have too." She looked at Leviathan. "Though he wasn't here all the time because he's a god, after all, I sense he was here often enough. And he was good to me." Her gaze drifted back to the couple as they faded. "I think he truly loved me as his own." She shook her head. "So what happened? How did I end up with the Celts?"

"More than that, how was a Celtic god able to do what your birth father did?" He frowned. "He should have never been here in the first place. This isn't his land, nor his people. Our gods would have never let him get this far."

"Maybe he had help even back then," Destiny speculated. "Maybe Mórrígan assisted him. Made him undetectable?" She thought about it. "With such a powerful ally lending her magic, I imagine he was convincing." She gave Leviathan a pointed look. "If he could fool my mother and her inner dragon, I'd say his disguise was impregnable." She frowned. "Though it still begs the question, why lay with a Norse dragon? My father," disgust flared in her eyes, "*monster* that he was, took mortal Celtic women whenever he pleased. So why risk war by crossing over into Norse territory?"

"Perhaps the risk was worth the gain," Leviathan murmured. "Perhaps his sole intention was to create a child that was half Norse dragon, half Celtic god." His gaze stayed with hers. "A powerful child that might aid him in some unknown way." He perked a brow. "Maybe even give him an edge if there was ever a war between the gods."

"Yes," she whispered, sensing something in that. "Not give him an edge, though. *Her.* Mórrígan…"

As if her words triggered it, another scene appeared.

One that showed them so very much.

-Leviathan-

Chapter Twenty-Five

DESTINY WATCHED THE scene, or latest memory, unfold with a sense of dread. "Is it me, or does something feel off? Sinister?"

Though nobody saw them in these flashbacks, Leviathan kept her close and pulled a blade free. "It does."

"Leviathan, come back in," little Destiny called out. She stood on the rocky shore, wringing her hands with worry while his dragon lounged on his back, floating in the ocean. "There's a bad storm coming."

"That storm's not right," Destiny murmured.

"No, it's not," he agreed, taking in the unnatural lightning. "The gods weren't warring then, though, and I recall no such lightning until the last decade or so."

"Storms don't hurt dragons," little Leviathan scoffed but made his way onto the shore anyway just to appease her. "If you shifted, you would know." He shook his wings, and water went everywhere. "I still don't understand why you can't. I know your parents say it will escalate your godliness, but so what? Dragons are stronger than gods."

"I don't know about that." Little Destiny shook her head, unconvinced. "Mother says I come from a very powerful god, so I must be careful. There's no way to know how I'll be if I embrace my dragon. How it might affect my blossoming godliness."

"That was a constant worry for her...me," Destiny murmured, recalling more and more by the moment. "Loki...*father* felt differently." She remembered calling him that, thinking of him that way. "Even though I was Celtic, he was convinced he'd be able to get me through it. Channel my powers. Help me cope." She sighed. "Like you, he wanted me to shift. Felt I would grow stronger if I did."

"And did you?" Leviathan asked, only for their attention to be pulled back to their younger selves.

More so, her mother, when she frantically rushed into the cave. She looked from the incoming storm to the children. "Return to your kin and stay there, Leviathan."

She scooped Destiny up, grabbed something out from under a pillow on the bed, and headed into a familiar tunnel. Not surprisingly, little Leviathan didn't listen but trailed along, worried about Destiny

"Was that…" Destiny followed them and narrowed her eyes. "Did she just grab my dagger? Loki's dagger?"

They stopped short when lightning shot across the sky, and a dark mass slid over the ocean in their direction. It looked like the shadow a cloud might make on the sea when it crossed in front of the sun. The air thinned and grew icy, freezing the sea along the shore, moments before a beautiful yet terrifying woman appeared. She wore a long dark clingy gown, and her reddish hair seemed alive, twisting and turning around her.

"Mórrígan," Destiny whispered.

She knew her, didn't she?

Her mother gave little Destiny the dagger, told them to run, and rushed out to confront the goddess. Perhaps even distract her.

"Leave her be," her mother roared, shifting into a dark blue dragon. "She does not belong to you!"

"She has *always* belonged to me." Though Mórrígan didn't appear to raise her voice, her words were deafening. Echoing. Her face contorted in rage. Her features flickered from beautiful to grotesque and back. "He conceived her for *me*." Her murky eyes narrowed to slits. "She has always been *my* destiny. *My* design. What *my* future holds."

Destiny's mother roared again and attacked, but unfortunately, little Leviathan was wrong. Dragons were not stronger than gods. Laughing all the while, Mórrígan snapped her mother's neck mid-lunge, and her dragon landed dead at her feet.

"Mother," Destiny whispered. She put a hand to her midriff, feeling the acute pain she'd felt back then. The terror and horrible sadness.

"Mother," little Destiny cried from inside the tunnel.

Fearful for her mother, she had not run like she'd been told

"You're trying to get to her, but my dragon won't let you pass," Leviathan murmured, remembering. "You dropped the dagger, but I gave it back to you..." He blinked, startled. "Before she died, your mother was speaking in my mind, saying the same words Revna did on Mt. Galdhøpiggen. 'Just grab it, Leviathan! Give it to her...she still has a chance! Hope!'" He looked at Destiny. "Then she said you should keep it with you always. Let no one know about it. Made by your father Loki to keep you safe, it's for your eyes only. It will bring you home someday if the right person wields it."

This was it. The moment from her dream. She'd been trying to get to her mother. Leviathan had blocked her. Somehow her mind had morphed it, though, seeing him as he was now. No doubt because of their time in Scotland and Ireland.

"And you did eventually wield the blade." She looked at him. "And it did bring me home." She narrowed her eyes. "You would've thought when I turned to the darkness, I would have shunned the dagger, but I didn't. Despite knowing it was my mother's, I never did away with it."

"Loki's magic is strong," Leviathan replied. "And he put much of it in that blade."

"You will *not* go near her!" Leviathan's little dragon roared, drawing their attention back to what unfolded when he raced out of the tunnel. He bared his teeth and stood as tall as his short stature allowed. "She is *my* mate, and I will keep her with me always. Protect her always!"

Mórrígan chuckled, rolled her eyes, and went to flick her wrist to snap his neck too, but little Destiny raced out first.

"No, please don't!" She leapt in front of Leviathan. "He is *not* my mate, just a daft child." Though her eyes shimmered with tears when she glanced back at him, she showed great courage. "He is not worth my time or yours."

"Then allow me to end him, child," Mórrígan replied, clearly impressed by Destiny already.

Little Leviathan grumbled something about not needing a girl to protect him but stayed put when Destiny glowered at him.

"Spare him, and I will go with you willingly," little Destiny pleaded with Mórrígan. Though her lower lip wobbled when she glanced at her dead mother, she kept her head held high. "Spare him, and I will become everything you want me to be. Your destiny. Your future."

"Yes, you will." Mórrígan's eyes narrowed on Leviathan. "But he will not be left alive. Daft or not, he cares too much for you."

She was about to flick her wrist again but stopped when thunder cracked overhead, and Thor's lightning hit the ocean behind her, turning ice to water.

"Loki's coming with help from Thor," Destiny murmured. "He's almost here."

"There's no more time." A blink later, Mórrígan grabbed little Destiny and pulled her away, out over the water.

"No," little Leviathan roared, cried, whimpered. "Shift, Destiny! Embrace your dragon so that you can stay! Fight!"

"I remember looking back at you." Destiny's throat thickened with emotion. "I remember you getting smaller and smaller until you vanished...until I vanished..."

"*Ja.*" Sadness filled Leviathan's eyes as he watched his little dragon fly after her, struggling against the wind shear, flapping his wings for all he was worth. "And I remember how my dragon felt when you snapped away into thin air. The horrible emptiness..."

"It was awful," she whispered. She rested her forehead against his chest and tried to navigate her emotions. The terrible grief she'd felt over the loss of her mother. The same emptiness Leviathan had felt when he realized they would be separated forever.

He cupped the back of her neck in comfort and rested his chin on top of her head. "I'm so sorry I forgot you, Destiny. So sorry that..."

When he paused, she realized he was looking at the shore.

They weren't alone.

"Loki," she said softly, suddenly overwhelmed with emotion, remembering even more now. What she'd sensed before was true. He had been good to her despite who'd sired her. He had, in fact, raised her as his own. "Father?"

"Yes, daughter." His gaze turned from the sea to her. "It is I." He held out his hand. "And I have missed you."

Though she knew Leviathan was wary of her going to him, she went anyway and embraced the god who should have been her biological father. The years seemed to fall away. Everything was just as it had been. His scent. The strength of his arms around her.

"You have been returned to me." Loki cupped the back of her head tenderly for a moment before gazing at her with nostalgia. "You look so much like your mother, only her eyes were much darker."

He brushed the pad of his thumb over her temple, and for a moment in time, she saw those eyes looking back at her. Recalled seeing them in Elsie's eyes when her dagger first appeared in Maine. It had been her mother helping her from the afterlife. Guiding her in the right direction.

A flash later, she saw her mother meeting Loki for the first time deep in the woodland. He'd been drawn by her inner strength and incredible beauty. Even the stunning creature that was her other half.

"I have never loved quite like that," he murmured. "Then you came…"

He didn't need to finish his sentence. She saw the truth in his eyes. How much he loved her despite her lineage.

"Like your mother, you had a way of bringing out the best in those of us who run darker." His gaze flickered from Leviathan to her. "I'm glad you found your way back to yourself, Destiny. Welcome home, daughter."

"Why didn't you say something before?" She shook her head. "When you came to me outside the cave?"

"Because I could not." He fingered one of her curls like he had when she was a child. "Not until you remembered more." His grateful gaze went to Leviathan. "Not until you were brought home all the way." He nodded once at her mate. "You did well, Leviathan. Your gods are pleased. *I* am pleased."

"Am I home all the way then?" Destiny sighed and looked at the sea. "Because I still don't remember everything. I'm still not entirely myself."

"No, you are closer to who you were always supposed to be," Loki replied. "Now that you're back among your people." He looked from Leviathan to her again. "Now that you are mated and forged in fire."

Speaking of that and all-things-dagger.

"What happened?" Destiny cocked her head. "How did Mórrígan and the monster who sired me not know about my dagger?" She frowned. "For that matter, why did my mother have it under her pillow to begin with?" She shook her head, brimming with questions. "And how did that monster trick my mother into thinking he was you? How did he get this far into Norse territory?"

"With help from the she-devil who killed my love," Loki sneered, confirming their suspicions. "To this day, I don't know how Mórrígan infiltrated our realm or got past me, only that she did. Her power combined with Donn Fírinne's was able to fool your mother. Able to accomplish something no god before them has."

"All so that she could have me," Destiny murmured. "What was her end game? Her ultimate goal?"

"This." Loki gestured at the heavens. "A foot in the door. A crack in the land of the gods that grows wider and lets more through. That causes endless war and countless deaths."

Though tempted to ask why Norse gods drained their own dragons, she refrained, for now, wanting her other questions answered first. "And the purpose of the dagger?"

"To protect and keep you safe," he revealed. "Mórrígan and the beast who sired you could not see such a blade. Not with my magic protecting it." His nostalgic gaze swept over the lair. "All of this was to protect you." He sighed. "I should have had you both here far sooner, but your mother wanted to stay with her tribe as long as possible. Eventually, between the attacks and knowing your dark magic would soon blossom, she relented."

"Attacks?" she murmured before she understood. "Like the one we witnessed in the Forest of Memories."

"Yes," he replied. "I ensured special warriors were with her whenever she traveled, but I didn't feel it was enough as time went on. As your magic seemed to lure your biological father ever closer."

"Dagr, one of my protégés, didn't think those warriors could stand against her father," Leviathan mentioned, curious before he seemed to realize. "Because they're designed that way…meant to seem less threatening than they really are."

"That's right," Loki confirmed. "Though it's doubtful one of them could have withstood the God of Death alone, together they would have subdued him long enough for me to get there."

"Well, I'm glad my mother finally relented," Destiny said, having no desire to see Loki go up against Donn Fírinne.

"As was I." Loki looked at Leviathan. "That's when Destiny's mother sought out your people for refuge. If any would not only protect Destiny but accept what she became, it was the Ancients."

Just as they had suspected.

"*Ja*," Leviathan agreed. "Especially Ancients back then. We would have valued dark magic, strength, and ruthlessness above all else. If anything, we would've both protected and revered her."

"And her mother knew that, so she went to your people to request safe harbor." Loki perked a brow at Leviathan. "It was yours and Destiny's unexpected first meeting that saw her request through, though. Or should I say, you yourself?"

"That's what you were doing at the Sigdir's attending a Thing," Destiny murmured, recalling little Leviathan's claim in her more recent dream. That he'd gotten this lair for her and her mother.

"Yes, and it worked," Loki confirmed. "With Leviathan's persistence, his kin allowed you and your mother to join the Ancients." His gaze went to the cave again. "For a time, it was good. I came as often as I could, and we were happy." He shot her mate a rather fatherly look. "Leviathan might as well have lived here for the amount of time you two spent together."

"Time we don't remember." Leviathan scowled. "Time stolen from us."

"Not stolen but hidden," Loki corrected. "Once Destiny was taken, I had no choice but to erase all memory of her and her mother." He gave Leviathan a look. "Especially yours, dragon. For as you now know, you had a very important fate ahead of you. People to bring together and help evolve. Sigdirs to mentor."

"If you hadn't done what you did, I would have gone after her," Leviathan murmured, realizing. "No matter what it took, I would have found my way into the land of the Celtic gods to retrieve her."

"Yes, and you would have died a swift death." He gestured at Destiny. "Instead, when the time was right, you found your way there anyway, did you not? Or at least as close as any Norse dragon has ever gotten."

"Because of the blade?" Destiny asked.

"No, because of you, daughter." Loki looked from the dagger to her face. "Only one dragon could have ever utilized my magic to forge you in fire. I designed the blade that way." He glanced from Leviathan to her. "While I would have chosen him anyway, Leviathan could've only ever done what he did if you and your inner dragon fully accepted him. Your souls had to be perfectly matched to allow the initial spark of fated mates."

She warmed at the look in Leviathan's eyes. How much he seemed to like the idea of them being so right for each other. More than that, based on his lair, on some level he hadn't acknowledged before, he liked the idea of being with just one dragon. Or so she hoped. Because she wouldn't share him with another. Refused to.

Which might make this whole fated mate business tricky.

She was about to ask Loki more about the war between the gods, mainly why they drained their own dragons to gain strength, but her father's attention turned north, his sudden anger palpable.

"Why does that lightning seem more vivid than usual?" But she already knew the answer. Could feel it in the air. Sense it closing in on far too many fellow dragons.

"Because it is." Loki's gaze darkened all the more. "The time is upon us...Mórrígan has come."

"Just like Revna said she would." Destiny clasped her hand over the hilt of her dagger. "She's come to end me and take this."

"She was," Leviathan growled. His gaze narrowed on the horizon. "But something else got her attention."

"You mean her wrath," Loki said. "First, she will have her revenge on the Ancients for sheltering you, Destiny, then she will—"

Destiny didn't wait to hear the rest of his response but acted on pure instinct. Pure adrenaline and a need to protect Leviathan's people. *Her* people. Mórrígan would harm them over her dead body. So she didn't think twice but raced along the craggy shore, leapt into the air, and did something she wished she'd done far sooner.

Chapter Twenty-Six

LEVIATHAN MIGHT BE enraged that Mórrígan thought to attack his Realm, but that didn't stop him from being awed by Destiny. Not because she rushed to save others, that was just in her nature, but because she finally, at last, embraced her dragon.

"Just look at her," he whispered, dumbstruck. Pearly white like her sheen, she glowed with an inner light as she launched into the air and spread her wings for the first time. "She's magnificent."

"And she's angry." Loki gave Leviathan a look before he vanished, his last words tossed into thin air. "Not to mention *alone!*"

That snapped him out of his stupor, and he launched into the air after her.

"I'm coming, mate," he said into her mind, speaking dragon to dragon for the first time. *"We will face her together."*

While part of him feared Destiny going up against such a powerful goddess, another part was proud. She was every bit the dragon he would want in a mate, lifetime after lifetime. Courageous. Putting others before herself. A protector and true leader. But could her dragon fight? He didn't doubt it for a moment.

What he refused to dwell on and put from his mind was that she might be carrying their offspring. Thinking thoughts like that wasn't going to help either of them or his people, so best to focus rather than panic.

Though she was fast and doing exceptionally well, considering this was her first flight, he was bigger and just as fast, so he caught up quickly. There was nothing quite so satisfying as sailing alongside her stunning beast. Connecting eyes for the first time in this form. Hearing her reply in his mind.

"You've grown since I last saw you." She sounded both aroused and amused, impressed as she eyed him. *"You're not that little dragon anymore."*

No. In fact, he'd become the largest of them all.

"This is amazing." She flapped her wings and shot forward faster, adjusting to her serpentine body so quickly he knew something was changing inside her. *"I don't think I've ever felt anything so good."* She tossed him a telling look, referring to their bed play. *"Well, almost anything.*

While tempted to flirt right back, his concern for her safety only grew.

"Land before fighting Mórrígan, Destiny." He eyed the black cloud front and soupy, sinister tornadic clouds forming over the Keep. *"Not only are you not experienced enough to handle turbulence, but you won't be able to withstand her power in the sky."*

"But that's where I need to be." She sounded certain. *"It's the only way to stop her."*

"And how, exactly, do we do that?" He scowled, trying to keep his dragon steady alongside hers in the roughening wind shear. *"Dragons have never gone up against the gods. Ever…"*

He trailed off, not just feeling but seeing the metamorphosis in Destiny as she whipped forward faster still. She was undergoing a rapid awakening. The return of great magic. Great power.

"Your godliness," he murmured.

Her eyes shined brightly and her scales even brighter as she became the first of her kind. A Norse dragon and Celtic demi-god. A dragon god the likes of which his kind had never seen. Humanity had never seen, for that matter.

"We are ready, brother," came an unexpected voice in his head. *"Let us face these gods once and for all!"*

Torc? He hadn't seen his brother in ages, but there he was, standing among a flight of dragons on the highest spires of the Keep. Standing among Múspellsheimr dragons, Ancients and Leviathan's Sigdir protégés.

"Brother," Leviathan replied, grateful he'd come to their aid but startled to realize the dome was down. They were all exposed. *"Where is the dome?"*

"Vicar saw it lowered, and I agreed." Torc roared at the sky alongside the others. *"These gods will no longer keep dragonkind cowering but feel our wrath!"*

A loud boom, then a wicked cackle reverberated from horizon to horizon as though Mórrígan laughed. Moments later, several dragons were struck with crippling lightning where others had their heads snapped.

"No," Leviathan roared, wishing he could get there faster. What was Vicar thinking? Was he out of his mind? *"Vicar, raise the dome. Protect our people!"*

No response. At least not from Vicar.

"I had him somewhat balanced until your brother showed up," Freya explained. *"Then everything just spiraled out of control. Like fire feeding fire. Way too much alpha male instigating alpha male."*

More like a complete breakdown of everything he'd taught them. Then again, the energy Mórrígan was putting off would have likely whipped his dragons into a frenzy regardless.

"Don't worry, though," Freya went on. *"Tor just arrived, so Vicar should be under control somewhat soon."*

"Hope so," he grumbled. *"Because this goddess is damn dangerous."*

"Don't worry," Destiny growled, her eyes narrowed. *"I've got this."*

Before he could stop her, she did what no dragon could and catapulted forward at a supernatural speed, her glow only brightening more. Like an angry comet streaking across the sky. Seething and unstoppable, her rage at Mórrígan for taking so much from her blazed for all to see.

"What the hell is she doing?" Liv said into his mind. *"Not to say she doesn't look impressive doing it."*

He had to agree with her there.

"I'd say she's going to fight that," Freya said, worried when a monstrous black dragon swooped down out of the tornado. *"That's one sinister beast."*

"Mórrígan is a coward then." But he was never so grateful she'd sent a minion to do her bidding. While he certainly didn't like the looks of the smoking dragon heading Destiny's way, it beat facing off with the goddess directly.

"Of course, she's a coward," Destiny growled. *"Tell the other dragons to stand down. I'm dealing with this one myself, then going after the bitch that spawned him."*

He couldn't help being amused despite his growing distress over her safety. He had liked the demi-god she was before but suspected he was going to like this new version of her even better. The perfect mix of good and bad, kind and tough.

Made to rule beside him.

Though Vicar evidently listened to Leviathan—or Tor got him under control—and the dome went back up, Torc had whipped the dragons into a frenzy of anticipation. Bloodlust and a need for revenge.

Leviathan might fear for Destiny, but he trusted her judgment. Knew his lot wasn't ready to face off with Mórrígan's minion. So he roared into each and every dragon's mind to stand down. If any disobeyed, they would deal with him personally.

"Let us help, brother," Torc bit back. *"We deserve our revenge too!"*

"A revenge that will come when the time's right," he replied. *"When Destiny and I know our people will not be so easily destroyed."*

"You would give a woman that much power, then?" Torc grunted, surprised. *"Over your own kin?"*

"I would give my queen that much power," he corrected. *"And with good reason."*

"And what is that?"

"Because she is my strength," he watched her rain godly fire down on the dome, fortifying it so his, *their*, dragons, couldn't leave its protection even if they tried, *"never my weakness."*

Destiny seemed a mighty butterfly breaking free from her cocoon as she raced straight up into the cyclone, barreling toward the enemy dragon. Fortunately, though she'd tried to hold Leviathan back with her magic, their connection allowed him to push past it and follow. The tornadic cloud bank was remarkably high, nearly thirty thousand feet, so it was a climb.

"Be careful, mate," she roared. *"He's not your average dragon."*

"Then this should be fun." Leviathan chuckled, reveling in the upcoming battle for no other reason than he was an Ancient. Built for it. *Lived* for it.

The air chilled, grew thinner, yet up they climbed until *slam*, Destiny crashed into the enemy dragon. Ready, bracing himself, Leviathan latched onto the black dragon's back when they tumbled past him.

Both thrilling in the attack and furious at any dragon who dared attack his mate, Leviathan tore into his neck, drawing blood. Meanwhile, Destiny and the enemy roared and clawed at each other. Their magic pulsed and lashed out, booming around them, echoing across the sky. Unnatural lightning zigzagged down at them, but the tumbling dragons stayed just ahead. Just out of reach of Mórrígan, thanks to Destiny's sheer speed dragging them down.

"Our dragons won't survive the impact if we hit land," he warned her. *"So aim us for the ocean."*

"You got it," she replied, her voice a little off. *"Mórrígan's put a lot of herself in this dragon, Leviathan. He's strong. I'll be able to take him down, but it might...come at a cost."*

He tensed at that. *"What kind of cost?"*

They kept spinning, battling the beast with claws, talons, teeth, and even their tail spikes. Everything at their disposal as they catapulted downward.

"The kind of cost there might be no coming back from." Her dragon eyes met his over the enemy's shoulder. *"If you don't feel it yet, you will."*

Her pupils flared in distress, in what he realized was love. For a split second in time, they were back on the rock in Ireland before he ended her. Back when their eyes connected in the fire. Then further still to when he lost her to Mórrígan then to when he popped his head over the edge of his ship as a child and first locked eyes with her. Then back, full circle, to being forged in fire.

That's when he realized she had returned.

Destiny remembered everything.

Only this time, things would be reversed.

"This time, it's my turn to save you, Leviathan, so you can lead your people to victory." Her pained eyes never left his as they whipped downward. *"I will see you again next time around, fated mate."*

He didn't understand until he did. Until he felt the enemy's blood trickle down his throat, and everything slowed. His limbs became sluggish, hard to move. Though it wouldn't kill him, the enemy's evil godly blood had tainted him.

Temporarily crippled him.

"No," he roared, struggling to hold on, to pull the enemy away from her. *"Don't do this, Destiny. Flee and come back to fight another day. Fight when you have all of us behind you!"*

"There is no fleeing this dragon," she said softly. *"He has to go down if we have any hope of winning this war."*

Though he howled in denial, the enemy easily flung him from his back the next flip. Barely able to keep his wings spread, never mind flap them, he kept his gaze locked on Destiny and the enemy as they battled all the way down. The severe turbulence from the cyclone made him teeter and nearly go off course, but sheer willpower kept him on target enough that he kept Destiny in sight all the way to the bottom.

All the way to the fateful moment the enemy locked onto her neck hard, and they crashed into the sea.

Chapter Twenty-Seven

D ESTINY KNEW THE minute the enemy's strong jaws clamped down on her neck and dragged her beneath the rough waves, her only hope lay in finishing him before he finished her. Yes, her godliness might be back, but she fought a creature saturated with Mórrígan's essence. Brimming with godly power.

Far darker power at that.

Nonetheless, its blood didn't weaken her like it had Leviathan, so she would fight until the end. Fight with everything she had. Which, as it happened, was quite a bit. But then she fought for Leviathan. For his people. Those they had lost.

For all that had been taken from her.

They slammed into the ocean floor, started rolling, and resumed fighting. She might be new to this dragon thing, but it all came so naturally. From the moment she first shifted to now. Leviathan being by her side every step of the way made it even better. Gave her strength and confidence.

She was glad she'd been able to soar alongside him just once. To see the approval and pride in his eyes that she had finally shifted. To witness the desire he felt when he looked at her beast. The possessive gleam that promised they'd enjoy these forms in the bedroom as much as their human counterparts.

"Destiny," he echoed in her mind, struggling to stay strong when the enemy's blood had so weakened him. *"Do not do this, mate. Don't leave me."*

She didn't respond because there was nothing to say.

He knew how she felt. Had seen it when they locked eyes that last time. Saw the love. Knew it was real. She could say it was love born from being fated mates forged in fire but knew better. It had started long before that when they were children. Best friends who were destined to become more someday had it not been ripped away from them.

Now here they were about to be ripped away from each other again.

She was losing far too much blood.

Though dragons could survive underwater for a time, it was limited. Therefore the longer she kept her enemy down, the better. He had to die with her. Which meant he needed to be fatally wounded. So she bought time, fighting, clawing, struggling, hoping for the best only to achieve just what she needed.

She ripped her throat from the enemy's grasp long enough to scramble her feet on the ocean floor and whip rocks up into his face. Then she swooshed her body back and forth several times, frothing bubbles and sand all around them, blinding him.

Now time to drive it home. Or so she hoped.

Drawing on every last bit of godly speed she could muster, she swooped under him, aimed hard and true, and shot the spike on the end of her tail up under his scale straight into his heart.

He roared with fury and crunched down on her neck again before she could get away.

This was it.

The end.

But she'd gotten him too. Now their magic and life force drained together. While it wasn't Mórrígan's life force, it *was* a great deal of her magic pouring into the ocean around them via her enemy's blood. Not fast enough, though. Not quick enough to diminish his strength as he held fast and clamped down harder.

The world dimmed more by the moment.

The ocean around her began to fade.

"Destiny," Leviathan roared. *"Don't go. Fight it...please."*

She heard the pain in his voice just as she had that day so long ago when Mórrígan dragged her away. Anguish as she went where he couldn't follow. Off to another plane of existence beyond his reach.

"I can't," she whispered into his mind when she meant to remain silent. It seemed, however, when met with the end, she wasn't strong but selfish. Needed his connection and the comfort he could offer until the very last moment.

Until the ocean around her shifted colors and sharpened.

Until Helheim came for her.

"I don't think so," she heard Maya's voice say from far, far away. *"Not like this."*

"I agree," came another unexpected voice.

Had she heard correctly? Could it be true?

"Mother?" she managed but got no response.

Instead, a pulse rippled through the water, and the enemy was ripped away. She blinked through the frothing bubbles as he was slammed to the ground and held there not only by Maya's unmistakable energy but by her mother's phantom dragon as well.

"Thank you," she whispered but wasn't sure anyone heard. She was fading too fast.

"Stay on that side, daughter." Her mother's eyes met hers. Transcended worlds. Filled her with love. *"It's not your time yet."*

She tried to respond but no longer had the strength. All she could manage was watching the last of her enemy's life leave him until she couldn't keep her eyes open anymore.

"Do not go, daughter," Loki whispered into her ear, part of the microscopic ocean life all around her. She felt his pain. Fear that she would leave him yet again. *"You are too needed. Far too important. Too...cared about."*

She understood that while Loki was capable of love, actually saying it wasn't always easy.

I have no choice, she imagined responding. *It's too late.*

Or so she thought until four dragons dove into the water.

"Leviathan," she managed, hoping he heard her. That she came through.

Though she cracked her eyes open to a remarkably dimmed world, she sensed him close. Healed. Stronger.

"Did you think I'd let you go that easily, mate?" He rubbed his neck against hers as another dragon came close and touched his forehead to hers. Dagr and Thorulf remained close as well. Thorulf to

give her Celtic godliness strength, Dagr to keep Helheim and death from encroaching any closer.

"Tor," she murmured to the dragon pressing his forehead to hers, *"what are you doing?"*

"Bringing you back, my queen."

She closed her eyes then opened them again when healing warmth washed over her, spreading from her forehead all the way to her tail. Deep crimson hazed her vision as the world shifted from vivid and crisp—a glimpse of Helheim—back to the duller colors of Midgard.

Strength slowly but surely filled her limbs and her neck wound burned before the pain faded.

"Thank you, Tor," she managed when he finally pulled back and met her eyes. *"That was...more than godly in its own way."*

His dragon peered at her with a wisdom to match his human half before he and Thorulf left. Dagr lingered a moment, his angry gaze on the underwater grave of their enemy.

"You see him, don't you?" she asked. *"You see our enemy's spirit leaving his body?"*

"Nothing leaves his body but dark, corrupt magic." Dagr's eyes were as turbulent as his emotions. *"Magic that came at a cost."* His gaze softened unexpectedly. *"A cost to very good magic."*

Before they could ask him what he meant, Dagr shot up out of the water, and they were alone.

"Come, mate." Leviathan rubbed his cheek against hers. *"You need oxygen to regain your full strength."*

"Are you well?" She looked him over with concern she hadn't allowed herself earlier. *"Are you still wounded? Did Tor get all the enemy's blood out of you?"*

"All's well, Destiny," he assured. *"I'm fully healed, as are the dragons Mórrigan attacked before we engaged her minion."* He nudged her along. *"Now, oxygen."*

Though she wanted time alone with him, a chance to tell him she remembered everything, she obediently did as asked. Not just because she knew it was for the best but because she liked him ordering her around while touching her. He chuckled and pursued her, promising more where that came from as they swam upward, broke the surface, and launched into the air to the last thing she expected.

Dragons roaring far and wide.

From the ground to the highest turrets of Leviathan's Keep.

The storm had vanished, but fire still rained down as Ancients, Múspellsheimr dragons, and even Sigdirs gave cries of victory. Roars of pride and approval.

"What is this?" she asked as they headed for shore.

"This is for you, mate." He sailed alongside her. *"You have proven your worth. They accept you as their queen and celebrate your great victory."*

Proven her worth? *Queen?* She'd heard Tor call her that but hadn't paid much attention.

"Land beside me." He headed for a wall walk high above the crowd in the courtyard. Women, children, and elderly who hadn't shifted during the battle because the danger had been too great. *"Land and address our people alongside me, mate."*

"No." She met his eyes as they sailed closer. *"I'll have no one below me."*

Understanding and approval flared in his eyes. *"As you wish, my queen."*

Though she startled at him addressing her that way, it felt right.

Where she was supposed to be.

Meant to be.

So she landed alongside him in the courtyard, back where they'd begun. Or at least one of their beginnings. She didn't shift right away but remained a dragon and let the children come close, touch her godly scales, do what she would have wanted to at their age.

She met the eyes of all, as many as she could, before she shifted back to human. Leviathan followed her lead and did the same. Again, taking her time, letting silence fall, she met many eyes, letting them see her as both dragon and human.

Dragons were everywhere. Perched on the gate, on every wall walk and turret, waiting, silent, wondering what she would say.

"We won today," she finally cried out, waiting for the expected roars of approval to rise and fall before continuing. "It was but a battle in a much larger war, though." Where she could never have imagined speaking to people like this, rallying them to a cause, it came naturally. Easily. "Though I," she looked at Leviathan, *"we* ended a vicious dragon today, he was but a fraction of a very powerful Celtic god. One that we intend to fight and destroy."

While most roared with approval, there were still murmurs of dissent. After all, this was a tribe of dragons who, despite how far Leviathan had led them, still thought like beasts from another world. With distrust. A warring sense of mind.

"What does this god want from us?" someone cried out. "Did you draw it here?"

While tentative, as though not wanting to test their limits, another voice followed. "You are a god too, yes? A *Celtic* demi-god at that?"

"*Ja.*" Leviathan's dark gaze cut over the crowd. "One who just saved you. All of you." His eyes narrowed. "So think twice about what you ask. How you treat my mate when—"

"When nothing," Destiny cut him off. She nodded at him in thanks for standing by her but wanted their support on her own merit. "I was born to a Sigdir dragon, but I was also born to Donn Fírinne, the Celtic God of Death," she confirmed, giving it to them straight. "While I'm proud to be Sigdir, I must accept that I am Celt too." She shook her head once. "I cannot change that." She ground her jaw, not wanting to say it, but it needed to be said. Acknowledged. "Nor, for all the heartache it's caused me, would I want to."

When everyone gasped, she said it like she saw it.

"Though I have no use for the monster who sired me, I took from him what I needed before vanquishing him." She met each of their eyes again, meaning every word. "I'm a proud Norse dragon and Celtic demi-god who understands the enemy. Understands the gods who cause unrest in the heavens." Her gaze swept over the lot of them again. "Therefore, I have the power to stop them."

Whether it was true or not, she meant it.

She *would* see it through before all was said and done if it was the last thing she did.

"Because we're now mated, Leviathan knows everything I do about the gods, and so will you." She nodded at Thorulf and Dagr. "And you." Then her gaze went to Liv, Freya, and Tor. "All of you." She looked up at Vicar, his fierce red dragon unmistakable as he peered down haughtily from one of the highest turrets. "Because every last one of you are my kin. My *people.*"

Though Thorulf, Dagr, and Freya roared their approval without hesitation, Liv and Vicar let the moment stretch before both finally offered mere nods.

They would stand by her. At least for now.

It seemed having the backing of her Sigdir kin did the trick because the crowd roared with approval once again until a hush of wonder fell at who appeared.

Someone who sealed her fate as Queen of the Dragons.

-Leviathan-

Chapter Twenty-Eight

L EVIATHAN HAD SEEN reverence in his people's eyes over the years but never as much as when Destiny gave her rallying speech. Where some remained cautious, most were too impressed by what she'd done to question her. Then, to top it all off, a massive flaming dragon appeared on the rampart above them.

"I am Loki," he roared. He swept one mighty wing, and his fire whipped down and around Destiny. "I give you my daughter." His fire whipped around Leviathan. "And her mate." Then his fire gusted over everyone, creating a sizzling wind that had eyes wide with wonder. "Your king and queen in this war. The god's war. *My* war!"

Despite the havoc the gods had reaped on them, all had the good sense to fall to a knee and lower their head.

Where Leviathan thought for sure Loki would make some grand exit, he did the opposite. Instead, he dropped down beside Destiny and showed them his human form. Came eye to eye with their people just as she had. While his naturally haughty look and innate way of humbling mortals didn't allow them to think him their equal, he made it clear he was an ally.

Leviathan and Destiny's ally.

"This night, you will not drink in Valhalla," he roared. "But in Leviathan and Destiny's Keep alongside me, *Loki*." He grinned, tipped a horn of ale that appeared out of nowhere, then drank deeply. "*Your* god in this war. One who will not drain you of power but *give* you power. So much power you shall defeat *all*!"

Roars of approval boomed far and wide as Loki made a hand flourish that Destiny precede him into the hall before he fell in beside Leviathan.

"My father is...ambitious," Destiny conceded into his mind, sensing his hesitation. Making an alliance with a god was no small matter in these trying times. Making an alliance with one like Loki? A god with a penchant for creating chaos?

Either brilliant or very, very foolish.

"We need to talk to him," he replied as he and Loki strode alongside her. *"We need to understand what happens next. How we win this war."*

"I couldn't agree more."

"But first..." He stopped and cupped her cheeks, searched her eyes. *"Are you all right after seeing your mother like that? Because I know she was there holding the enemy down."*

"She was, and I am," she assured, but he didn't miss the gratefulness in her eyes that he cared enough to ask. *"Believe it or not, it gave me closure of a sort. It's good to know she's still out there one way or another. That she's got my back."*

"And she does," Loki confirmed in their minds. *"We both do."*

When Destiny offered Leviathan a small smile of reassurance, he knew she really *was* okay. He could feel it. Sense it. Seeing her mother hadn't been easy, but it gave Destiny the closure she needed. Peace of mind that she still existed and helped them from the other side of this war.

They entered the chamber where the hierarchy commenced. This time, that meant Destiny, Loki, the Sigdirs, and, as it turned out, his brother Torc.

"It's good to see you again, brother." Setting aside how Torc had rallied his people into a frenzy because he still followed their Ancient ways, Leviathan clasped him on the shoulder. "It has been too long."

"It has." Torc glanced from Destiny to Liv, who merely narrowed her eyes in return. "But the time has come that I be here. Help you." He nodded once at Leviathan. "You will need me and mine."

Technically, Torc's were Leviathan's, but now wasn't the time to bicker.

Now was the time to stand together.

"We need to understand what we face, Father," Destiny said to Loki before looking at Leviathan. "At least now I remember Mórrígan, so that can only help us. I might even be able to use it to our advantage." She frowned. "At one time, I was as close with her as Donn Fírinne, so trust me, like you saw, she can be damn scary." She shook her head. "As far as I know, she only ever had one weakness. The same one that can also be her greatest strength."

"Men," Leviathan murmured. "Because she's also the goddess of sexuality."

"Exactly," Destiny confirmed. "Which makes her more obsessed with the opposite sex than most. Even the same sex sometimes." She shrugged. "Either way, while she typically remains in control, I've seen her let down her guard with those she's particularly obsessed over."

"That could come in handy," he mused.

"Yes, it could." Destiny looked at Loki. "Donn Fírinne and Mórrígan have occasionally been lovers, but their alliance, above all, has always been one that serves their own ends. While I never heard word of it, likely with good reason, Mórrígan wanting to defeat the Norse gods would make sense. She's always been power-hungry. Loves war. Enjoys being revered. So the more worshipers, the better."

Destiny's gaze skirted over the room before she continued. "Mórrígan might have supported my disdain of being half dragon, but I think she did it to appease me. My guess, based on her chosen minion? She admires dragons for their pure strength. The idea of being worshiped by such powerful creatures would hold great appeal."

"Why do you suppose they bothered telling you that you were half dragon?" Freya kicked in. "If Mórrígan rid you of all memory of Leviathan and this place, why let you keep memories of your mother? Because you remembered her, right?"

"I remembered a warped version of her," Destiny corrected. She narrowed her eyes and thought about it. "While I don't know for sure, I sense Donn Fírinne wanted me to have select memories of her. Wanted me to hate her if it meant strengthening the bond between him and me." She shook her head. "As to being a dragon, that knowledge was always mine. I think Mórrígan helped repress it a lot, though. After all, had I shifted, my dragon might've put a kink in her whole plan to rule over the Norse and become one of their gods." She shook her head. "Because I have little doubt that's what she ultimately desires."

"And now you've shifted and become what she feared," Liv said, however begrudgingly, but Leviathan imagined Torc's presence was already affecting her. Making her finally see Destiny as less of a threat. "You are a strong demi-god dragon who has made a powerful alliance with Leviathan and *will* ruin Mórrígan's plan to take over."

"If it's the last thing I do," Destiny vowed, clearly grateful to finally have Liv backing her without the attitude. Horns of ale were handed out, and her attention returned to Loki. Back to questions, they all sought answers to. "Why are the gods draining their own dragons to accomplish their goals? What do you think we can expect from Mórrígan going forward in this war? Because I know she's not defeated, just weakened." She glanced from the Sigdirs back to Loki. "And how do my new friends in the future tie in with all this?"

"A question I'd like an answer to as well," Elsie said into Destiny's mind, yet Leviathan heard too. *"Because that was some terrifying stuff back there."*

"The gods draw on dragons because the energy they used to gain from worshipers has waned considerably," Loki explained. "The warring between my fellow gods and the Celts has unnerved our worshipers. Lessened their faith in us." He shook his head. "So, though we do not wish it, we've had no choice but to gain strength from our dragons."

Frustrated, Loki downed his entire horn of ale before continuing. "Thor and I have long thought there was another way, though." He eyed the woman who refilled his horn with lustful appreciation. "We believe we should fight alongside dragons and humans. In doing so, we would give everyone not only the chance to fight but restore their faith in us which, in turn, would strengthen us." He shook his head. "We would no longer need to prey on dragons."

Though Leviathan saw the logic in that, it could go both ways, and Destiny called Loki on it.

"Or," she countered, "if you falter and don't fight as well on Midgard, the people might see their gods aren't as strong as the Celts, hence giving you no extra strength."

"We *are* as strong as they think us, though," Loki assured. "Especially in our territory." He glanced at the Sigdirs. "The added power you and your mates will bring when forged in my fire will only aid in our war. Perhaps even be the key to winning it."

"And why is that exactly?" Leviathan asked.

"Because the spark of dragons becoming fated mates is one of the strongest powers imaginable," he replied. "Between Tor's prophecy and how you have prepared your protégés, they are ready." Loki's gaze returned to Destiny. "As you theorized, your twenty-first-century sisters were directly affected by you being forged in fire. It was, in its own way, a call to arms. They are souls suited to this war."

"I affected their varying vibrations or frequencies, though, didn't I?" Destiny frowned. "Because I went from being such a dark demi-god to a better one? From negative to positive?"

"Yes," Loki confirmed. "But it was needed for the forge. For their role in this war." His gaze rose to the endless windows above as though he saw something beyond them. "Predestined roles mapped by your inner dragon, Destiny. Lines of energy burned in varying shades of dragon fire." His eyes dropped to them. "My fire."

"The ley lines," Destiny murmured, looking up. Her dragon eyes flared in surprise. "I can't see them yet, but I feel their frequencies. Their varying vibrations leading to different sisters." Her eyes returned to Loki. "That's why I saw different shades of fire when my dagger returned to me in Maine, isn't it? Because of the sisters' part in this?"

"Yes." Loki's gaze drifted over the Sigdir men then returned to Leviathan. "As your Great Serpent foresaw, though, it will be your protégés who rise up and fight this war above all others. That means they must control the dagger and harness the flames." His eyes flickered to the ley-lines they couldn't see. The sisters at the other end of them. "And that may not be as easy as you think."

"Nor something they might have needed to face," Destiny exclaimed, glancing at Leviathan. "What if Leviathan had decided to end me on Mt. Galdhøpiggen? What if he'd done it sooner in Ireland, then…"

She trailed off when she realized.

"Now you understand," Loki murmured. "Leviathan would have never ended you, Destiny. He's incapable."

"You planned this." Her eyes narrowed on Loki. "You knew Mórrígan would take me and that someday Leviathan would seek me out. When he did, we would start the forge. One that required four more couples influenced directly by him and me."

"Understand this, daughter." Loki closed the distance and cupped her shoulders. "I'm not the monster who sired you, forcing you to embrace evil, making you forget all. I am the father who would have done anything to stop Mórrígan. Yet, I knew how powerful she was. That there was a good chance she would take you before I could stop her."

His gaze dropped to the dagger then rose to her face again. "If she did, *when* she did, it only made sense to put something in place to help defeat her down the line. To keep you safe the only way I knew how." His brows arched. "You did well avoiding her wrath once you turned good, Destiny. Staying one step ahead. Because you and I both know it was only a matter of time before she caused more havoc."

"It was," she murmured, searching his eyes, suddenly understanding something only she could see. "But then I wouldn't have been able to do it without the dagger. Without the magic you infused in it. A magic that allowed me to separate myself from her and put distance between us."

"I believe you would have been able to do it with or without the dagger," Loki murmured. "But, yes, everything you said is true from start to finish."

Destiny continued searching his eyes, weighing what she saw there. How much was fact and fiction. What she should take from all of it. In the end, it seemed she realized her choices were limited. All of theirs were.

If anything, Loki and his long-hatched plan was their only hope. Their best hope.

"Then we must move forward," Destiny finally said, showing admirable strength and good leadership as far as Leviathan was concerned. "Though I'll admit I'm not overly thrilled about forcing four other couples to become fated mates."

She eyed the Sigdirs for a moment before she continued, saying what needed to be said. What Leviathan knew she truly felt.

"Setting aside our forgotten time as children, the Celtic goddess I was could have never imagined mating with Leviathan, never mind becoming fated mates." Destiny's gaze stayed with his protégés. "But by the end of our journey, some part of me knew. Understood. Saw something in him I didn't yet understand." She nodded once in reassurance. "So do not fear the forge." She met Leviathan's eyes, her love for him clear for all to see. "I promise you it'll be *well* worth it in the end."

"I've yet to come across a dragon who didn't enjoy finding their fated mate," Loki added. "Some might struggle with the idea initially, but all find great fulfillment in it." He looked at Destiny and Leviathan with pride. "And with you two helping them navigate it, I imagine that will not change now."

"No," Destiny agreed. She might be championing their cause, but it was clear she preferred to keep things honest. To remind his protégés exactly what lay ahead so that they could ready themselves. "How do we navigate the sisters' varying energy levels through all this, though, Loki? Through what this place might throw at them?" She shook her head. "Poor Raven can barely move around freely, let alone travel back in time, she's so crippled by low vibrations."

"Yet she's not the one we need to worry about most right now," Elsie said softly.

"Maya," Destiny murmured aloud, sensing it. "She's struggling, isn't she?"

"Yes," Dagr and Thorulf said at the same time.

Detecting his protégés' mutual interest in Maya, Leviathan perked a brow at them. "Care to elaborate?"

"I caught a glimpse of her human spirit beneath the sea," Dagr divulged. "Not only was she greatly affected by the negative energy of Mórrígan's minion, but her soul ended up crossing into Helheim when it shouldn't have."

"Dagr saw her, but she reached out to me telepathically," Thorulf added. "She was courageous but frightened."

"Why would she have reached out to you?" Dagr frowned at his cousin. "When it's my world she crossed into?"

"Uh, oh," Destiny said into Leviathan's mind. *"Should I be worried about these two?"*

"They might be close, but they've always been competitive," he granted. *"I don't see it affecting what they need to accomplish, though. Because one way or another, they're quick to forgive each other."*

And that would be the key when Maya ultimately chose one over the other.

If, that is, one of them was even meant for her.

"Let them compete all they want," Elsie said. *"My main concern is can they help her? Because Raven isn't as steady when Maya's not at her best. When Raven isn't steady, Jade gets pulled down and tends to wreak havoc which leaves poor Trinity to clean up her messes."*

"Messes?" Destiny asked.

"Yes, messes," Elsie confirmed. *"Jade's already caused several bar fights, stolen someone's boat, and riled up every animal from here to Massachusetts if the never-ending dog-barking is anything to go off of."*

Destiny flinched. *"Sorry to hear that."* She looked at Leviathan and spoke aloud. "Do you think Dagr and Thorulf can help somehow?"

"Or me." Fully dressed now and quite amiable, Vicar flashed Destiny a winning smile. "Nice to meet you."

She nodded hello, and spoke to Leviathan telepathically again. *"I take it this is his other personality?"*

"Yes," he confirmed. *"Tor finally got him back to his Sigdir side. Coaxed him down from what riled him up."*

"Which was Torc," she replied, having followed everything pre-battle.

"Ja," he grunted. *"As you saw, he appeals to Vicar's other personality, his primal side. Ancients and Múspellsheimr dragons aren't built to back down. So if Torc and Vicar declared it was time to take a stance, well, you saw what happened."*

"Yeah, and it can't happen again," she replied. *"Mórrígan's seriously no joke."*

"Agreed."

While Torc and his men certainly brought much-needed strength to their upcoming battle, it would become a delicate balance as they moved forward. Tor would need to stay with Vicar as much as possible to keep him where he needed to be.

"Because they had direct contact with her," Leviathan said aloud, speaking to all, "I think Dagr and Thorulf should go to the twenty-first century and help calm things down. See if they can help Maya."

Determined that she rule alongside him, he looked at Destiny. "Do you agree?"

She nodded. "Absolutely."

"They will need to take your dagger with them," Loki informed Destiny. "By defeating Mórrígan's minion, you weakened her, which means the gateway between the gods' worlds closed a great deal. Fortunately, that bought us time, but it's only that. *Time.*" His gaze went to the Sigdir men. "When the next pre-destined moment comes, the dagger will ignite the forge."

"Won't Mórrígan come looking for the dagger again?" Torc asked. "That was her purpose here today, right? To defeat Destiny, take the blade and gain control?"

"Yes, and she will come again," Loki confirmed. "Though Destiny and Leviathan are best equipped to fight her, all must learn how to hold their own with the dagger. Which, thanks to Leviathan, the chosen Sigdirs do."

"Because of their own godliness," Destiny murmured. "I knew that was going to be important in all this."

"Yes," Loki confirmed.

"What about Tor, then?" She frowned and glanced from Tor to Loki. "He possesses no godliness."

"No." Loki nodded once at Tor in approval. "Yet he displayed more strength than his kin today, did he not? Great power?" His gaze returned to Destiny. "So do not fret, daughter, but remain confident. Have faith." His gaze returned to her dagger. "Meanwhile, you must hand over the blade, for the forge is precarious. It depends on the right elements and the correct dragons coming together. Those best suited to be fated mates. So it *must* be in the right hands when the time comes." He shook his head. "And those are no longer yours."

"Who should I give it to?" Destiny considered those who had volunteered to see to Maya. "Dagr or Thorulf?"

"Whomever you choose." Loki looked between the men. "Either way, it will end up in the right hands when it's meant to."

Destiny nodded and eyed the blade, her attachment to it every bit as strong as Leviathan's.

It had seen them through a lot. Brought them together, then ripped them apart before once again bringing them together. While it had devastated them, it had also saved them. Made them remember.

Stronger. Just like it would others. Those it knew were right for each other. That could find the kind of love they had. So, without overly dwelling and showing them sentiment they didn't need to see right now, Destiny handed it to Dagr for no other reason than he was closest.

"I'll take good care of it, my queen." Dagr understood it hadn't been easy for her to part with. "I won't let you down."

"Nor I," Thorulf agreed, joining them. He glanced between her and Leviathan. "We will find our mates and see this war won."

"Thank you." Destiny gave them a grateful smile. "Travel safe."

They nodded, bid everyone farewell, and strode out, heading for the Fortress and Ulrik's fiery tunnel.

Satisfied they'd covered everything they could for now, everyone finally commenced to celebrating a victory and new alliance with Loki. Leviathan pulled Destiny close often where he wouldn't have before. Not only because he couldn't help himself but because it was a better example to set for his protégés, considering they needed to claim mates too. Strength in battle might be crucial, but love and affection need not be considered a weakness.

Not anymore.

In fact, it should be promoted considering the power of mating.

"Now, *how* am I going to get a collar around Liv's neck?" Freya pondered mischievously in passing sometime later. Her hair already matched Liv's and Torc's. She grinned and winked at Destiny. "Somehow, I don't think it'll be half as easy as getting one around yours."

Before Destiny could reply, Freya vanished into the crowd, getting ready to work her magic. Liv and Torc hadn't gone near each other yet but certainly eyed one another. Now, with Freya at the helm, who knew what was in store.

"It should be interesting watching those two come together," Destiny remarked. "Probably a little scary."

Leviathan chuckled. "That might be an understatement."

"Right, but at least…" Her amusement died as she watched them. As she saw what might lay ahead for a fellow Sigdir and Ancient. "I'm glad how far you and I have progressed, Leviathan. That we found each other…but I still worry."

It took no time to figure out what troubled her.

"You worry about me aging and dying eventually," he murmured. "Because you're a demi-god once again."

"But a changed demi-god," Loki kicked in, following their conversation easily enough from his woman-ridden perch nearby. "One forged in fire."

When they looked at him in question, he explained.

"You and Leviathan are now *one* in this lifetime," Loki revealed. "Which means you will age at the same rate as him, Destiny." He shook his head. "Neither of you will live much longer than the other."

Destiny breathed an audible sigh of relief. "Really?"

Loki nodded. "*Ja*, really."

"I can't tell you how good that sounds." She cuddled back against Leviathan. "Because honestly, I was never a fan of being immortal."

"You will still live remarkably long lives," Loki warned. "But at least you will have each other as time goes on."

What he didn't say and neither wanted to dwell on at the moment were children.

How they would most certainly outlive them.

"So when can we make our great escape?" Destiny eventually murmured in his ear. "Because I'm dying to—"

"Right now." He cut her off before she continued envisioning what she wanted to do to him. She'd been at it for hours, putting off her sweet scent, and it had been brutal. He was yet again, as always when it came to her, near his breaking point.

"Upstairs then?" she asked, the lust in her gaze just as strong.

Loki perked a brow. "Or perhaps somewhere else?"

"Somewhere else sounds wonderful." Relief flashed in her eyes when she realized what he meant. "Absolutely perfect."

"Then I say to you once again," Loki flicked his wrist, and they ended up right where they wanted to be, with the god's voice echoing off the rock, "welcome home, daughter."

-Leviathan-

Chapter Twenty-Nine

DESTINY SMILED WHEN she and Leviathan ended up back in his lair next to the sea.

Their lair.

Back where it all began.

"And back where we will stay," he murmured, pulling her close. They would still go to the lair at their Keep, but this would always be their preferred spot.

Her mother might have died in this cave, but she had done a lot more living here first. Loved her family in this lair. Created cherished memories that would always stay with Destiny and Leviathan.

Before she had a chance to respond, to tell him this was where they'd stay, where they belonged, his lips fastened over hers, and any thoughts she might've had vanished.

All that mattered was this moment.

Being in his arms.

With him the way they were always meant to be.

They chanted their clothes away at the same time, hungry for more. Desperate for everything they could make each other feel. This time, at least at first, it seemed he intended to go about things differently.

Less rough.

More loving.

He scooped her up until she straddled him, then carried her to the bed where he lay her down and came over her. Loved her with his eyes. Worshiped her with his lips and hands. Gentle, exploring, he memorized her with every touch and stroke. Suckled her nipples and fondled her breasts, growling with approval before he thought to go lower.

"I don't think so."

She rolled him on his back and took control, exploring and sampling him with equal fervor. Lusting after him just as well as he'd lusted after her. From his broad chest downward, she kissed and tasted until she took his cock into her mouth and pleasured him that way. He groaned and clenched her hair, enjoying every minute, thrusting, taking her as she took him, nearly finding fulfillment until she warned him to stop.

"Did I give you permission?" She gave him a naughty look and kept him on the edge as she slowly worked her way back up his body. Kept him desperate for fulfillment until she straddled him and rocked her center back and forth over his rigid arousal. Teased until his body was trembling and his jaw locked tight. Until his eyes were half-mast with desire and his fingers twitching with the need to grab her.

Take her.

Make her his yet again.

Slow-like, brushing her nipples against his chest first, she finally lowered, trailed the tip of her tongue along the seam of his mouth, before licking her own lips, teasing, taunting, pushing her limits. Then she froze, waiting, relishing his groan of impatience mixed with frustration. The leap of his eager cock seeking entrance. The way he humbled himself and growled his need to take her.

Yet still he waited.

Then, and only then, did she finally murmur in his ear, "Now."

She'd tempted him to such a degree that he pulled her down hard onto his shaft and let go so strongly, his body shook, and his muscles jerked. She was so aroused that when she twirled her hips ever-so-slightly to add to his pleasure, her own release hit her with a walloping punch. He groaned with approval when she clamped down hard then lost herself to a long, full-body release that left her liquefied.

"It's hard to believe I ever thought I would dislike this," he rumbled minutes later when she was halfway coherent. She sprawled across his chest with him still deep inside her.

"Dislike what?" she murmured drowsily, enjoying the way he massaged her ass.

"This," he murmured. "Being mated. Only wanting *one* mate."

"Do you then?" She met his eyes, hopeful. "This will be enough for you? *I'll* be enough?"

"One mate would have always been enough if I'd had it from the beginning," he said softly. "*You* from the beginning." He stroked her hair. "I think I only ever wanted more because I was searching for you. Trying to find my way back to what made sense."

"Which some might argue would've been trying to stick with one woman beforehand," she teased.

"Not if she wasn't the right one." He flipped her onto her back without pulling out and met her gaze so tenderly she knew he was all hers. "Not if she wasn't you."

He gave her no chance to respond but thrust hard, his bounce-back time admirable. She wrapped her legs around his waist and eased into his thrusts, drawing out the experience.

This time was slower.

Unbelievably loving.

She hadn't thought a dragon like Leviathan capable of it, but he was, his heart in his eyes as they moved together. Took each other somewhere neither had gone before.

Somewhere that drove home exactly what it was to be fated mates.

Every movement was perfectly orchestrated as they loved one another. Drowned in what the other had to offer. Lost themselves to the building desire. The fire that seemed to forever burn around them. Within them. Fiery red and blazing hot. Eventually, they moved faster, racing toward their pinnacle. Friction increased. Steam rose.

Yet, they never stopped.

Never slowed.

Not until they flew over the edge and dove head-first into pure sinful pleasure together.

She lost track of how many times they made love after that. All night, into the wee hours. Mostly rough. Dominating. Sometimes loving.

Always fulfilling.

At some point, they must have dozed off because something jolted her and Leviathan awake at the same time hours later.

"What *was* that?" she murmured, looking around, groggy.

Was someone here? Had trouble arrived again so soon? As far as she could tell, they were alone.

Leviathan's brows pulled together in confusion before he went perfectly still, and his dragon eyes flared.

"What?" she whispered.

"Shh." He put a finger to her lips, cocked his head, and listened more closely.

Seconds later, they both heard what had awakened them and his gaze shot to her belly.

"Was that a heartbeat?" He made his way closer to her midriff until his gaze aligned with her naval. Then they waited with bated breath, his gaze so intent on her womb, she couldn't help a small smile. He wanted to have heard correctly, didn't he?

As if responding to his proximity, his very eagerness, it happened again.

And again.

"Ja!" Such wonder filled his eyes when he placed his hand on her womb that she teared up. He smiled at her. "You are with child, mate. *We* are with child."

"Got that," she whispered, emotional. She placed her hand over his as the beat, heard only by dragons, finally leveled out and remained steady.

It took mere seconds before telepathic congratulations poured in from his kin, yet one voice came through the strongest.

Revna's.

"A new dragon perfectly suited to you," the seer said, giving them news almost as good as what they'd just received. *"Made by a demigod and Ancient forged in fire, your offspring will live a life in accordance to yours. Age as you age and live on after you as is the natural order of things."*

"Truly?" Destiny couldn't help it. Tears fell. *"Are you sure?"*

"She is," came Loki's proud voice in their minds. *"So said the children in your womb."*

As in *plural*?

Moments later, as the sun sliced over the sea into a new day, a second beat sprang to life.

Grinning from ear to ear in a most anti-Leviathan fashion, her mate kissed her belly twice before he closed his lips over hers, and they embarked on a whole new journey together.

An existence they never could have imagined.

They had battles to lead, a war to fight, but had no doubt they would conquer all. How else could it be when they'd never felt stronger? More alive? More in love?

Their story had been a long one full of sacrifice and unlikely outcomes. Of putting others before themselves. Making a difference in countless lives. Yet in the end, Fate, or as some would say, *Loki*, found a way to give Leviathan his Destiny.

A woman who would rule well by his side and love him until the end of time.

The End

Dagr
Coming Soon

Maya always knew she was meant to travel through time to help humanity in some unknown way. She would never have guessed it was to keep them safe from warring gods. Nor that she would straddle two worlds, caught between life and death, her only hope a Viking from the distant past she craves but can't have. A dragon prince with too dark a lineage.

Determined to make Maya his, Dagr Sigdir heads to the twenty-first century only to discover she's half immersed in Helheim, the Norse Underworld. Son to its ruler and certain he's her fated mate, Dagr's the only one who can free her from its dark hold. Or so he thinks until someone far more challenging than mere death stands in his way. His closest friend and brother-in-arms, Thorulf.

Will Dagr step aside if Thorulf and Maya are destined to be together? Or will he fight to claim his mate and risk his people's safety? After all, if Maya doesn't end up with the dragon meant for her, they won't harness the power needed to battle the deities. Find out as Dagr, Maya and Thorulf embark on a mystical super-steamy adventure for the ages.

-Leviathan-

Midgard Locations Glossary

Ancient's Lair– Ancient dragon lair.

Cave Catacombs– Network of interconnected caves across Scandinavia.

Cave of Memories– Cave born of Forest of Memories.

Dragon Lair– Sigdir dragon lair.

Forest of Memories– Powerful forest that captures traumatic events or memories and replays them.

Hvergelmir's River– A river in Níðhöggr's Realm that pours from the well that nourishes all life.

Hvergelmir's Spring– Spring that feeds Hvergelmir's River.

Maine Ash– Níðhöggr's ash tree in modern-day Maine.

Mt. Galdhøpiggen's Peak– Home of the seers.

Níðhöggr's Ash– Great serpent's ash tree in Scandinavia.

Níðhöggr's Realm– (AKA the Realm) Home on Midgard to Ancients and Múspellsheimr dragons.

Place of Seers– Magical location only those with seer blood can go.

Viking Fortress– Sigdir stronghold once ruled by King Heidrek, now ruled by King Sven.

Viking Keep– Stronghold once ruled by King Bjorn, now ruled by King Soren.

The Realm's Keep (AKA Leviathan's Keep)– Castle in the Realm.

Deities and Dragons

Author's Note: The following gods are known for several things. The descriptions given below are for the purpose of this series.

Loki– Cunning Norse god known for creating chaos. Though not blood-related, considered father of Destiny, Queen of the Dragons.
Thor– Norse God of Thunder and Lightning.
Mórrígan– Celtic Goddess of War, Fate, and Sexuality. Sometimes seen as a crow.
Donn Fírinne– Celtic God of Death. Biological father of Destiny, Queen of the Dragons.
Carman– Celtic Goddess of Evil Magic. Leaves destruction in her wake.
Dub, Dother, and Dain– Carman's sons. Darkness, Evil, and Violence.

Dragons

Sigdir dragons– The MacLomain Clan's Viking ancestors. Dragons born on Earth/Midgard.
Ancient dragons– First-generation Midgard dragons. Parents born on Múspellsheimr, dragonkind's homeworld.
Múspellsheimr dragons– Dragons born on Múspellsheimr who now live on Midgard.

Series Cast

Author's Note: Characters will vary from book to book. This provides a general overview of main couples, allies and enemies within the series. Various parents/elders may make appearances based on particular hero/story.

Leviathan– King of the Dragons and an Ancient. Mated to Destiny.
Destiny– Queen of the Dragons. A Sigdir. Biological Daughter of Celtic Death. Mated to Leviathan.

Elsie– Aunt of the modern-day sisters. Dragon psychic. Motherly, calming disposition.
Maya– Highest frequency sister dragon. Very kind. Super positive. Lifts her sisters emotionally.
Trinity– Second to highest frequency sister dragon. Can tap into various vibrational levels. Ultimate peacekeeper.
Jade– Second to lowest frequency sister dragon. High-strung. Soaks up and helps sisters release negativity. Bit of a trouble maker.
Raven– Lowest frequency sister dragon. Needs to be in areas free of too much negativity so she isn't susceptible to death or evil.

Dagr– Sigdir demi-god Norse dragon. Son of Eirik, Kenzie, and Goddess Hel. Battles with fine-honing his inner Helheim magic.
Thorulf– Sigdir dragon. Possesses some Celtic godliness. Son of Soren, Agatha, and Ava. Heir to his own throne. Has trouble harnessing the power of his inner god. Half-brother to Vicar.
Vicar– Sigdir dragon. Possesses some Celtic godliness. Son of Soren and Ava. Split personalities. Half Sigdir, half Múspellsheimr dragon from former life. Half-brother to Thorulf.
Tor– Sigdir dragon. No godliness. Even disposition. Medium and healer. Son of Sven and Emily.

Allies

Freya– Cupid dragon. Brings mates together. Daughter of Davyn and Shea.

Liv– Warrior dragon. Strong personality. Daughter of Rokar and Tess. Fated for Torc.

Torc– Leviathan's brother. Adheres to Múspellsheimr's more primal ways. Fated for Liv.

Ulrik– Sigdir dragon. Controls fiery gateway tunnel. Husband to Frida. Son of Håkon and Sage.

Frida– Wife of Ulrik. Helps protect Ulrik's magic.

Revna– Head seer. Half seer, half fire demon. Daughter of Magnus and Vigdis.

Vigdis– Former head seer.

Magnus– Leader of the fire demons.

Loki– Cunning Norse god known for creating chaos.

Thor– Norse God of Thunder and Lightning.

Sven– King of the Sigdirs. Tor's father.

Emily– Queen of the Sigdirs. Tor's mother.

Heidrek– Elder. Thorulf and Vicar's grandfather.

Cybil– Elder. Thorulf and Vicar's grandmother.

Enemies

King Ødger- King of rival Viking tribe.

Mórrígan– Celtic Goddess of War, Fate, and Sexuality.

Donn Fírinne– Celtic God of Death.

Previous Releases

~The MacLomain Series- Early Years~

Highland Defiance- Book One
Highland Persuasion- Book Two
Highland Mystic- Book Three

~The MacLomain Series~

The King's Druidess- Prelude
Fate's Monolith- Book One
Destiny's Denial- Book Two
Sylvan Mist- Book Three

~The MacLomain Series- Next Generation~

Mark of the Highlander- Book One
Vow of the Highlander- Book Two
Wrath of the Highlander- Book Three
Faith of the Highlander- Book Four
Plight of the Highlander- Book Five

~The MacLomain Series- Viking Ancestors~

Viking King- Book One
Viking Claim- Book Two
Viking Heart- Book Three

~The MacLomain Series- Later Years~

Quest of a Scottish Warrior- Book One

-Leviathan-

Yule's Fallen Angel- Spin-off Novella
Honor of a Scottish Warrior- Book Two
Oath of a Scottish Warrior- Book Three
Passion of a Scottish Warrior- Book Four

~The MacLomain Series- Viking Ancestors' Kin~

Rise of a Viking- Book One
Vengeance of a Viking- Book Two
A Viking Holiday- Spin-off Novella
Soul of a Viking- Book Three
Fury of a Viking- Book Four
Her Wounded Dragon- Spin-off Novella
Pride of a Viking- Book Five

~The MacLomain Series: A New Beginning~

Sworn to a Highland Laird- Book One
Taken by a Highland Laird- Book Two
Promised to a Highland Laird- Book Three
Avenged by a Highland Laird- Book Four

~Pirates of Britannia World~

The Seafaring Rogue
The MacLomain Series: A New Beginning Spin-off
The Sea Hellion
Sequel to The Seafaring Rogue

~Viking Ancestors: Rise of the Dragon~

Viking King's Vendetta- Book One
Viking's Valor- Book Two
Viking's Intent- Book Three
Viking's Ransom- Book Four
Viking's Conquest- Book Five
Viking's Crusade- Book Six

~The MacLomain Series: End of an Era~

A Scot's Pledge- Book One
A Scot's Devotion- Book Two
A Scot's Resolve- Book Three
A Scot's Favor- Book Four
A Scot's Retribution- Book Five

~Viking Ancestors: Forged in Fire~

Leviathan
Dagr
Thorulf
Vicar
Tor

~Highlander's Pact~

Scoundrel's Vengeance
Scoundrel's Favor
Scoundrel's Redemtion

~Pirate's Intent~

Rescued by Passion
Taken by Sin

~The Lyon's Den Interconnected World~

To Tame the Lyon

~Calum's Curse Series~

The Victorian Lure- Book One
The Georgian Embrace- Book Two
The Tudor Revival- Book Three

~Forsaken Brethren Series~

-Leviathan-

Darkest Memory- Book One
Heart of Vesuvius- Book Two

~Holiday Tales~

Yule's Fallen Angel
+ Bonus Novelette, Christmas Miracle

About the Author

Sky Purington is the bestselling author of over fifty novels and novellas. A New Englander born and bred who recently moved to Virginia, Purington married her hero, has an amazing son who inspires her daily and two ultra-lovable husky shepherd mixes. Passionate for variety, Sky's vivid imagination spans several romance genres, including historical, time travel, paranormal, and fantasy. Expect steamy stories teeming with protective alpha heroes and strong-minded heroines.

Purington loves to hear from readers and can be contacted at Sky@SkyPurington.com. Interested in keeping up with Sky's latest news and releases? Visit Sky's website, www.SkyPurington.com, join her quarterly newsletter, or sign up for personalized text message alerts. Simply text 'skypurington' (no quotes, one word, all lowercase) to 74121 or visit Sky's Sign-up Page. Texts will ONLY be sent when there is a new book release. Readers can easily opt out at any time.

Love social networking? Find Sky on Facebook, Instagram, Twitter, and Goodreads.

Want a few more options? "Follow" Sky Purington on Amazon to receive New Release Kindle Updates and "Follow" Sky on BookBub to be notified of amazing upcoming deals.

Made in the USA
Middletown, DE
15 October 2021